False Profits

False Profits

Patricia Smiley

NEW YORK   BOSTON

Copyright © 2004 by Patricia Smiley
All rights reserved.

Mysterious Press
Warner Books

Time Warner Book Group
1271 Avenue of the Americas, New York, NY 10020.
Visit our Web site at www.twbookmark.com.

The Mysterious Press name and logo are
registered trademarks of Warner Books.

Printed in the United States of America

First Printing: November 2004

10 9 8 7 6 5 4 3 2 1

Library of Congress Cataloging-in-Publication Data

Smiley, Patricia.
    False profits / Patricia Smiley.
        p. cm.
    ISBN 0-89296-790-0
    1. Physicians—Crimes against—Fiction. 2. Business consultants—
Fiction. 3. Consulting firms—Fiction. 4. Women detectives—Fiction.
5. Divorced women—Fiction. 6. California—Fiction. I. Title.

PS3619.M53F35 2004
813'.6—dc22   2003068606

For Susan Josephson
Always reading
Always laughing
Always believing

Acknowledgments

the author wishes to acknowledge the assistance of the following people: William Solberg for his steadfast support and
his talent for turning a phrase; fellow writers Patricia Fogarty,
Barbara Fryer, Peggy Hesketh, Steve Long, Elaine
Medosch, Reg Park, Tim Polmanteer, and T. M. Raymond for
keeping me on the true path; Michael Levin for his insightful cri-
tique; Anne McCune for providing information on the consulting world; Kerry Kidman, Esq., for his knowledge of the law;
Vicki Sabella for her willingness to brainstorm anytime, any-
place—even on the bumpy road to Avalon; James E. West II,
black belt in kenpo, for coaching me in self-defense; my buddies
at Pacific 14 for letting me hang out with them; and my angel
dogs, Dottie and P.J., for teaching me *joie de vivre* the Westie way.

My enduring gratitude goes to Elizabeth George for her brilliant mind and her generous spirit, and for teaching her students
not what they should write, but rather how to take what they've
chosen to write and to make it better.

I also thank the following extraordinary people: my agent,
Scott Miller of Trident Media Group, my editor, the late Sara
Ann Freed, and editorial assistant Kristen Weber.

False Profits

1

i woke up with a twenty-pound dog wrapped around my head like an Easter bonnet. His name is Muldoon, my mother's West Highland white terrier. She bought him used from new parents with an allergic baby, so you can understand why the little guy has abandonment issues that only a shrink could sort out. Unfortunately, he'd decided that sharing my pillow was all the therapy he needed. And who could blame him? Sometimes it seems we spend half our lives finding that pillow, and the other half trying to recover after it's yanked out from under us.

It was mid-November, on a Monday morning, golden with autumn sunlight. Muldoon and my mother were living with me in Zuma Beach, just north of Malibu, in one of the few beach cottages in the area that hadn't been replaced by a starter mansion. I inherited the place from my grandmother. It's not much, just a little brown shoebox on the sand, but I love it unconditionally.

My mother's stay was temporary—just until the owner of her Los Angeles apartment building repaired some old earthquake damage. A week or two. She'd promised. But that was three months earlier, and despite the mother-daughter bonding opportunities, she and Muldoon were feeling less like visitors and more like squatters.

It wasn't that I didn't like company in general, or my mother and Muldoon in particular, but I had my own psyche to worry about. I wasn't concerned just because, at age thirty, I'd already been divorced for two years. No, I'd managed to downplay the failure of my marriage, because my ex and I were still friendly. It was my career that concerned me more than anything else.

For the past seven years, I'd been working in a downtown Los Angeles firm as a management consultant, a sort of business doctor handling everything from financial facelifts to red-ink bypasses. After what seemed like an eternity, I was finally being considered for a partnership in the firm, competing against two colleagues, both men. It was a make-or-break moment in my career: According to the law of the corporate jungle, the losers were expected to resign or fade into the wallpaper. Aames & Associates had been my first job out of business school, and the most stable thing in my life since my marriage had flatlined. I just wasn't prepared to flunk another of life's little tests. I wanted to stay with the firm as a partner, not as wallpaper.

The problem was, I had less seniority than my two competitors, and I took more risks. That made people nervous. And for at least one voting partner with a festering Napoleon complex, I was, at five feet nine, simply too tall to be a partner. I wasn't a stranger to uncertainty, but the situation at work had left me feeling more vulnerable than at any time in my career. So when I heard Muldoon's stomach gurgling in my ear, it was another solemn reminder that I could still wake up on a warm bed every morning, or, if I wasn't careful, on a burlap sack in the garage.

I was unsympathetic to the leg lifter's demands for more snooze time, because my hair smelled like the Green Room at the Westminster Kennel Club's dog show, and washing it would make me late for work. I rolled out of bed, showered, spritzed some lavender room deodorizer on my head, and put on a borderline prissy white blouse and a navy blue suit because looking corporate was important to my career right now. The skirt exposed a tad too much leg, but at least I'd never been criticized on that front. I completed the outfit with a pair of flat shoes, just for General Bonaparte.

In less than two hours, I was scheduled to meet with my boss, Gordon Aames, founding partner of Aames & Associates, for one last interview before the promotions committee announced its final decision. My performance had to be flawless. I'd overcome a lot of obstacles to get to this crossroads, including a few flaky clients, a streak of stubborn independence, and a neurologist named Dr. Milton Polk.

I'd first heard about a client named Polk in early August, after he sidestepped the customary chain of command at the firm. He'd called Gordon directly, dropped a couple of powerful names, and pushed his project to the head of the line. Polk was passionate about expanding his neurodiagnostic testing center. But expansion plans need more than passion. For starters, Polk needed money, and he wanted someone at Aames & Associates to give him the tools to raise it. He claimed that he'd already developed a group of potential investors through personal contacts and memberships in several medical organizations. Now he needed something in writing to convince them that his ideas were going to make them rich. Fortunately for him, our firm specializes in just that kind of writing.

In reality, the business plan Polk wanted us to research and write wasn't difficult. It would have made a straightforward project for any ordinary consultant. However, when Polk whispered the names of those powerful people in Gordon Aames's ear, he got himself assigned not to an ordinary consultant but to a senior manager, and that senior manager turned out to be me, Tucker Sinclair.

I don't care much for people like Polk, who throw their weight around, but I'd dealt with individuals like him before. The truth was, not all clients came to us with a clear understanding of business or a grasp of adult behavior. Anyway, I could hardly have said no to Gordon. With a partnership hanging in the balance, there was too much at stake. At the time, Polk seemed like the final barrier in my quest for the Holy Grail.

So naturally, I called him immediately to set up a meeting. Polk suggested we get together for lunch at the Auberge, a restaurant in the trendy section of Melrose Avenue. The place reminded me of the cottage in the Alps where little Heidi idled away the days, yodeling and braiding her hair. I arrived early to make sure we got a good table, and found a gas fire hissing in the fireplace and the air conditioner cranked up to snow. In L.A., faux ambiance is everything, but give me a break—it was August, and that fire–air conditioner combo felt a little too bipolar for me. I asked for, and got us, a table on the patio.

That was a mistake. Midday August sun and a business suit turned out to be a bad combination. It must have been ninety degrees outside, with no trace of a breeze. Even under the table's umbrella, I felt the sun tattooing a new crop of freckles on my face and homing in on my dark hair like a heat-seeking missile. I waited forty-five minutes while an intermittent procession of Lexus convertibles, Range Rovers, and the odd Rolls Royce pulled up to the valet parking sign. Not one of the drivers was Polk.

I was getting ready to leave when a dusty blue Mercedes eased up to the curb. You rarely see a dirty car in L.A., especially an expensive dirty car, so this one caught my eye. I half expected to see a bumper sticker that read, *My Other Car Is a Minivan.* The chassis lifted visibly as a barrel-chested man somewhere in his fifties rolled out of the driver's seat. He was of medium height, with black hair, graying at the temples, and an impertinent grin on his face. He was wearing a chocolate brown polyester suit, and as he walked up the patio steps past my table, I noticed an unidentified yellow crumb clinging precariously to his matching brown and beige tie. I'm only a rookie in the fashion police, but I suspected that beneath all that polyester lurked a short-sleeved shirt. After a brief conversation with the maître d', the guy strolled over to my table and sat down. For a brief moment he looked at me as if I were a tall, cold mug of beer.

"So," he said, drawing out the word. "You're Gordon's girl wonder."

I focused on the small crescent-shaped scar on his chin to keep myself from telling him that I might have been Gordon's girl wonder forty-five minutes ago, but after sitting in ninety-degree heat for the better part of an hour, I felt more like a moist towelette. Instead, I smiled and extended my hand. "Good to meet you, Dr. Polk."

"So, shall we get this show on the road?" Polk tried to get the waiter's attention by sweeping his arm back and forth like a windshield wiper, exposing a couple of snags on the arm of his jacket. I was actually enjoying the breeze he'd created until our waiter arrived with two menus and a stony smile. We ordered lunch. I had a salad, while Polk picked at but never finished an entrée and several side dishes that looked like enough potluck for the entire nation of Namibia.

From the moment Polk sat down until well after the dishes had been cleared away, he regaled me with ideas for his business. I gathered from what he said, but mostly from what he *didn't* say, that he was in the process of frittering away his Sherman Oaks neurology practice through neglect. His passion for day-to-day patient care had shifted to a passion for expanding NeuroMed Diagnostic Center, a testing facility he'd opened the year before, where noninvasive tests were administered to patients with disorders of the brain, such as tumors, epilepsy, and learning disabilities.

Polk had a small administrative staff plus five technicians, but he wanted more. He loudly proclaimed high tech as the key to unlocking the secrets of neurological disorders. He seemed to feel he could conquer the world if only he had more floor space, more state-of-the-art equipment, and more centers all across the country, maybe across the world. It wouldn't have surprised me if he planned to go galactic.

I'd done some PubMed research before our meeting, but I hadn't run across any articles about the ultrahigh-tech testing equipment he was talking about. That made me nervous. Still, his ideas seemed coherent. And one or two of his claims sounded interesting.

Even after lunch, he continued drinking endless cups of coffee and droning on about brain stem auditory-evoked response and brain electrical activity mapping until I almost felt a tumor sprouting on my own frontal lobe.

"That all sounds very exotic," I said. "I'm envisioning some guy with a personal computer in Lard Lake, North Dakota, running a wand over his head while Internet software reads his brain and beams the diagnosis back to your office in L.A."

Polk stopped sipping his coffee and blankly stared at me. I wasn't sure if the sudden trickle of perspiration I felt running down my chest was from heat or panic. The last thing I wanted was for him to think I was poking fun at his ideas. It surprised me when he let out a wheezy chuckle that reached all the way to his eyes. For the first time, I noticed that they were brown, like mine. My grandpa Felder had always told me that my eyes were the color of Old Grand-Dad Kentucky bourbon. Polk's were darker, like Kahlúa.

"That's good," he said. "At least Aames didn't stick me with some putz, did he?"

It was getting late, and I had to get back to the office, so I maneuvered the conversation around to the business plan. I told him it would basically be a sales pitch to investors, backed up by solid research and financial and statistical analyses aimed at convincing them to invest their money with him and not somebody else. The plan, I told him, was the key to raising the funds he needed, so it had to be convincing and it had to be credible, and for that I'd need his full cooperation.

"I've done some preliminary demographic research on Neuro-Med's current location," I said. "The good news is that the potential patient population has grown by twenty-seven percent in the past five years. The bad news is that in the next three to six months, two major employers in the area are moving operations out of the state, which means unemployment, loss of health insurance, and a likely decrease in population. That will hurt you, even if the trend doesn't continue. I'll do similar studies on Newport Beach as well as the other locations you plan to open."

He frowned. "Hey, you're running up my tab with numbers that don't mean diddly-squat. You're guessing."

"Maybe so, Dr. Polk, but it's educated guessing."

Business plans aren't very sexy for most people, and talking about statistics frequently makes a client's eyes roll up into the back of his head. With Polk, that discussion seemed to irritate rather than confuse him. I could tell by his fidgeting that he preferred to dwell in the abstract rather than the concrete. In my experience, that was generally not a good sign.

"I'll also need profiles of all your key management people," I told him.

"What for?"

What for? Either he was naive, or he hadn't listened very carefully to my pitch about cooperation. "Because investors want to know who they're dealing with," I said.

"My investors already know who they're dealing with. Listen, I'll tell you what I told them: I'm going to make them millionaires, Tuck. Can I call you Tuck?" He didn't wait for an answer. "When I get this equipment, patients will be clawing at my door."

As hard as it was to smile sweetly with my teeth clenched, I managed it. "I hope that's true, but we have to show them that your people have the depth of experience to handle everything, including rapid growth."

He motioned impatiently to the busboy for more coffee. "Okay, okay. What else?"

"As for your major competitors—"

He interrupted, clearly upset. "Let me educate you about something. Neurology as a specialty is a dead end. Everybody is coming out of the woodwork, horning in on our patients— chiropractors, massage therapists, you name it. Diagnostic testing is where the future is. That's where the money is, too. Like I said before, I'm going to get rich from it, and I plan to take a lot of people there with me. As for competitors, I don't have any. That's why I want to move on this now."

I barely kept the frustration from my voice. "Maybe you don't have competitors now, but you will. And as you well know, Dr. Polk, everyone in the health care industry is your rival for patient dollars."

His eyes were hyperalert, juiced up by caffeine and nervous

tension, and his breathing was getting louder and faster. Maybe I was hitting him with too much too soon.

"Look," I went on, "why don't I outline a few issues for you to think about? Meanwhile, I'll do some further research, and then you and I can meet again in a week or so."

"I don't need a damn thesis. I need a marketing tool. Forget the research. I'll tell you what to write."

"It doesn't work that way, Dr. Polk."

"It works the way I want it to work."

My jaw muscles tensed. "You're not listening to me. Aames and Associates is respected in the industry because—"

"Jesus, how long have you been in this business?"

I had a creepy feeling that the question was rhetorical, but I answered anyway. "Seven years."

"Then you should know what the hell you're doing. I don't want outlines and issues. I want results."

"You'll get results, Dr. Polk, but I can't make this stuff up. I told you the research has to be credible. That takes time."

His eyes narrowed. "I've got news for you: I own you and your time."

I sat for a moment, staring at him, clenching and unclenching my fists. I took a deep breath and repeated to myself over and over, *Partners bring in business; partners do not blow off business*—but it didn't quiet my anger. The guy was a horse's patootie. And if I wanted to spend my afternoon looking at the wrong end of a pony, I'd have become a jockey. Polk had crossed a line. I couldn't let him get away with it. Slowly I pushed my chair away from the table and stood.

"You know something, Dr. Polk? I think you might be better off working with somebody else. Somebody you can communicate with. I'll ask Gordon to reassign you to another consultant."

Polk's mouth inched open wide enough to neigh if he'd wanted to. He studied me for a moment, as if calculating what to do next. A few tense seconds passed, while a little voice inside my head screamed, *What were you thinking?*

Finally, a knowing smile appeared on his lips. "That's the only stupid thing you've said all day, and you don't look stupid. Your boss won't be impressed."

He waited for that to sink in. So did I, and it didn't take long. He was right about one thing: Gordon wouldn't be impressed with my handling of the situation. For the past seven years, he'd pulled me aside—more than once, I admit—whenever I displayed what he called my "tendency to be too direct." And here it was again, practically smacking me in the face. It was time to fade into the backfield and punt or pass or something, but I didn't know what to do with the ball. Thankfully, Polk did.

"Look," he said. "I'm in a hurry. I don't have time to break in somebody new. Sit down. Let's get this meeting over with."

For reasons I didn't want to think about and couldn't have explained, but for which I thanked Glinda the Good Witch, Obi-Wan Kenobi, and the patron saint of lucky breaks, whoever that was, Polk seemed to be offering me a temporary cease-fire. It would have been career suicide not to accept it. I sat and immediately pulled out our standard Aames & Associates contract as well as our Terms & Conditions Agreement, a document that basically says: We'll give you the best advice we can, but don't blame us if things don't pan out. I wanted to get Polk's signature on the papers before I did anything else to blow this situation. Polk skimmed through the pages, and then signed both documents. Afterward, he put my pen in his pocket and pushed back his chair.

"I have to go. I have a one-thirty patient."

I glanced at my watch. "Gosh, it's two-fifteen."

"Don't worry. He'll wait." He grabbed the check and studied it for a moment. Before I had a chance to tell him that Aames & Associates never allows clients to pay for lunch, he patted his back pants pocket.

"I must have left my wallet somewhere," he said. "Do you mind? I'll catch the next one." He handed me the bill. "I love spending Gordon Aames's money. Let's do it again, and soon." He winked and headed toward the street.

While I waited for the waiter to return my credit card, I watched Polk arguing with the valet. I presumed he was testing his missing-wallet theory again. Whatever the doctor was complaining about, his forcefulness proved too much for the poor valet, who eventually threw up his arms and relinquished the keys to Polk's Mercedes. The doctor sidled into the car, which shortly thereafter slipped into the vortex of Los Angeles traffic.

Polk's valet caper confirmed my worst fears: The doctor was going to be a nightmare to work with. I could deal with his take-no-prisoners attitude and his entrepreneur's oversize ego, I thought, but if he ever called me Tuck again, he was going to end up with prosthetic kneecaps.

The following morning, I'd cleared my calendar so I could put all my efforts into the NeuroMed project. Like Polk, I wanted the plan finished quickly. I was on the computer, researching a bill before Congress that threatened to ax Medicare reimbursements—and cut into NeuroMed's profit potential—when I received a telephone call from the doctor.

"I was out of line yesterday," he told me, "with some of what I said. The stuff about owning you. The thesis bit. What can I say? I get intense. No offense meant. From now on, I promise to be good."

His apology left me feeling bewildered and somewhat suspicious. Was his act of contrition sincere, or was he manipulating me? Finally, I decided that his motivation didn't matter all that much, because at the time, maintaining a good relationship with Polk was good for the firm and good for my career.

"Maybe I overreacted," I said. "I'm sorry."

Those had been our first apologies, but they certainly weren't our last. Despite our good intentions, over the next two months we continued to butt heads over everything from whose ideas were more strategic to whose turn it was to buy coffee. He was gruff, bullheaded, impulsive, and sometimes fun to be with.

As insistent as Polk was that I finish the plan quickly, he wasn't always focused on that goal. He frequently interrupted our meetings to rant about his pet peeves, like when he claimed the *New England Journal of Medicine* had gotten it all wrong in an article on balance testing protocols. I quickly learned that if I wanted to get any work done, it was better to indulge his tangents for an hour or so than waste a day denying that I was closed-minded or—what was worse—boring. That "boring" accusation always hit too close to home, because not counting my marriage, I hadn't had a date since the Spice Girls' last hit record. My ex-husband, Eric, and I continued to see each other after the divorce, but those weren't actually dates. They were more like supervised visits to see who got the salad spinner.

I hadn't always liked Milton Polk, but eventually I found things to admire about him, and I knew he felt the same way about me. The guy was an original. He was tireless, like an oversize hummingbird fueling up in a field of wildflowers. Not only that, but he could hold my attention with an idea. So over time, we formed a curious kind of bond.

I won't say that completing the NeuroMed business plan was

all fun and games, but by early October I had completed it. After that, Polk and I didn't see much of each other. At first we kept in touch by telephone, but even those phone calls tapered off as the days rolled by. I went on to other projects for other clients, and Polk presumably went on to sell his expansion ideas to investors.

On that November morning when I dressed for what I thought was imminent success, it had been about a month since I last heard from Polk. I was still high-fiving myself for surviving the experience, glad that the NeuroMed project was behind me. Before heading for work, I made sure that Muldoon's water bowl was full and checked my outfit one last time in the bathroom mirror. Of course, if I'd had any idea what was in store for me when I arrived at the office that day, I would have chucked that prissy blouse and the flat shoes for combat boots and a flak jacket.

2

my employer, Aames & Associates, occupied the fifteenth floor of a smoky-glass high-rise on Hope Street, a building that could only be described as a boring footnote in some architect's fading career. But the building's exterior didn't matter to Gordon Aames. What did matter to him was keeping his overhead low, which he was able to do thanks to a favorable lease agreement.

In addition to the personnel in human resources, marketing, information technology support, and administration, the firm employed around a hundred consultants, a number that had remained relatively stable over the years because Gordon Aames made it his personal mission to avoid layoffs by constantly trolling for clients. Most of our competition hired employees when big projects came into the firm and laid them off when those projects ended, but at Aames & Associates, everybody stayed as long as everybody hustled. If you survived long enough and hustled hard enough, like me, you went from consultant to manager to senior manager until, finally, you got a shot at partner and a move from a small, windowless cubbyhole off a central hallway to an office with a view and potted plants that needed watering, not dusting.

Actually, my office wasn't all that bad, even if it was the only spot of color in a sea of wishy-washy beige. A few months back, the partners had the whole floor redecorated to make the decor more uniform. The new look was fine if you liked paintings that matched the carpet, but to me it felt like working in a sensory deprivation chamber. That's why I smuggled in a colorful Moorish area rug, and a dark wicker lowboy to hold my books and a few tchotchkes. So far, no one had forced me into the United Front for the Elimination of Color, which was good. I wasn't much of a joiner.

I pulled the latest Serrano Seafood profit-and-loss statement from the file cabinet. Gordon was going to love what I had to show him. The company's problems started when Benjy and Gino Serrano's father died, and the brothers each left their respective jobs to take over the family business. Unfortunately, Benjy taught high school French and Gino repaired refrigerators, and neither of them knew much about selling squid. By the time they realized that they were in over their heads, the company was all but pushing up daisies. That's when they'd called me.

When I first brought the Serrano working contract to my firm's managing partners for approval, they thought it spelled failure with a capital *F*, but in the end, they okayed it because they didn't like to turn down business. Once I figured out the Serranos' problem, I set up a new computer system to track their inventory and developed a risky little marketing plan with an ad campaign featuring a grumpy clam in a vat of chocolate—don't ask—and the rest was fine-tuning. In less than five months, the seafood company was showing a healthy profit. The brothers were, shall we say, most grateful. Gordon would be, too, when he saw these figures.

I put my mind into interview mode and headed for Gordon's office, thinking that the only other obstacle I'd face that day was his executive assistant, Marsha Bennett, an officious woman in her mid-forties who needed an antifreeze cocktail just to crack a smile. Frankly, I found her intimidating. There was nothing in Marsha's job description that required her to be nice, only to protect Gordon's flank, and she had that technique down to a science. So even though I had an appointment, I wasn't surprised in the least when she kept me waiting in Gordon's anteroom for ten minutes in an oversize mushroom-colored wing chair that made even *me* feel petite. Marsha had spent too many years in the halls of power not to know a few maneuvers of her own.

When she finally signaled me to go into Gordon's office, I found him with a pained look on his face, rummaging in his desk drawer, obviously looking for something. A moment later, he pulled out a bottle of antacid and popped a couple of tablets in his mouth.

Gordon was sixty-one and a lean five feet ten. He looked tanned and fit, but he was a worrier, and that had taken a toll on him. For a long time, he drank too much—claimed it helped him relax—until an ulcer finally convinced him to stop. Recently, he'd developed an artificial bald spot on the crown of his head from a nervous habit of pulling out his hair. That made a lot of people cringe, but not me. In a way, I felt sorry for Gordon. He took his responsibilities to his clients and employees very seriously, and lately, I'd sensed that the pressure was getting to him.

When Gordon looked up over the top of his wire-rimmed glasses and noticed me standing there, he frowned. That struck me as a little odd, but I ignored it because I was jazzed about the Serrano financial statements and knew he would be, too. I laid the reports in front of him and waited for a few well-deserved *attagirl*s. He thumbed briefly through the pages.

"Nice job," he said.

Nice job? I mean, come on. I thought my chocolate-covered clam deserved better than that. I sank into a leather chair in front of his desk, disappointed by his reaction but determined to maintain a positive attitude. I smiled and waited for my first interview question. When it came, it wasn't at all what I expected.

"Have you ever heard of Mo Whitener, DDS?" he said.

"A dentist named Mo Whitener? You've got to be kidding. Is that short for Molly or Morris?"

"From the letter I got in the mail this morning, I'd say it's short for money." Gordon removed his glasses and massaged the bridge of his nose. "Dr. Whitener represents a group of people who invested heavily with one of our clients. Now they aren't too happy about it. They've hired a lawyer."

"Wow. Mo Whitener, denture capitalist."

Gordon didn't even crack a smile, and that's when I knew I was in trouble.

"The client is Milton Polk," he said.

When I connected the dots—investors, Polk, lawyers—I felt a jolt of alarm. I thought back to our first meeting at the Auberge. It was the only time he spoke specifically about his backers. What did he say? Something about investors already knowing whom they were dealing with. I wondered if Whitener was a friend or colleague who trusted enough to buy into Polk's hyperbole—that everybody was going to get rich from Neuro-Med—without reading my business plan.

"So what does Mo want?" I said. "A twelve-step program for buyer's remorse?"

Gordon put his glasses back on, which only magnified the tension in his eyes. "No. He wants the group's eleven million back, plus attorneys' fees."

I laughed. It was a nervous laugh, but a laugh all the same.

"Eleven million? As in dollars? That's a complete crock, Gordon. In fact, it sounds like Whitener's pulling some kind of scam. The NeuroMed deal was shaky at best. Polk understood that, and so did I. That's why we only asked for three million. Do you honestly believe any savvy investor's going to say, 'Forget three million; I'd rather lose eleven instead'?"

"Polk signed our standard agreements?" Gordon asked.

"Of course."

"And the master copy?"

One by one, I ticked off on my fingers the original Neuro-Med documents that were filed away in my office. "Contract. Terms and Conditions Agreement. Master copy of the final business plan, with Polk's signature on a cover letter and his initials on each page of the document. They're all in a maroon document envelope in my file cabinet."

Gordon didn't respond right away. Finally, he said, "Take a look at this."

He handed me a gray booklet with the firm's logo on the cover, which I assumed was a copy of the NeuroMed plan. I flipped through it until I got to the five-year profit projections. That's when I realized something was wrong. The totals didn't make sense at all. I turned back to the section on strategic issues, which summarized the company's goals and objectives. I felt as if my head were floating away from my body as I read the text. It claimed that NeuroMed had developed revolutionary software that performed complex neurological testing on patients in remote areas via the Internet! It further stated that the company planned to raise twenty-five million dollars to launch NeuroMed.com, and estimated that the initial public offering of stock would generate a minimum of two hundred million dollars on the first day of trading.

"This isn't the report I wrote. Internet testing might be possible down the road, but for now it's science fiction, and so is NeuroMed dot-com. This is all bullshit."

"Yeah, Whitener thinks it's bullshit, too," Gordon said. "He also thinks that since those reports were sent through the U.S. Postal Service it's a little more than that. He thinks it's mail fraud. Whitener claims he invested in NeuroMed based solely on your name and the firm's reputation. He holds you responsible for falsifying this report, and the firm for failing to catch you at it. It's all in the letter, Tucker. He wants the money back by Monday, one week from today. If he doesn't get it, he'll call in the feds."

I saw Gordon's lips move, but I couldn't process the message. All I could think of were a few choice *F* words: *FBI, felony,* and *federal prison.* It wasn't until I read the letter myself that the gravity of Whitener's threat finally sank in. To a business consultant like me, nothing short of claiming that I'd poisoned the entire office staff with my apple brown betty could be worse than an accusation of fraud. Why? Because over the past few years, both individuals and entire companies had been toppled by similar charges. And even though Whitener's allegations were false, they could still damage my reputation and destroy my career at Aames & Associates. If that happened, it would also end my prospects of getting hired at any other consulting firm. I could even lose my house. The best I could hope for was a one-shot book advance for my fall-from-grace memoir.

"Who in his right mind would invest in a dot-com right now?" I said. "Doesn't Whitener read the newspapers? This has to be some kind of horrible mistake."

"Perhaps." Gordon's voice was a low monotone that could only be described as creepy. "But there was a lot of pressure on you to make Polk happy, Tucker, especially with the partner vote coming up. So if you wrote this business plan, I'll understand, but you've got to tell me now."

I suppose Gordon was obligated to ask me that question, but it still hurt. He had always been my champion at the firm, even when it caused problems with the other partners. I didn't think he'd desert me now, but I had no illusions. When push came to shove, he'd protect the firm first, because he had to. It was the one thing he couldn't allow to fail.

"Give me a little credit, Gordon. I try to please all my clients, but I don't invent harebrained rip-offs so they can dot their *Is* with happy faces."

He paused as if weighing his response. A few moments later, he nodded. "Okay, that's a good start. Now, I want you to tell me everything you know about Milton Polk: what you said to him, what he said to you. And, Tucker? Don't leave anything out. Am I making myself clear?"

I tried not to sweat on the leather as I told Gordon as much as I could remember. He stared out the window without saying a word, until I mentioned how the Internet idea had come up at that first meeting.

"Could any of your notes about the Internet have gotten into the final report?"

"I didn't take notes, Gordon. Polk and I were just talking. I made a joke. He laughed. That was the end of it. No way did he have the money to develop that fantasy. Besides, do you actually think I'd deliver a final project to a client without reading it?"

"Obviously, somebody tampered with the data. Who had access to your computer?"

I scanned my brain for a list of names. "Anybody who was alone in my office."

"Did you discuss the Internet scenario with anybody else?"

"A couple of technical people. I guess they could have mentioned it to others."

I didn't tell Gordon, but that included the two other candidates for partner, both of whom had a lot invested in seeing me fail. Only, Mark Ross wasn't conniving enough. He was basically a nice-guy bean counter suffering from imagination deficit disorder. On the other hand, Richard Hastings was a glad-handing sneak who had the ethics of a guy who'd gotten his MBA from a matchbook cover. He was always sniffing around my office, looking for screwups he could exploit. Hastings would love to discredit me, but I didn't think he'd railroad me into federal prison just to beat me out of a promotion.

"Gordon, don't you think the question we should be asking is, who stood to gain the most by tampering with that data?"

"Unfortunately, Whitener has already answered that question, Tucker. He thinks it's us."

My breathing felt thin and shallow as I organized my thoughts and tried, but failed, to suppress a growing feeling of doom. I placed a high value on loyalty to friends, which made what I had to say next even more difficult. Milton Polk and I hadn't exactly locked pinkie fingers and sworn to be best buds forever, but we had developed a friendship of sorts, based on mutual respect. I hoped my hunch was wrong, but at that moment, it was the only one that made sense.

"Look," I said, "I didn't tell you before, Gordon, because I thought it was handled. Polk wasn't happy about my report at first. In fact, he was pretty upset. He didn't think investors would be interested if the projected profits weren't higher. He asked me to add a few zeros. I refused, and he backed off. He finally signed off on the report, but I'm wondering if maybe he decided later to go back and do the math himself."

Gordon's lips looked pale and dry as they slowly parted. "My God, Tucker, what have you done?"

"I told you. I didn't—"

He interrupted. "A client asks you to falsify financial data, and you don't tell me? Why didn't you come to me for help? Don't you understand that Whitener's lawyers can twist that information, make it seem like you were bargaining with Polk?"

I felt as if I had a two-ton hippo sitting on my chest. My mouth was dry and my tongue felt boggy as the words clicked against my palate. "I don't see how anybody can twist anything, Gordon. The point is, the report I wrote—the real one—was well researched and professional. No one could have mistaken the data or my conclusions. Look, I should have told you about Polk. I'm sorry. But when he backed down, like I said, I thought it was handled."

I realized how foolish that explanation sounded now. Obviously, Gordon did, too. "It always amazes me," he said. "People know they can't turn back the clock, but they still make the big mistakes, don't they?" He closed his eyes for a moment, as if he was drawing from some inner strength. When he spoke again, his voice sounded old and defeated, and that frightened me more than anything. "I don't have to remind you who sent Polk to us."

"No, Gordon, you don't."

Wade Covington had been labeled both saint and sinner, depending on who was doing the labeling. I thought of him more as a sinner, especially since I'd discovered that he was lobbying for Richard Hastings to make partner over me. Covington controlled SBI International, a multibillion-dollar conglomerate that relied heavily on consulting services. Our company had just bid on a contract to get some of that business, and like every other consulting firm in the country, the partners would gladly have canonized Covington themselves if they thought it would help their cause.

"If Covington gets wind of any FBI investigation," Gordon said, "we'll lose that bid. Not only that, but we'll lose other clients, too. You know the climate out there, Tucker. It's open season on consultants. Nobody is going to stick by us if we're accused of fraud. The vultures will pick at us until there's nothing left but bones. Reputations, livelihoods—everything will be destroyed."

I thought about my administrative assistant, Eugene Barstok, and my friend and fellow consultant Venus Corday. Both could lose their jobs because of me. Venus would find other work, but Eugene was fragile. What would happen to him? I felt sick.

"Gordon, believe me, okay? I didn't change that report. Not for Polk. Not for anybody."

After a moment, he dredged up a smile, but it wasn't convincing. "I do believe you, Tucker."

I could see he was trying to make me feel better, but the truth was, Whitener's threats could be devastating to all of us. And no one had more to lose than Gordon—except me.

He turned toward his computer and began tapping on the keyboard, searching through what appeared to be an address database. I sat numbly, listening to the click of the keys and staring at an antique pocket sextant he kept on his desk. I'd given it to him for Christmas my first year at Aames & Associates. I'd heard that Gordon's greatest passion, aside from the firm, was a powerboat he kept at a yacht club in Marina del Rey. I was trying to make a few brownie points, I suppose. Right now I wished the thing could navigate me out of the mess I was in.

Gordon's tone was all business now. "Our insurance company won't come near this if the FBI starts breathing down our necks.

We've got to meet with our attorneys, this afternoon if we can. You check in with Marsha later. In the meantime, bring me all the NeuroMed documents ASAP. If we have a little luck, we should be able to head off a crisis. We have to stick together on this, Tucker, convince Whitener and his lawyers that this isn't your work."

The intercom buzzed. Gordon picked up the phone and listened intently before saying, "Let me know the minute he gets here." When he looked up, I saw that a deep crevice had formed between his eyebrows.

"Wade Covington wants to talk to me," he said. "He's on his way over."

I felt a sudden flip in my stomach. "You think he knows about Whitener?"

"I guess we're about to find out. Those documents, Tucker—I need them now."

I turned to leave, but Gordon stopped me.

"By the way, let's keep this Whitener business to ourselves. The only people who need to know are you and I, and the lawyers."

I nodded, but what was Gordon thinking? That I was going to send engraved announcements to the members of the promotion committee? Then it dawned on me. The promotion committee. This meeting was supposed to be my final interview with Gordon before he made his recommendation on my promotion. As I headed back to my office, I tried to stay calm, but all I could think about were leg irons, chain gangs, and cell mates named Spike. Things couldn't get any worse. Not even a chocolate-covered clam could help me now.

3

my administrative assistant wasn't at his desk. In fact, Eugene Barstok wasn't my personal administrative assistant. I actually shared him with three other consultants. But they'd all been in Arizona on a job for the past two months, and during that time he'd adopted me as his personal project. According to office scuttlebutt, the team might stay in Phoenix to open a branch office when their project was finished. If so, Eugene would soon be all mine.

In a way, I was relieved he wasn't around. He always sensed when I was upset, and right now I didn't need any mothering. His absence would give me time to find the NeuroMed documents before he came back and started applying cold compresses.

I was walking toward the file cabinet when I spotted a pink message slip propped up next to my telephone. It was a call from my father's sister, Sylvia Branch. Just what I needed, more trouble. There was only one thing Aunt Sylvia could want: my house.

My beach cottage had been in my father's family since the forties. In the early days, it had been used primarily as a summer getaway, but for the past ten years or so it had been rented out, which is why it had never been remodeled.

Neither my mother nor I had had any contact with my father's side of the family since he died, two months before I was born. My mother is an actor. The Sinclairs never approved of that or her, so when my father passed on, they made it clear that she and I were on our own. Fine. We survived.

My problems began when Grandma Sinclair died eighteen months ago and left the beach house to me. Maybe she felt guilty about all those years of neglect. Maybe she just forgot to ax my name from her will. I guess I'll never know. In any event, Aunt Sylvia apparently couldn't stand the thought of my name on the deed. At first, she'd claimed that the will was invalid because one of the witnesses was underage. When that proved to be false, she said my father had borrowed money from the family that he'd never returned. She argued that I was obligated to repay his debt to the estate, which, with thirty years of interest, turned out to be—surprise—just about what the house was worth. She couldn't prove that bogus debt theory, either.

The sad thing was, she didn't care about the house or its history. What she cared about was the sand that the house sat on, which was worth a couple of million dollars, maybe more. I didn't care about the value of the land, because I never planned to sell the place. For me, the house was hallowed ground because it was my only concrete link to my father.

"That came to my voice mail by mistake." The voice startled me. I looked up to see Venus Corday leaning against the door-jamb, eating chocolate chips from a bag of trail mix. Venus is a foodie and a chocoholic. We'd been friends for five years, ever since the firm recruited her for her expertise in manufacturing. She's in her late thirties, has long, tightly coiled black hair and expressive round eyes the color of French-roast coffee. Men love her, but she's commitment-phobic. However, that didn't stop her from occasionally lecturing me about my own failures with men.

"New client?" she said.

"No. Old aunt."

I didn't know what Aunt Sylvia was up to, and frankly, I didn't want to know. Probate was closed on my grandmother's estate. There was nothing she could do to get the house back now, so I fired up the shredder and made pink confetti.

Venus sat down and draped her arm across the back of the chair. "I heard about the Serrano P and L," she said. "That chocolate clam's going to give Ross and Hastings a bad case of indigestion."

I didn't have time to chitchat, so I headed for my computer. "Yeah, I got lucky."

"Luck?" she said, followed by a hoot of laughter. "Don't play humble with me, honey. You raised Lazarus from the dead. If the Serranos want you to make partner, the committee better listen or somebody is gonna wake up with a horse head in his bed."

I wanted to believe her, but I wasn't the safest choice for partner, even before I had the FBI breathing down my neck. I had the requisite MBA, not from Harvard or Wharton but from UCLA, which was good in a West Coast kind of way. And even though I had a string of successes and happy clients, the race was going to be close. I reminded Venus of all that. What I didn't mention was that if Gordon couldn't fend off Mo Whitener, the race would be over, at least for me.

She just said, "Ha!" and then, "Here, want some?"

I glanced over my shoulder. She had the package of trail mix in her hand, and as she opened the bag wider, a couple of raisins rolled onto the carpet.

"Thanks," I said. "I'll pass."

I copied the final version of the business plan from my computer hard drive onto a disk in case Gordon needed it, and then shifted my focus to the file cabinet, relieved to find the Neuro-

Med folder in its proper place. That relief quickly disappeared when I realized that the sealed envelope containing the signed report, the contract, and the agreement wasn't in the file. I dumped the file contents on my desk and thumbed through each page. Nothing. Nada. Zip. I took a deep breath. Okay, I thought, don't panic. The envelope could be misfiled. Only I didn't think so. Eugene was persnickety about keeping things organized.

"I went out with Anthony last night," Venus said.

I rolled my eyes, making sure she didn't see, and then mumbled, "Who's Anthony?" I didn't listen for her answer, because I was too preoccupied searching through my In basket. I didn't think the NeuroMed documents were there, but I looked anyway.

"Can you believe the first words out of the guy's mouth? 'You must be a parking ticket, cuz you have *fine* written all over you.' If I'd had a gun . . ."

I tore through the paperwork cluttering my desk, while Venus rambled on. I vaguely remember hearing "chocolate soufflé," or maybe it was "chalk it up to foreplay." I wasn't sure, and didn't have time to ask. I'd been in my own thought bubble for what seemed like an eternity before Venus's voice finally broke through.

"Excuse me, Tucker, but you're digging around this office like some dog burying a bone."

Without thinking, I whipped around and blurted out, "I don't have time for one of your date-from-hell stories, Venus. Can't you see I've got problems of my own?"

Her eyes got bigger and rounder, and her face took on that familiar stony pay-attention-or-pay-the-consequences look.

"Sorry," I said, softening my voice, "but a file's missing, and I have to find it—now."

Venus rustled in her chair as if fidgeting would help her decide whether to forgive me. Maybe she would, but not just yet, because her tone was tepid. "Well, I'd love to stay and watch you do that all day, but I've got work to do."

"NeuroMed's business plan," I said, "and the agreement, the one with Milton Polk's signature. Venus, they're missing."

"So?" She cocked her head and studied me intently. "Oh, I get it. You're hiding something from me. You'd better confess, Tucker, before you see my dark side."

"I can't."

She leaned her body toward me. "Let's put it this way: If something bad has happened to you, and I have to find out at the watercooler, your ass is grass and I'm the mower."

I couldn't tell her about Whitener's letter. Gordon would be furious. Then I asked myself, which one would I rather have mad at me: Gordon or Venus?

"Okay," I said, "but you can't tell a soul. Swear?"

She raised her right hand. "On a stack of Bibles, honey."

I closed my door and gave her the abridged version of my meeting with Gordon. She whistled when I told her about Whitener's fraud accusations.

"I hope you didn't do it, girl, because you're not getting any promotion from some cell at Lompoc."

I shot her a look. She held up both hands in defense.

"Ease off. I was just funning you," she said. "But just between you and me, Tucker? If Eugene's filing system is as screwed up as he is, you'll never find that report. I say, tell him to get his bony little ass in here and find it for you."

Venus and Eugene were classic examples of how opposites don't always attract, but she was right. He'd set up the files. He'd know where to look. As I headed for the intercom button on my telephone, the door burst open and Eugene came bustling into my office, wearing a charcoal sweater-vest he'd knitted himself.

Eugene was in his mid-twenties, five feet five, and as thin as a bedsheet in a cheap motel. He had a low tolerance for stress, which sometimes made him prickly, so his therapist suggested knitting as a way to unwind. Unfortunately, her suggestion had made me the beneficiary of an assortment of lumpy bedroom slippers and dozens of snoods, which I suspected would never make a comeback.

Eugene's lips were pursed. He wore a frown aimed directly at Venus as he scooped up her spilled raisins in a tissue he pulled from his pocket, and dumped the whole mess in a nearby waste-basket. He opened one of the file cabinets and ruffled his finger along the plastic tabs.

"Uh, Eugene?" I said. "Excuse me?"

He shrugged. "You're right. I listened on the intercom. Let's move on." He prodded me gently with his elbow. "Stand back. I'll find it."

Venus raised a disapproving eyebrow, but I always weigh grumpy Eugene against good-secretary Eugene and find that his willingness to dust the tchotchkes on my lowboy always tips the scales in his favor.

"So how long were you listening?" I said.

"Long enough."

Gordon had warned me not to tell anyone about the fraud accusations, but at the rate I was going, the whole office would know by the ten o'clock coffee break. Under Venus's disapprov-ing eye, Eugene looked through every file in every cabinet before finally giving up.

"I can't believe it's not here." His tone was flat and full of failure.

"Um-hum." It was all Venus said, but the message was definitely "I told you so." Eugene wasn't confrontational, but I didn't want to test him, so I decided to move things along.

"Okay," I said, trying to sound positive. "I remember when the printer delivered the reports. I compared them with the original document just to make sure that everything was in order, and gave you the master copy to file."

"That's right. A few minutes later you went to Gordon's office for a meeting."

I thought for a moment. "You're right. The Amsterdam project."

The firm had been hired to evaluate the operations of the Juliana Health Clinic and Spa, a chain of resorts in the Netherlands that catered to wealthy Europeans who wanted to stop smoking and get a peppermint foot soak all in the same weekend. The clinics were packed, but they were losing money. The owners wanted to know why.

Gordon was introducing me as the project manager at that meeting. The assignment was a big coup. Secretly I thought of it as my reward for surviving two months of Milton Polk. Either way, being chosen was good for my career. I'd even gotten my own company Visa card for travel to Amersterdam—platinum, no less—a privilege reserved only for partners. The gesture seemed prophetic, and I'd been distracted.

"I called the mail room just like you told me," Eugene continued, "and got Cherry to deliver the box of reports. I went to lunch, and when I came back, the box was gone."

An alarm went off in my brain. "Could Cherry have accidentally sent the original documents to Polk?"

"I don't think so, Tucker," he said. "I distinctly remember filing them."

Venus rolled out of the chair and stood. "Tell you what I'm thinking, Tucker. You suck up trouble like a Hoover."

I looked at Eugene. "Has anybody asked to see the file lately?"

He thought for a moment and then shook his head. "Not that I know of."

"Are you sure? What about Dr. Polk?"

He frowned. "No, I'd remember that."

One of the other consultants could have borrowed the file for some reason, but that seemed unlikely. They would have asked my permission. I wondered if Milton Polk had manipulated Cherry into bringing him the originals. Maybe, when she'd delivered the box of reports, he'd told her the originals were supposed to be included and sent her back to find them. Only, that didn't make sense. She wouldn't have taken documents from my office without telling somebody.

On the other hand, maybe Polk took the stuff himself. He'd been in my office on several occasions. He could have slipped in when I wasn't around, found the NeuroMed file between the *Ms* and the *Os*, and made off with it. The receptionist wasn't supposed to let people wander around unescorted, but Polk was a client, and receptionists weren't infallible. I just hoped Eugene hadn't screwed up and was afraid to tell me.

"Okay, let's eliminate Cherry as the culprit," I said. "Call her in the mail room and see if she remembers taking the documents."

Eugene paused. His face was the color of alabaster. "I can't. Cherry got an acting job. Friday was her last day."

I sank into my chair and propped my head in my hands. "Damn actors. This can't be happening."

Eugene leaned against the wall. His breathing was becoming quicker and more irregular. "What are we going to do?"

"I have to talk to Dr. Polk," I said, "and find out what he knows about this."

"Look," Venus said. "No one wants you to get out of this mess more than I do, but if the doctor is behind this, he's not going to tell you anything. And if you accuse him without any evidence, you're just gonna piss him off. Let Gordon and the lawyers handle it."

I tuned her out and dialed NeuroMed's number. The line was busy. I tried the number several more times to make sure I'd dialed correctly. Same annoying blare. That was odd for a business. I tried Polk's home number. A machine answered. I left a message.

I grabbed my purse from inside the desk drawer and threw the disk with the report I'd just copied into its place. A computer file wasn't worth much without the signed hard copies.

"I'm going to NeuroMed," I announced.

"Tucker, what you're doing is dangerous," Venus said. "If you go charging into Polk's office like Dirty Harry, believe me, it's not gonna make his day. Yours, either. Shit, what if he calls the police? I know you. I'm gonna flip on the six o'clock news and see a thousand cops chasing you and that yuppie car of yours down the 405."

"Oh, come on, Venus, don't get yourself all worked up. I can handle Milton Polk." My tone carried a lot more confidence than I felt.

She shook her head in frustration. "You're making a mistake." She held out the bag of trail mix. "At least take this. I just hope it's not your Last Supper."

There were one or two coconut swirls left in the bag, and a few dried-up old raisins. The chocolate chips were long gone.

I tilted my head and raised an eyebrow. "You ate all the good stuff."

"I thought you liked that health food shit." She gave the bag one final appraisal and threw it in the wastebasket.

"I'm so sorry, Tucker," Eugene said. "This is all my fault. I should never have gone to lunch. I should have watched your office more carefully, should have locked the file cabinets."

Eugene's hands were pressed against his chest. He seemed disoriented—a look I knew all too well. I saw snoods in my future. His angst seemed over the top to me, but it kept his therapist busy counseling him not to "should" all over himself.

"Relax," I said, gently patting his back until his breathing slowed. "I'm going to straighten everything out. You'll see. I'll drive over to NeuroMed, pick up the documents, bring them back here so our lawyers can show them to Mo Whitener and get me out of trouble."

I cracked open the door to make sure no one was standing outside. I didn't want Gordon to see me leaving the building, especially since at that moment I was supposed to be in his office with the NeuroMed documents. Obviously, I couldn't produce them just yet, and I didn't want to give him an opportunity to ask me why not.

"If anybody asks," I went on, "you don't know where I am."

I didn't want to worry either Venus or Eugene, but if Polk had those NeuroMed documents and wouldn't give them back, or worse yet, had destroyed them, it would be a disaster. Without the doctor's signature on the original business plan, the contract, and the Terms & Conditions Agreement, there was no way to verify that he'd approved a more conservative expansion strategy. No way to authenticate for Whitener's lawyers that the profit projections I'd calculated were much lower than the ones mailed to investors. No way to keep Whitener from filing a civil lawsuit to recover his money. He'd go after everybody but especially the deep pockets, and that was Gordon, but I'd be dragged into the long and costly legal battle as well. The firm would probably survive, but I'd be ruined both professionally and financially.

And that was the good part. If Whitener chose instead to report me to the FBI, I'd be investigated, maybe arrested, and maybe sent to prison. And while I was making license plates and eating off metal trays, Aunt Sylvia would find some way to get her hands on my house.

Okay, so I should have gone to Gordon when the problems with Polk first surfaced, but somehow I'd gotten the notion early in life that asking for help was a sign of weakness. Now what I'd always seen as strength—my independence—Gordon saw as a character flaw.

Charging off to confront Milton Polk was probably another one of those big mistakes Gordon had just warned me about, but I was convinced that Polk would respond better to me than he would to a pack of snarling lawyers. Besides, I couldn't just stand by and do nothing. I had to find out who was setting me up. If it was Polk, and he'd gotten his hands on those original documents, he was going to give them back, or I was going to take one of his cheesy polyester ties and wring his devious little neck.

4

oments later, as I left my office and headed for the parking garage, I tried to remember what, if anything, I'd done differently with Polk than I had with my other clients. It didn't take long to come up with an answer: everything. I'd babied, cajoled, compromised, and placated him far more than I had anybody else, because I wanted us both to succeed. So what had I done to make him angry enough to set me up for federal fraud charges? Unfortunately, I could take a stab at answering that question, too.

Gordon had just asked me to tell him everything about Milton Polk, but I'd spared him a few of the gorier details. The truth was that shortly after I started working on Polk's business plan, I realized that his vision for NeuroMed wasn't feasible, even with the money he hoped to raise. The equipment cost millions, and the major insurance companies had, so far, refused to reimburse patients for testing fees. With clever marketing, Polk could bring in some patients on a self-pay basis, but that wouldn't be enough money to interest investors.

I had advised Polk to scale back his plans, ask for a smaller amount of money, and concentrate on improving the existing facility before opening others. He refused. So by the time the final report was written, the singular NeuroMed Diagnostic Center had become the decidedly plural NeuroMed Diagnostic

Centers and looked less like Cinderella and more like her ugly stepsisters. I tried to talk to Gordon about the situation, but he was too busy with his own clients. In the end, his input didn't really matter, because nothing was going to put a better spin on the data.

I had known Polk would be livid when he read my conclusions. He might even refuse to accept the plan. If so, all my hard work would end up as a freeway pileup. Richard Hastings would gloat, and why not? He'd be partner, and I'd be wallpaper. I couldn't let that happen, so I decided to make one last-ditch effort to persuade Polk to listen to reason. It was against my own rules, but I was going to let him preview a copy of the final business plan. I thought that when he saw the truth laid out in front of him on twenty-four-pound bond, he'd finally listen and agree to change his approach. If so, he'd succeed rather than fail. I'd look like a brilliant strategist. Clients would clamber for my services. Oh—and one more thing: I'd be the newest partner at Aames & Associates. At least, that had been the plan.

I arranged for Polk to join me at what had become our favorite meeting place, a small coffeehouse in Venice with thrift store tables, Toulouse-Lautrec posters, and a series of teenage counter clerks who looked like dropouts from the same cut-rate drug treatment center. Luckily, the coffee was bitter, so we generally had the place to ourselves. Polk was in good spirits when he arrived, but, as I suspected, when he read the business plan his pleasant expression turned into an angry scowl.

"What the hell are you trying to pull here?" His tone had been quiet but menacing. "This makes me look like a loser."

"None of this information should come as a surprise to you. We've been discussing it for weeks. Listen, there's still time to downsize your short-term goals. If you give investors a healthy return on their money in this first phase, it'll pique their interest for the next—"

Polk interrupted. His face was flushed, and his voice was taut with righteous indignation. "Slow growth makes sense if some schmuck is running the show. But this is *me* we're talking about. I have the energy of ten tight-assed CEOs getting five-million-dollar-a-year bonuses for doing nothing but screwing over stock-holders. You know that."

"Look, I admire your confidence and your energy, Dr. Polk, but investors want more than—"

"Profit projections are estimates!" he roared. "I paid you to estimate in my favor. Instead, you're trying to destroy me, to kill me. That's what you want. You've already stabbed me in the back. So go ahead. Finish the job."

He held his arms out in surrender, as if he expected me to pick up a plastic stir stick and lunge for his carotid artery. I'd never seen him so angry. I kept my hands clasped in my lap under the table because they were trembling. He ranted for what seemed like an eternity. Finally, the clerk came out from behind the counter and shouted, "Hey, man, chill, okay?"

That distracted Polk long enough for me to say, "I'm sorry. Obviously, you're not happy. I'll ask Gordon to waive my fee. You can go to another firm."

Polk stopped shouting, but I could see that he was still seething inside. He threw down a ten-dollar bill that he'd pulled from his wallet, and stood to leave. Paying for the coffee without our usual skirmish unsettled me more than anything. I sensed that an important balance had been upset that would never be made right again.

His eyes looked angry and wounded. "You screwed me over,

lady," he said. He stared at the NeuroMed plan lying on the table. A moment later, he picked it up and stormed out the door.

It's always bad news when you make a client angry, but even worse news when someone as important as Wade Covington refers that client. I knew Polk couldn't make a case against the research or conclusions in my report. They were both solid. But he could cause problems by complaining about my attitude to Gordon, or worse, to Covington.

But as I'd just explained to Gordon, Polk had backed off. In fact, he called me the following day, calm, almost chipper, and told me he'd decided to accept my slow-growth proposal. I was to revise the plan and send him a hundred copies as soon as I could get them printed. When I asked why he'd changed his mind, all he said was, "I thought about what you said, and you were right."

His sudden flip-flop smelled fishy, but it wasn't the first time Polk had made me feel like a yo-yo on a string. I figured, why look a gift horse in the mouth? I gave the guy some good advice, and he took it. So I retooled the plan to make the goals and financial projections more reasonable, printed a hundred copies, and had Cherry deliver them.

Now I wondered if Whitener knew about that draft report and had somehow misconstrued it. Maybe he thought I had kept revising and revising until I came up with the phony Internet idea. Whatever. There was no time to speculate about that now. I had to get to NeuroMed and talk to Polk about those missing documents.

It took only minutes to get from my office to the parking garage. At ten o'clock I slid into the front seat of my Boxster, still feeling a twinge of guilt for leaving Eugene in the middle of one of his panic attacks.

I put the top down to get some air. Polk had always given me a bad time about the silver Porsche, accusing me of overcharging him in order to pay for it. He was joking, but he'd gotten under my skin a few times. In reality, the car had been a surprise gift from my then-husband, Eric Bergstrom, who'd thought that my ten-year-old Toyota Camry wasn't sending the right message to my clients. I'd been upset when I found out what he'd paid for it, but after a cooling-off period, I had to admit, my heart melted. I was in love. Not with Eric, of course—with the car. Eric and I lasted a couple more months before calling it quits, but the Boxster and I were in it for the long haul. Besides, if the Milton Polk fiasco meant the end of the road for my career, at least I'd have gotten there in a zippy car.

The wind was surprisingly chilly as I jockeyed my way through the downtown traffic onto the 10 Freeway toward L.A.'s Westside. My problems aside, it was a beautiful fall day. The sun beat down on the Hollywood Hills, making the houses dazzle against the hillside greenery. A half hour later, I pulled into the hospital's parking garage.

NeuroMed was located in a back wing of Bayview Medical Center, just north of Venice Boulevard in West Los Angeles. The hospital had a sterling reputation, but because of stingy insurance reimbursements from HMOs and PPOs, Bayview had begun to suffer from a corresponding number of IOUs. So for a modest cut of the gross, the hospital leased space to Polk and allowed him full use of the facilities. Access was through the main hospital lobby, so few patients suspected that the two weren't one and the same. Polk felt that gave NeuroMed a symbiotic credibility, a competitive edge. I agreed.

The hospital's lobby was permeated by dueling odors: acrid disinfectant from a mop bucket·and sweet carnations from the nearby gift shop. A half-dozen people waited in uncomfortable-looking plastic chairs, some watching television, others reading or staring into space. When I got to NeuroMed, the door was locked. First the busy telephone line earlier, now the locked door. Not good signs. I knocked.

"Hello. Is anybody in there? Francine. It's Tucker Sinclair."

Francine Chalmers was Polk's office manager. I'd interviewed her briefly for the business plan. Around Polk her behavior fell somewhere between schoolgirl crush and hero worship. With me she'd been helpful but distant. I hadn't seen her in a couple of months, but I was sure she'd remember me. I knocked harder on the heavy wooden door, calling her name again.

Finally, it opened a crack, and Francine's face appeared. She was an attractive woman in a 1950s kind of way. Her fine blond hair was salon teased and sprayed; I wondered how she kept the shape between appointments. She was a tad on the plump side, but I could see through the crack in the door that the drape of the lavender silk jacket she was wearing camouflaged any serious flaws. The overall impression was flattering.

"What do you want?" Her voice was brittle.

Not exactly a hale and hearty hello, but I could work with that.

"I have to talk to Dr. Polk," I said. "I called earlier, but the line was busy."

"He's not here." Her hands were pushing against the door, and her periwinkle blue eyes seemed focused on keeping me out. I wondered why.

"Then where is he?" I said. "It's important."

"I don't know."

Yeah, sure, I thought. I pushed gently on the door and pressed my face to the opening to get a better look. She pushed back. If she slammed the door on my mouth, I knew I'd end up with a permanent case of fish lips.

"Francine, let me in," I demanded.

She was strong, but my flat shoes gave me better traction. I shoved until the wedge widened enough to accommodate my foot. One last push, and I was inside.

I scanned the office, starting in the waiting room, traveling across the reception counter to the front office. "Holy shit! What happened in here?"

Office supplies and medical charts were strewn about, nearly concealing the linoleum floor. It looked as if a minitornado had blitzed through the room. Either that or someone had been looking for something. I sure hoped it wasn't the NeuroMed documents. I had visions of Mo Whitener on a search-and-destroy mission, trying to get to them before I did.

Francine followed close behind me as I walked through the open door that separated the waiting room from the front office. Inside, on a nearby desk, a telephone button blinked on hold. The receiver lay on a chair. When Francine saw me eyeing that, she became defensive.

"I just couldn't talk anymore. When I came in this morning, this . . ." Her arms flailed helplessly, jangling the gold bracelets on her wrist. "I canceled patients and sent everyone home."

"Anything missing?"

"I can't tell yet."

The break-in at the Center was one more banner headline in a bad-news day. I took a couple of deep breaths, trying to stay calm and objective, because I didn't want to believe that this mess had anything to do with Milton Polk or the missing NeuroMed documents. I walked into a small storage room off the front office, where the patient medical charts were kept, and set my car keys and purse on top of a file cabinet. I used my foot to flip over several files on the floor, hoping to see that familiar maroon envelope. No luck.

"You think somebody was looking for drugs?" I asked hopefully.

"We don't keep drugs here," she informed me. "There's nothing to steal except the equipment, and it's too heavy to move. It was probably one of the doctors looking for a chart or something. Some of them have short fuses."

"A doctor would do this?" I asked. Visions of that kindly TV doctor, Marcus Welby, flitted through my memory. It was an image I couldn't quite reconcile with the mess in front of me. Francine must have it wrong.

"Talk to a few nurses," she said defensively. "They'll tell you. Sometimes anything—even a misfiled patient record—will set them off."

I stepped over a plastic box filled with computer disks that had been overturned, its lid cracked.

"Have you called hospital security?"

"No, and I'm not going to." Her voice sounded determined.

Her position was hard to understand. The place was a shambles. Even if it did turn out to be a histrionic doctor, the hospital should know it had granted privileges to some nutcase. So why didn't she want to tell anybody? It didn't make sense . . . unless she was hiding something.

Francine walked around the room, randomly picking up a couple of dozen medical charts, fumbling to keep the metal cover brackets from snagging the silk of her jacket. Then she slipped them into the drawer of a nearby desk.

"I don't think we should touch anything," I warned. "I think we should find Dr. Polk."

Francine paused for a moment. Near her foot was a coffee cup with its handle broken off. It read, *Worrier Princess*. She picked it up, along with the broken handle, and set it on a cart.

She frowned in frustration. "I told you, I don't know where he is."

"Have you called his home?"

Francine reached to quiet a tic that had begun pulsing under her left eye. "I called his wife, for all the good it did." The comment had a clear implication, as in *she-devil, wife from hell*. "She was in Santa Barbara for the weekend and just got back. She claims she doesn't know where he is."

"You sound like you think his wife is lying about his whereabouts."

"I didn't say that. She probably doesn't know—or care."

I could barely keep the panic out of my voice. "Wait a minute. Are you telling me nobody knows where he is? What about a pager? A cell phone? A homing pigeon? Help me out here."

Her eyes filled, and a tear splashed onto her cheek. She dotted it away with a middle finger. I noted she was careful not to smudge her blush.

"I tried his pager. He won't answer." She began searching in the folds of lavender silk for something but came up empty. Still sniffing, avoiding my eyes, she located a box of tissue on a nearby desk. The box was crushed but still dispensing.

I softened my voice because I felt guilty for making her cry. "When was the last time you saw him?"

"Friday," she said, kneading the tissue. "Dr. Polk left early. He seemed upset. Said he'd come back, but he didn't. When I came in this morning, his tux was still hanging on the back of his office door. That's when I knew something was wrong."

Friday was three days ago. My mouth felt dry, but I managed to say, "From a tux on a door?"

"He had a dinner on Saturday," she said. "An important one. Black tie."

Attending a formal dinner with his wife out of town? Not unheard of, but a little odd. Polk had never discussed his family or anything else about his personal life with me. Maybe he and his spouse had an open marriage, or maybe Francine had her information wrong. Wrong or not, it was strange that Francine seemed to know more about the doctor's schedule than his wife did.

"He could have changed his mind and worn a suit," I offered.

"He wouldn't have done that. He was meeting someone."

"Like who?"

She formed a cage around her mouth with her fingers and stared at me for a moment. "I don't know. But this feels bad."

My palms felt sweaty, and I had to remind myself to breathe. I didn't need to hear "bad." I needed to hear "good." "Bad" was not good.

"Have you called the police?"

"What good would it do?"

"It would do good if it's bad," I said. "Maybe he was in a car accident, in the hospital, can't remember who he is, crying out your name."

I was working myself into a hissy fit. I imagined finding Polk on his deathbed with me at his side, whispering in his ear the last words he'd ever hear: "WHY ARE YOU TRYING TO RUIN MY FRIGGING LIFE?"

Francine moistened her lips and swallowed audibly. "I don't want the police."

Did she have police phobia or just a case of denial? Hard to tell. I didn't buy her crazed-doctor theory, but I didn't have time to worry about it, either. If Milton Polk had the original Neuro-Med documents, I had to get them back, and the only way to do that was to find him. Maybe Francine had misunderstood about the dinner. Maybe Polk had gone to Las Vegas to hustle showgirls. But a horrible feeling had begun churning in the pit of my stomach, telling me I wasn't going to find him anytime soon.

By now, Francine's tissue was in shreds. She looked completely defeated, and for a moment I wondered if there was more than employee loyalty that kept her tied to the doctor.

"Go ahead, then," she said. "Call the police if you want, but I don't want them coming here."

Didn't want them coming here? Did she actually think I could control the Los Angeles Police Department? Not even the chief could do that. The truth was, I didn't know if someone would take the report over the telephone or in person. All I knew as I dialed the number was that my hands were trembling.

A female officer answered my call. She asked a lot of questions that I couldn't answer, like what had Polk been wearing when he disappeared, and who had seen him last. In the middle of describing the scar on Polk's chin, I was abruptly transferred to a detective named Kleinman. Francine clamped her lips together as she listened to a long series of "uh-huhs" before I hung up.

"What's the matter?" Her voice was strained. "Why didn't you finish? What did he say?"

"He doesn't think Dr. Polk's missing," I said cautiously.

"What do you mean? Where is he?"

"Someone's coming over. They want to show us some pictures."

"Pictures?" she said. "What on earth for?"

Well, that was the hard part: the "What on earth for?" Poor Francine. Poor me. Amazing how much deeper the shit I was in had just become.

5

I'd told Francine that the police were coming to the Center to show us some pictures, but I hadn't told her everything Detective Kleinman had said, especially not the part about a body that had been found on the beach near the Venice pier late Sunday evening, and definitely not the part about Kleinman suspecting that the body was Milton Polk's. I didn't tell her, partly because it was hard enough to deal with my own shock over Polk's death. Francine had been devoted to him, and I didn't know how she'd react. I decided to let the police handle it.

Lucky for me, Francine didn't ask any further questions about my conversation with Kleinman. She was obviously in denial. After I hung up the telephone, she stepped up her efforts to tidy up the office. I tried to persuade her to let the police look around first, to make sure we weren't contaminating a crime scene, but she was adamant that there had been no break-in. It was true that there were no signs of forced entry. So maybe she was right. Still, I felt apprehensive, even as I pitched in to help her sort through the debris. After a while, Francine took a stack of patient charts, walked down the hallway to her office, and closed the door. I left her alone.

I'd been gone from my office long enough to be missed, so I used my cell phone to check in, but Gordon was out and

Marsha-the-Popsicle-queen hadn't heard anything about the attorney meeting. I gave her my number, but she seemed on edge, so I didn't keep her on the line. I wasn't sure what to tell Gordon anyway. He didn't even know that the NeuroMed documents were missing—maybe permanently missing. Even if they were still around somewhere, with Polk dead, finding them and getting Mo Whitener off our backs was going to be difficult if not impossible.

At least an hour or more had passed since I'd spoken with the detective. Francine was still in her office, and I was beginning to wonder if Kleinman had forgotten about us when I heard two quick taps on wood. Before I could react, the door opened and a man entered. He was on the far side of forty, five ten, thinning brown hair, and a neat little mustache on a face with enough crags and crannies to qualify as interesting. He was wearing sharply creased black slacks, a matching houndstooth check sports jacket, and a tie that looked snappy but not flashy. As a package, he wasn't all that bad, except for his hairstyle, which definitely needed an update to one of the more recent decades.

"Detective Duane Kleinman, LAPD," he said. "Are you . . . ?" He consulted a small spiral notebook.

"Tucker Sinclair," I said.

He looked up from his notebook and studied me. The hint of a smile trailed across his lips, as if he liked what he saw. Then he pulled a business card from his pocket and handed it to me. When I read his title, a tingling sensation crept up my neck.

"This says you're a homicide detective."

"That's right."

"You think Dr. Polk was murdered?"

"We don't even know if it's your missing doc yet," he said. "Like I told you on the phone, he wasn't carrying a wallet. I'd like you to take a look, but I have to warn you, he's a little banged up."

I didn't want him to think I was a wuss, so I said, "Don't worry about me."

Kleinman pulled a Polaroid photo from his coat pocket and placed it on the desk in front of me. I leaned over to get a better look. The face of the man in the picture was gray. No, not gray exactly. It was more like colorless, except for a purple, gooey hole in the forehead. The features were barely recognizable. Part of his nose was missing. His eye sockets were empty, gaping holes. His mouth stretched into a macabre grin. He was wearing off-the-rack brown polyester that could have belonged to any of a thousand men, except that it didn't. Even if I hadn't spotted that familiar crescent scar on his chin, I'd have known by the suit that the man in the photo was Milton Polk.

Ambient noise in my head blocked out all other sounds. A blend of fascination and revulsion kept my eyes fixed on the picture until my face contorted and my throat began to close. Only one question stormed through my head: Was the trashcan within barfing distance? Firm hands gripped my shoulders and guided me to a chair.

"That him, ma'am?"

I looked into Kleinman's hazel eyes and nodded. "Where's his nose?" This was good. This was investigative reporter stuff.

"Fish," he said. "Looks like he was in the water for at least twenty-four hours."

"What happened?"

"He drowned, according to the autopsy."

I'd never seen an autopsy, but imagining Polk on a dissecting table brought back painful memories of tenth-grade biology, a dead frog, and what I had to do to get an A.

"He's got a hole in his head." I said it as though I were telling Kleinman something he didn't know.

His voice was gentle, more so than I expected. "Body gets tossed around pretty good in the surge. Could have hit something sharp while he was down there. Like rocks or debris."

While I impressed the detective with my clever incisive questions, Francine had slipped out of her office and moved to a position behind my chair. She stood in freeze-frame, wide-eyed and silent, gaping at the picture. Her hand clenched the lavender jacket close around her throat. I heard low, guttural keening and felt air rushing past by my cheek. Kleinman managed to catch her just before she melted onto the floor.

Needless to say, that put a damper on Kleinman's interview, but didn't stop it altogether. After a brief delay to allow Francine to compose herself, he resumed asking questions. He seemed particularly interested in finding out why Polk's wife hadn't reported him missing. Francine was in no shape to theorize, and I explained that I'd never met the woman. The only concrete information Francine offered was Mona Polk's name and home telephone number, which she recited from memory. After an hour or so, Kleinman finally gave up and allowed Francine to lock up the office and go home.

I didn't want to think about Milton Polk's death anymore, but Kleinman seemed bent on continuing his interview. I had no choice but to grab my purse and allow him to nudge me into a quiet corner of the hospital cafeteria. While he thought I wasn't looking, he straightened his tie and hiked his pants over the hint of a paunch. He bought us each a cup of tepid coffee. I hadn't eaten since breakfast, so the oil slick floating on the surface of the java didn't look exactly appetizing. The detective pulled up a chair for me beside his and then studied me carefully.

"Calvin Klein," he said. I waited for the punch line. "Your suit. Looks like Calvin Klein. I used to be a ragman. Know what that is?"

I raised my palms in the international you-got-me sign.

"Apparel business. Doctor told me to get a job with less stress, so I joined the Department." He shook his head and chuckled.

Then he asked if I minded if he took a few notes. Notes, I thought. Why did he need to take notes? I didn't know anything about Milton Polk's death. But he didn't wait for my answer, just took out a pencil and the same tablet I'd seen earlier and asked me to spell my name. Then he took down my address and phone number, too. It gave me the creeps that my personal statistics were going to be in a police file somewhere.

"I just can't believe he's dead," I said. "What was he doing at the beach anyway?"

"Like I told you before, we don't know. He was alive when he went in the water. Could be accidental drowning, or maybe suicide. You think the doc was the type to kill himself?"

I paused, but not for very long, because the notion was ridiculous. "No. I mean, he had his ups and downs, but he was an entrepreneur at heart. What sends the rest of us into therapy was just a day at Magic Mountain for him."

Kleinman rocked back in the chair and tapped the eraser end of a pencil on his knee, like a drummer. He asked me if Polk had been in poor health, or despondent over a loss or a death in the family, or had marital problems. Every "I don't know" reminded me how little I'd actually learned about the man.

It was only when Kleinman asked if Polk had had any financial difficulties that I paused. Telling Venus or Eugene about Mo Whitener's accusations was one thing, but telling Kleinman was quite another. I tippy-toed around the subject by explaining that Polk had wanted money to expand NeuroMed and that I'd helped him write a business plan to present to potential investors. Aside from that, I told him that there were no other financial pressures I knew about. I didn't see how Whitener's charges of fraud could possibly relate to Polk's death, unless Whitener compensated for being a bad businessman by being a good hit man. That seemed a little far-fetched. On the other hand, if Polk's death wasn't an accident or suicide, then someone had killed him. That was a sobering thought.

Kleinman's tablet remained on the table, but he didn't make any more notes in it. He just continued nodding and drumming and rocking in his chair, listening politely to whatever I said. His hazel eyes sparkled with interest, but his facial muscles remained slack, betraying no emotion at all.

"When was the last time you saw the doc?"

"A few weeks ago, I guess."

His mouth turned up in a reassuring smile. "You didn't see him or hear from him at all this past weekend?"

I told him no, that except for a trip to Trancas Market for tomatoes and mozzarella cheese, I'd stayed at home all weekend, mostly alone, mostly working. I almost told him that no one had called, either, but that seemed a little too pathetic.

After a few more questions he smiled again. "Sure appreciate your cooperation." Then he added, "By the way, is there anything you think I should know that I haven't asked?"

I knew I'd paused too long when I saw him frown.

"I think somebody broke into NeuroMed over the weekend," I said.

All rocking and drumming stopped, as well as any smiling or polite questioning. Kleinman's facial muscles hardened.

"And you're just getting around to telling me now?" He sounded irritated.

I used an airy tone to cover my nervousness. "Better late than never."

He frowned but listened without interrupting while I told him what Francine had said about the tux, the dinner, and Polk's mystery meeting. This time he took notes, lots of them. His response to Francine's theory that the office had been tossed by a doctor having a temper tantrum was a chilly "You don't really believe that's what happened, do you?" and I had to say, "No."

"You destroyed evidence." His voice was stern, almost angry, and rightly so, but what was I supposed to do, wrestle Francine to the ground to keep her from contaminating his crime scene?

"I didn't destroy anything," I countered.

"It's called aiding and abetting, ma'am," he said. "You may have just helped a killer get away."

Not me, you dickhead, I thought. Francine helped a killer get away. I wanted dull-but-pleasant Kleinman back. Badass Kleinman was getting on my nerves. He continued grilling me, asking me over and over again: Why had I come to NeuroMed this morning? When did I arrive? What did the room look like when I got there? Who else did I see? My prissy white blouse got so damp from nervous perspiration that I found myself wishing dress shields were back in style. When he finally finished scribbling in his notebook, he slapped it closed and told me that either he or his partner would be in touch.

As he stood to leave, I said, "By the way, you got the wrong Klein."

He looked annoyed. "Beg your pardon, ma'am?"

"My suit. It's Anne, not Calvin."

He looked at me for a moment, then smiled, but the sparkle in his eyes was now less of interest and more of suspicion. "Bad call, I guess."

"Yeah. Tell me about it."

Detective Kleinman abandoned me to the smell of old French fries and a feeling of dread. Maybe he and I could be friends if we really tried, but at this point Jimmy the Greek wouldn't have taken those odds.

It was after five, but I tried once more to reach Gordon. I got only voice mail and more frustration. I dumped the coffee and headed toward the exit. Maybe my life would have been better if at the moment of conception my parents had been watching *Breakfast at Tiffany's* instead of groping each other in the backseat of a Corvair, listening to a National Public Radio special on Sophie Tucker, the "last of the red-hot mamas." Then my name might have been Audrey. Audrey was a stand-alone name. Nobody messed with it. There would have been no Tuck, Tuckie, T-bird, or Friar, and no temptation for creative rhymesters. If my name were Audrey, I'd be hustled by Hollywood's hunk du jour, not macho jerks whose nicknames were Bulldog or Spud and whose idea of a romantic gift was a nose-hair trimmer. This is the kind of deep thinking I do when I'm looking for my car in parking garages and trying to forget my troubles.

When I finally found the Boxster, I reached into my purse to get my keys, but they weren't there. I checked my pockets. Nothing. I tried to remember where I'd last seen them, but with all the confusion, I couldn't recall. I walked back to the cafeteria and looked around the table where Kleinman and I had been sitting. They weren't there, either. Just what I needed—an eighty-buck round-trip cab ride home so I could search my desk drawer for spare keys I hadn't seen since I got the car.

The smell of onion rings from the cafeteria was making me so woozy, I actually thought about offering to buy Kleinman dinner in exchange for a ride home. I was reaching for my cell phone to call him when I remembered something. I hurried toward NeuroMed, knowing that everyone was gone for the day, but hoping to find a maintenance worker or someone with a key to let me in.

The outside door was closed, but just as I always check the coin tray in a pay phone, knowing it will be empty, I turned the knob. To my surprise, it was unlocked. Maybe Francine had come back. Maybe it was the cleaning crew—or maybe someone else. That thought created a fluttering sensation in my stomach. I wondered if Kleinman had left the building yet.

My breathing stopped as I listened for any sounds. There was nothing but silence. The broomlike weather stripping brushed against the floor as I quietly pushed open the door. The waiting room was dark and empty, but from what I *could* see, everything seemed just as we'd left it. The door leading to the front office was still propped open. I made my way past the receptionist's desk, dragging my hand along the nubby wall to guide me in the dark. At the end of the hall, I saw a thin ray of light from Dr. Polk's office, spiking out across the hallway floor. Then I heard the faint sound of rustling papers. To call out or to sneak? Well, what were rubber-soled shoes for anyway? I tiptoed back to the front office and picked up an electric pencil sharpener from one of the desks. I wrapped the cord around the thing and hoisted it to my shoulder like a shot, just in case. Pencil sharpeners aren't exactly cutting-edge weaponry, so I gritted my teeth, hoping that it made me look scary. I wanted whoever was in Polk's office to think I was a cyborg hit woman, not a Cro-Magnon cavegirl stalking woolly mammoths. Then I cautiously headed back toward the light.

The door was open wide enough for me to see the back of a tall man wearing an impeccably cut gray suit. From the age spots on the back of his hands, and the roughness of the skin on his neck, I put him somewhere in his sixties, but fit and trim. His brown hair was well manicured, but the color looked too dark for his age, as if he'd dyed it one shade beyond believability. The evenness of the hue made it seem brittle under the fluorescent light.

From a nearby filing cabinet he pulled out a manila folder, and thumbed through the papers inside. For the second time in as many days, someone had come to NeuroMed searching. For what? As he turned his head slightly, I recognized the profile and relaxed. He was no burglar.

I'd met him several times. I'd never worked with him before, but Venus had, and so had Richard Hastings. Most of what I'd heard about him came from newspapers and gossip. Rich. Powerful. To some, a caring philanthropist, to others, a poster boy for all the bad isms. He, Gordon, and Hastings were all alumni of Luther Mann, a private college whose graduates made it their calling to network within the "club." He was also the man who could guarantee our firm's success with one stroke of his pen. What I didn't know was how Wade Covington had gotten into this office, and why he was rifling through a dead man's files.

"Can I help you find something?" I said.

He apparently hadn't heard me enter, because he spun around, dropping the folder on the floor.

"Sorry, I didn't mean to startle you."

I cleared my throat to conceal the tremor in my voice, and reached down to pick up the folder he'd dropped. Unfortunately, he had the same idea, and we nearly bumped heads. This wasn't going well. I scooped up the file and handed it to him. "I promise not to do that again." I extended my hand. "I'm Tucker Sinclair." He didn't take the bait. I hesitated, watching him, hoping he wouldn't associate my name in a negative way with Gordon or the firm.

"I know who you are." His voice was deep and intimidating and echoed through the small room. I wondered what, if anything, Hastings had told him about me. Whatever it was, it couldn't have been good. Covington's pale blue eyes glowered at the lethal-looking pencil sharpener I still held in my hand. Apparently, I wasn't winning him over with my chirpy smile or my choice of weapons.

"The door was open," I said, putting the sharpener on the desk. "Francine locked it. I mean, I thought she locked it. Someone broke in earlier. Well, maybe not 'broke in' exactly. You must be looking for Dr. Polk? I guess you haven't heard. Of course not. How could you have? He's dead."

Even *I* knew I was babbling. We locked gazes for a moment as he assessed me. His face was taut, as if all the wrinkles had been stretched smooth by a surgeon's hand. His expression was hard to read. His face seemed placid until the mouth widened and the lips parted. It was subtle, but still, it looked strangely like a smile.

"Guess one of his bad habits caught up with him," he said.

He wasn't exactly overcome with grief, and that made me feel defensive. "Which bad habit was that? Scuba diving without a tank? I'll be sure to mention your theory to the cops."

As soon as the words slipped out, I realized I'd gone too far. The scowl on his face told me that he didn't buy the idea that one flippant remark deserved another. His mouth set in a hard line as he roughly jammed the file back into the drawer. Luckily, I was spared having to construct another heartfelt apology. Without warning, the overhead fluorescent lights in the hallway flipped on, flooding the whole office with light. As I spun around to look, I heard a gasp and then a female voice.

"Jeez, you scared the shit out of me!" she said.

A young woman stood just outside Polk's office door with her hand on her chest, staring at us. Her dark brown hair was twisted on top of her head and held with a butterfly clip that left an uncluttered view of a round, pretty face. It was Dolores Rod-riguez, one of NeuroMed's medical technicians.

"What are you doing here?" I said to her.

"The hospital called me for an emergency EEG. I came to pick up my machine." Her brown eyes narrowed. "Who's he? How'd you two get in here?"

"If you ladies will excuse me," Covington said, "I'll leave you to discuss your security concerns in private." He flashed a smile that held no mirth, and before I could ask him what he'd been looking for, he picked up a black textured briefcase from the floor and walked out. Wade Covington was everything I'd re-membered: arrogant and just a little intimidating. He hadn't asked one question about Milton Polk's death. Maybe he didn't care, or maybe he preferred to get the information from someone in his own socioeconomic group.

Dolores mumbled something that sounded suspiciously like "asshole" as a pager clipped to her uniform pocket went off. She checked the readout panel and then hurried toward the door.

"ICU," she said. "Catch that light. I'll lock up."

"I have to find my car keys," I said. "I left them when I was helping Francine this afternoon."

She paused for a moment as if to weigh priorities. "I thought you were done working here."

"It's a long story," I said. "Francine will explain. I'll only be a minute."

She shrugged. "Lock up when you leave."

She quickly walked to an EEG cart parked in one of the test-ing rooms and adjusted some knobs. Despite the fact that she car-ried no more than ninety pounds on her five-foot frame and looked barely strong enough to push the contraption, she bent her upper body forty-five degrees and used the traction of her white nurse's shoes to start the cart rolling down the hall.

After Dolores left, I checked the cabinet in Polk's office in the hopes of locating the file Covington had been looking at, but it was impossible to tell which one it had been. Most held testing protocols or reprints of journal articles. Not very enlightening. I turned off the lights in his office and went looking for my car keys. I found them on top of a file cabinet in the storage room, just where I'd left them. I put the keys in my pocket and doubled back to douse the rest of the lights.

My finger was poised to flip the switch in Francine's office when I noticed the corner of what looked like a blue patient chart poking out of a drawer in one of her filing cabinets. The more I stared at it, the more it looked untidy. Francine had just spent hours straightening up the place. It was almost like my duty to pop that puppy back inside the drawer. But more than that, the file looked out of place. Why was a patient chart filed in her office? It was supposed to be kept in the storage room where I'd left my car keys. That made me suspicious. Francine had been locked up alone in her office all afternoon. Maybe she'd been misfiling all sorts of things—maybe even the NeuroMed documents. I owed it to myself to find out.

I wasn't sure how long it would be before Dolores returned from the intensive care unit. I didn't want her to find me here snooping around, but I was in curiosity overdrive. After locking the outer door to eliminate any more surprise visitors, I returned to Francine's office and opened her file drawer. It was filled with patient medical charts. I pulled the one that had been sticking out of the drawer and thumbed through it. It seemed like standard stuff. No ahas! No alarm bells sounded, which made me wonder if I was missing something. I continued searching through the entire drawer, and then the one below, but found nothing but more patient records, detailing results of various neurological tests performed at the Center. Except for the fact that they were filed in Francine's office and not with the others, the files were one big routine yawn. I was searching the last drawer, feeling I'd wasted my time, when I came across a chart toward the back that made the breath catch in my throat. I pulled it out, staring in disbelief.

The file contained six separate reports detailing test results. Inside was a statement addressed to what looked like an apartment on Rexford Drive in the flats of Beverly Hills. A green sticker near the bottom read, *Your insurance has been billed. This statement for your information only.* The balance due was $3,987.00. My finger traced across the patient's name, neatly typewritten on a white label along the side of the file. It read, *Tucker Sinclair, 30-year-old right-handed woman.* Okay, so lots of people had told me I needed my head examined, but I was sure I hadn't had it done at NeuroMed, and not to the tune of four grand.

I considered the odds of finding another thirty-year-old Tucker Sinclair in the Los Angeles area and came up with slim to none. Maybe it was just some bizarre coincidence, but if not, that meant only one thing: Someone at NeuroMed was using my name to commit insurance fraud. I wondered if Polk had been so desperate for money that he'd sucked me into not one but two white-collar crimes. With Mo Whitener's threats hanging over my head, it would be a disaster if I had to fight off charges of insurance fraud as well.

I knew that NeuroMed used an outside billing service to process insurance claims, but even so, Francine had to know about this. She managed the office. Maybe she was even involved, which would help explain why she hadn't wanted the police at the Center and why she'd cleaned up before they got there. For all I knew, she was also Polk's partner in the investor scam. She didn't strike me as the girl-genius type, but she and the doctor together could probably have pulled it off. If so, I had to find out, because I'd worked too hard and given up too much to let Milton Polk or Francine Chalmers ruin my life. Tomorrow Francine and I were going to have another little chat.

It was already five-thirty, but with Whitener's deadline only a week away, I didn't have any time to waste. I decided to check out my clone on Rexford Drive. Beverly Hills was less than eight miles away, but it was rush hour. It would take me a good twenty to thirty minutes to get there, just enough time to meet the other Tucker Sinclair before the end of happy hour.

I stuffed the blue patient chart into my bag, turned out all the lights, and locked the door. The door felt secure, but I didn't. Earlier, I'd discounted the theory that Whitener was involved in Polk's murder, but what if the killer *had* been one of the investors or else someone tied to this insurance fraud? My name was connected to both scams now. I wondered if the creep had any other names on his hit list—like mine. That thought didn't make me feel secure at all.

6

ifteen minutes later I was on the road, headed toward Beverly Hills. An enormous peach movie prop moon dominated the sky as I followed the great Milky Way of rush-hour taillights on Olympic Boulevard, crawling along until I got to Rexford Drive. The address listed on the insurance claim was located in an area lined with mature trees and even more mature apartment buildings. Most were six- or eight-unit two-story post-war transitional architecture with small, well-manicured front lawns. When I got near the address, I took one of the metered spots across from a Starbucks and set off on foot.

I wandered up and down the block for at least five minutes before realizing I had passed the address, mainly because it wasn't at all what I expected and because the number was jammed in with dozens of other signs plastering a large plate-glass window. Signs that read, *Open 24 hours, UPS, FedEx, FAX, Copy, Western Union.*

The address on the statement belonged to Mail Companion, a commercial mailbox rental store. A poster with a cartoon Pilgrim, his arm around a Thanksgiving turkey, hung on a glass door that opened into a small lobby. Inside, the space was divided in half. On the left side, banks of mailboxes covered two walls. On the right side, partitioned off behind a wall and a second glass door, was a retail shop selling limited office supplies and packing boxes.

The patient statement was addressed to number 218, so I went to the left side of the room and looked for the corresponding mailbox. Some of them had strips of black plastic label tape identifying the owners, but not 218. I peeked through the window. It looked as though there was mail inside, but the opening was too small and it was too dark inside for me to make out any names.

I tried the door of the retail shop, but it was locked. I could see through the glass that the walls were covered with movie posters: *Thelma & Louise, Legends of the Fall, Meet Joe Black, Seven Years in Tibet.* It took me a minute or two to figure out the unifying theme: Brad Pitt.

A woman in her late fifties was still inside the shop, doing whatever clerks do at the end of the day. She was a few pounds beyond voluptuous and had a florid complexion, made more dramatic set against long bleached-blond hair. She'd gathered a clump of hair into a skinny ponytail on the top of her head and harnessed it with a floppy grayish bow that looked like a dead pigeon. I knocked on the glass to get her attention. She looked up, annoyed by the intrusion, gesturing toward the Closed sign on the door. I gestured back with praying hands. She waved as if batting at a fly as she walked toward me. She wore a white ankle-length chiffon skirt and an oversize pink sweatshirt. The outfit was accessorized with white tights and tennies. A light from behind her exposed the outline of a pair of chunky thighs. It wasn't a pretty sight. As she got closer, I noticed a plastic name tag pinned to her sweatshirt that identified her as the owner. Rosie Glenn. It sounded like some housing development in Calabasas.

"Closed!" She shouted through the glass with an accent that sounded southern. Again she pointed to the sign.

"I want to rent a mailbox," I responded.

"Come back tomorrow." She turned to leave.

"I need a specific box. Maybe you could save me a trip and tell me if it's available? Number two-eighteen."

"I don't keep all them numbers in my head," she said, annoyed. "Come back tomorrow. I gotta be somewhere."

Where? I wondered. A chili cook-off? Well, too bad, sweetie, I thought, it'll just have to start without you.

"Oh, gosh, maybe you could just check for me quick before you go." I aimed for an irresistible yet desperate tone in my voice.

For a moment she looked as if she were weighing the gross revenues of the rental against the throbbing of her swollen feet. Guess the revenues won out, because she unlocked the door and let me in. She sauntered over to the counter and pulled a ledger book from the drawer, thumbing through a list of numbers.

"Two-eighteen's taken," she said, flipping through a couple more pages. "Give you four-twenty-three."

"Oh, wait," I said. "Sorry. Not two-eighteen. That's my friend's box. Tucker Sinclair? We want to pick up each other's mail, so I need to get a box close to hers."

She glared at me as if I was testing her patience.

"Try again," she said. "There's no Tucker Sinclair in two-eighteen."

"Really? I'm sure that's what she told me," I said, searching for a way into her heart and her ledger book. "You sure? What does it say?" I leaned over and tried to read the entry.

"That's confidential." She closed the book with a slap.

"Oh, right." I paused and then gestured toward the posters. "You a Brad Pitt fan?"

She eyed me suspiciously. "Yeah."

I flashed my pearly whites and nodded. "Me, too."

The woman looked flushed as she glanced up at the *Legends of the Fall* poster.

"Near wore that video out, looking at it," she said.

"My mother's an actress. She worked with Brad before he got famous. She told me that for fun he signed some of those posters, but really small so you couldn't see it right away. Guess his autograph on one of those old guys would be worth a fortune now. Look. See down there in the corner of *Thelma & Louise*? It almost looks like a *P-I-T-T*." I squinted for effect and pointed, trying not to feel guilty for telling her a big one.

"Nah, that's just a smudge."

"Next to the smudge," I said. "You have to look really close. See the squiggles?"

"I don't know . . ." She sidled over to the poster and examined the corner.

"Did I mention he wrote really, *really* small? Like magnifying glass small?"

There was a brief silence, as if the woman was questioning her better judgment. Then she said, "Hold on a minute," and headed toward the back room. As soon as she was out of sight, I quietly opened the ledger book, turning the pages until I found number 218. The entry read, *Sunland Manufacturing*. I'd never heard of the company before. I closed the book and pulled my hand away just as Rosie came back, carrying a magnifying glass the size of a Chihuahua.

She studied the poster for a moment. Talk about gullible. She was probably the type who thought those boys on Sunset Boulevard had nothing for sale but maps to the stars' homes. When she turned around to look at me, her face clearly registered disappointment.

"Told you," she said. "It was just a smudge."

"Tough break. Thought for sure I recognized his handwriting."

It didn't appear that I was going to collect any more information here, so I decided to leave. Just then, Rosie Glenn's eyes opened wide. It looked like the birth of a brilliant idea to me.

"Hey," she said. "Find out your friend's box number. Maybe I could move her and get the two of you side-by-side boxes."

"I don't know," I said skeptically. "I'd better check with her first. I'll let you know."

As I stood on the sidewalk waiting for the traffic light to change, I noticed Rosie Glenn out of the corner of my eye. She was moving from poster to poster, inspecting every line and squiggle. It almost made me wish I'd been telling her the truth.

It was already six-fifteen and too late to research Sunland Manufacturing, so I decided to head for home, where my mother and her goofy dog were waiting for me. I love my mother, and Muldoon's okay, but the two of them have a knack for complicating my life, and at the moment, that was the last thing I needed.

7

the moon cast a shimmering trail of light on the ocean as I turned left off Pacific Coast Highway and drove down the hill toward my house, past a cactus garden planted on the public hillside by one of my well-meaning neighbors who suffers from a succulent fixation that I call the Scottsdale syndrome. A lime green Beetle convertible was parked in my driveway. The car belonged to my mother, aka Pookie Kravitz, star of stage, screen, and infomercial. Pookie isn't her real name, of course, but early on she'd decided that none of her prior names—Mary Jo Felder, Mary Jo Sinclair, or Mom—had what you'd call star quality.

I entered the house from the back door and made my way to the kitchen, which is one of those small apartment-type arrangements with an open counter separating it from the living room. I like the way it's set up, because while I'm doing my least favorite thing, cooking, I can do my most favorite thing, looking at the ocean through my French doors.

I hadn't done much to change the place since I moved in. I kept the few pieces of furniture that belonged to my grandmother, including an iron headboard and an old steamer trunk. Most everything else had either been trashed or stolen by renters. I'd also added a few touches of my own: a round hooked rooster rug in the kitchen, an overstuffed living room couch and chair covered in a rose and celery floral print, and hand-painted seashell tiles above the kitchen stove. I'd also bought fake white wicker furniture for the deck. The place might never make the cover of *Architectural Digest,* but it was all mine.

I called out to Pookie, but she didn't answer. Across an end table in the living room lay a hat that looked like the leafy part of a celery stalk. It was from a commercial she'd done for Lettuce Entertain You, a produce co-op owned by some actor friends. Scale plus vegetable headgear. What a life.

I laid the blue patient chart on the kitchen counter and pushed the rewind button on my message machine. I heard Venus's voice, asking me to call her. She probably wanted to hear about my meeting with Polk. I was eager to speak with her, too, because manufacturing was her specialty, and I was hoping she could tell me something about Sunland. I pressed the speed-dial button next to her name, but the line was busy. There were no messages from Gordon. I was relieved. Maybe he'd been so tied up with Covington that he hadn't noticed I'd left early and without bringing him the NeuroMed documents.

I thumbed through the Tucker Sinclair medical chart again, hoping to find some confirmation of her identity. Most of the registration page had been left blank. There was no social security number, no driver's license, nothing.

All that bad hospital cafeteria coffee was wreaking havoc on my stomach, so I checked to see if there was any seltzer in the refrigerator. There wasn't. The fridge door was still open when I realized I was cold. Not refrigerator cold. *Cold* cold. I turned toward the living room and let out a short, high-pitched noise that sounded like one of Muldoon's yippy barks. The French doors leading to the deck were wide open. After the kind of day I'd just had, I didn't need any more surprises. I walked cautiously out into the dank night air and scanned the beach.

"Pookie? You out there?" My voice sounded squeaky.

There were no sounds except for the waves hissing against the sandy shore. I went back inside, locked the doors, and tried to convince myself that Pookie's absence was no big deal. She'd probably taken Muldoon for a walk. Only, she should have locked the door. My mother grew up in a small town in Washington State where people are still basically good at heart. But she'd lived in L.A. for years now. You'd think she'd have developed a healthier sense of distrust.

A tap on glass made me jump. I looked toward the French doors and saw Pookie standing on the deck, shivering. She had on a quirky Drew-Barrymore-meets-Indira-Gandhi outfit, which wasn't meant for a chilly November evening.

My mother has short blond hair, blue eyes, and stands five feet three. At fifty-one, she weighs a hundred five pounds and has the body of a thirteen-year-old boy, which is good because, as an actor, her looks are her livelihood. Standing side by side, it's hard to believe that the two of us share the same gene pool.

As soon as I opened the door, she hurried inside and kicked her shoes off onto a nearby rug. Muldoon followed close behind her, his wet paws leaving a trail of gritty sand on the tile floor. The guy was a sneak pee-er, so I kept an eye on him.

"Pookie, I've told you before, don't leave the door—"

She interrupted. "I love you, sweetie, but don't start with the door thing again. I'm trying my best to stay centered."

More to the point, she was trying to stay centered because she hated to fly. Unfortunately, she was leaving the next morning for a week-long retreat to the backwoods of British Columbia to explore her shamanic powers. That was a little woo-woo for me, but what the hell. If you asked me, I was the one who needed centering, because in a serious lapse of judgment, I'd agreed to baby-sit for Muldoon.

The leg lifter and I had an uneasy truce. I objected to that pretty-boy hold-me, need-me, love-me look he always used to charm Pookie into excusing the yellow wee-wee stains on my couch legs. Once my mom was gone, Muldoon was going to find out that batting his baby browns wouldn't work on me.

Pookie looked tense as she turned on a lamp near the couch. The heat from the lightbulb activated the lemony-smelling oil ring she'd installed. The aroma was supposed to heighten serenity or shrink kidney stones; I couldn't remember which. She took a couple of whiffs and began packing the clothes stacked on the couch into a vintage Samsonite suitcase.

She frowned. "You got a phone call today."

"I know. Venus."

"It wasn't Venus."

"Really? There was only one message on the machine."

"I took the call." She hesitated for a moment. "It was from Sylvia Branch."

My jaw tightened. "She called me at work, too, but I shredded the message. Aunt Sylvia and all her baggage is the last thing I want to deal with right now."

"I think you should hear what she—"

"Pookie, please, it's been a rotten day. Can't we talk about it later? Come on, I'll help you pack."

She hesitated but didn't say any more. Muldoon jumped up on the couch and circled three times. I barely rescued a blue rayon bowling shirt with *Min-Da-Lanes Mamas* machine embroidered on the back before he settled in for a snooze.

Pookie picked up a pair of chartreuse palazzo pants and held them up to her waist. "Remember these? Oregon. That cute lit-tle thrift shop. Do you still have that Nehru jacket I bought for you there?"

Of course, she knew the answer was no. That was the sum-mer between my junior and senior year of high school, and the last thing I wanted was a Nehru jacket to remind me. Pookie had been cast as Peter Pan off-off-off-Broadway, which in layman's terms meant dinner theater in Eugene. For a month while she rehearsed, I stayed in a second-floor room at the Motel 6, watch-ing *The Brady Bunch* and pretending that Florence Henderson was my mother.

"You said you had a bad day," she said. "What happened?"

While she finished packing, I told her about the mail fraud charges, Milton Polk's death, and the Tucker patient chart. I tried to put a lighthearted spin on it because I didn't want to spoil her trip by letting her know how concerned I was. But even before I got to the good stuff, the Brad Pitt part, she stopped packing. She went to the refrigerator and filled two wineglasses with a liq-uid that looked like something from a car engine after a long stretch between tune-ups.

I studied the slime pattern on the glass. "What's this?"

"Secret sauce," she said. "For nerves."

Secret sauce for nerves? Sounded therapeutic except for one thing: In less than twenty-four hours I expected to find my mother in a sweat lodge with a bunch of aging hippies, drinking her own urine. So if her secret sauce was supposed to make me feel less nervous, it wasn't working. In fact, it was making me slightly hysterical just trying to figure out where she'd gotten the recipe. We clinked glasses, but I barely let the liquid graze my upper lip.

She rinsed her empty glass under the faucet and then turned

toward me with a determined look on her face. "I'm canceling my trip."

"What for?"

"You say this doctor was murdered," she said. "What if the police think you did that, too?"

That hit a nerve. What if Detective Kleinman found out that I'd met with Milton Polk at the coffee shop in Venice? He'd be positively giddy to hear that Polk had accused me of trying to kill him. Of course, that had only been a figure of speech. Polk had meant I was killing his dreams, killing all the millions he'd planned to make. Whatever. I just hoped no one had overheard the conversation, and if they had, I hoped they couldn't pick me out of a lineup.

I tried my best to sound offhand. "Nobody's going to think I killed Polk. And even if they do, what's the worst that can happen? The minute the jury sees how horrible I look in those county jail jumpsuits, they're going to acquit me out of pity."

"Tucker, this isn't funny. Mail fraud, insurance fraud. Those are serious crimes. But murder . . . I'm afraid for you. What are you going to do?"

"Whoa," I said. "The police will find out who killed Polk, and that phony patient chart is just another little snag. I'm checking in to it. Meanwhile, Gordon is arranging a meeting with our attorneys."

She put her hands on her hips and cocked her head. "What do you mean by 'our attorneys'?"

"The firm's attorneys."

"You mean Gordon's attorneys."

"You're being cynical."

She shook her head in disapproval. "You need someone representing you, Tucker. Not Gordon. Not the firm."

"If I lose, Gordon loses," I told her. "He has nothing to gain by screwing me over."

"Trust smarter, not harder," she said. "I don't want to see you caught up in some power struggle. It's you who'll lose."

"My knees are shaking."

Her eyes flashed. "Go ahead, Tucker, have your fun."

She was miffed, so I softened my tone. "Pookie, don't worry. No one's struggling for power here."

"I just wish you'd get out of that business you're in. There are too many sleazy, backstabbing little people. Watch yourself, okay?"

That was a funny thing to say, considering the business she was in. "Ditto," I said.

Pookie finished packing while I nuked some vegetarian lasagna from the freezer and made a salad. A gray funk hung over her in the room, and I suspected that the little "watch yourself" pep talk had deeper roots than she cared to share with me. At dinner she picked at the cheese and sorted the tomatoes, but she didn't eat much. Muldoon had grown tired of begging and fell asleep under the table, with his head resting on my foot.

"You know," I said, "you don't have to *fly* to Vancouver, if that's what's bothering you. There's probably a train."

Despite the worry that had worked tiny lines around her mouth, she looked way younger than her years. She stared at me without speaking. When she finally said something, her voice was unusually subdued.

"Tucker, we have to talk about Sylvia Branch."

I sighed. "Okay. What kind of game's she running now?"

"She found another will," she said softly. "In a safety deposit box no one knew about. It was handwritten by Mrs. Sinclair and dated two weeks before she died. Apparently, she changed her mind, Tucker. She left this house to your aunt, not to you. Sylvia is planning to sell the place. She told me all the money is right-fully hers, but she's willing to reimburse you for moving expenses."

My heart began to pound, but I managed to keep my voice calm. "Look, even if this new will is real, which I doubt, probate is closed. I don't even know if she can reopen it legally. I say, let Aunt Sylvia contest till the cows come home. This house is mine."

"She has lawyers, Tucker, high-priced lawyers."

Muldoon was still sprawled under the table, but he was now whimpering from a puppy dream. I petted him until he settled down, and then leaned forward in my chair, hoping to make my-self look confident and self-assured.

"Don't worry, Pookie," I said. "The only way Sylvia Branch will ever get this house is over my dead body."

The only problem was, I'd seen my aunt in action before. She was a woman with considerable resources and a history of get-ting what she wanted. I was guessing that my dead body might suit her just fine.

8

emperatures in the mid to low seventies. Winds out of the west at fifteen miles per hour. Early morning fog along the coast . . ."

It was 6:45 a.m. As I reached over to turn off the radio alarm, my foot nudged a lump on the bed. Muldoon was at my feet. His paws were up, and he was snoring. Pookie had probably left for the airport. I rolled out of bed, made some coffee, and went into the bathroom to shower. Taped to the mirror was a list of explicit doggie care instructions, along with the places that carried Pookie-approved dog food.

Before I dressed for work, I scanned the *Los Angeles Times* for any word of Polk's death, finding only a small article in the California section.

BODY FOUND IN VENICE IS IDENTIFIED

The body of a man found in Venice was identified Monday as that of Milton Raymond Polk. Authorities said the body of Polk, 56, was discovered about ten o'clock Sunday night by a tourist walking on the beach. Homicide detectives are conducting a routine investigation to determine if there was foul play.

Foul play? That sounded a little Agatha Christie. According to Kleinman, Polk's body had been in the water for at least twenty-four hours. If Polk had been found at ten p.m. Sunday, he must have died some time on Saturday. That wasn't exactly higher math. It was a good thing no one was counting on my keen deductive reasoning to solve this crime. I decided to switch to something I was good at, so I called Eugene to tell him I'd be late for work.

I wanted to stop by NeuroMed and find out if Francine Chalmers knew anything about the Tucker medical chart I'd found. After that, I'd try to get the scoop on Sunland Manufacturing. The company's profile would be in one of the databases at work, but I didn't want to invite questions about why I was looking. There had to be another way.

There were two patients in NeuroMed's waiting room when I arrived. Neither one looked terribly stimulated by the murky fish tank or the selection of disease brochures. The Center's secretary, Janet, was at her desk, transcribing from a tape. The door to the front office was no longer propped open, so when I asked to see Francine, Janet had to buzz me through.

I found Francine in Polk's office, sitting at his desk. Her makeup was carefully painted on, but it looked slightly caked under her puffy, red eyes. She wore the same gold bracelets I'd seen the previous day, but her black dress, though appropriately funereal, was a little low-cut for an office.

She didn't seem particularly surprised to see me, but she wasn't hostile, either. Obviously, Kleinman hadn't been back to see her, or she'd have known that I'd blabbed to him about the break-in at the Center. She nodded but continued filling the wastebasket with what looked like business correspondence. It made me uncomfortable not knowing what she was throwing away.

"What are you doing?" I said.

"I assume someone's taking over for Dr. Polk," she said. "I

thought I'd straighten out his desk. Get it organized. Can I get you some coffee or tea?"

"No, thanks," I said. "I can't stay long."

"Well, then, I think I'll have some myself."

I followed her to a coffee station next to the sink in the storage room and watched as she poured java into the Worrier Princess cup. The handle had been glued back on; you couldn't tell it had ever been broken.

"One of the reasons I stopped by," I said, "was to ask if you still had any of the NeuroMed business plans here at the office. The original is missing, and I wondered if it was sent to Dr. Polk by mistake."

She thought for a moment as she emptied a bag of sugar and a heaping spoonful of creamer into her cup and stirred it with a plastic stick.

"No. I don't remember anything like that, but I didn't open the box when it came, and Dr. Polk took it away that same day. It was a long time ago."

Yeah, six weeks was an eternity, all right. I had better recall of my flossing history. She took a paper napkin and carefully wiped away a spill and a few sugar granules.

"By the way," I said, "I left my car keys here yesterday. When I came back to get them, I found a man in Dr. Polk's office, looking through his files."

Her back was toward me, so I couldn't see her expression, but her answer came back in an artificially light and airy tone.

"Probably Dr. Hernandez," she said.

"No. It was a man named Wade Covington. Happen to know how he got in?"

She seemed almost relieved as she turned toward me. "Oh, Mr. Covington. He has a key."

My eyebrows darted up in surprise. "Really? Dr. Polk never told me Covington was connected with the Center."

"He isn't," she said. "He's a friend of Dr. Polk's. I hope you're not thinking he tried to steal something, because I can assure you—"

"Oh, no," I said. "I'm not saying that at all. Somebody did kind of leave a mess in *your* office, though, but it was probably the cleaning people. But don't worry, I straightened things up."

She bit her lip and frowned. "You shouldn't have—"

"No problem. Funny thing, though. I came across a patient chart with my name on it."

Maybe it was the steam from the coffee, but I thought I detected a film of moisture collecting on her upper lip. She went back to sprucing up the coffee station until it could have passed an FDA inspection.

"What a coincidence," she said.

"Yeah, it's such an uncommon name."

"Maybe it was a typo."

"Gosh," I said caustically. "The whole name?"

"Well, I can check it for you, if you'd like."

I followed Francine back to her office, where she pulled out a breadboard-type tray from above the top drawer of the desk. Taped to it was what looked like an employee address list. She set down the coffee, entered my last name on her computer keyboard, and pressed search. There were several Sinclairs, but no Tuckers, not even any *T*s.

"We have several doctors dictating test results," she said. "Some of them are hard to understand. Maybe when Janet was setting up the file, she misunderstood and typed the wrong name. I'll see it gets corrected."

Part of me wanted to believe that the name was a transcription error, because, the truth was, her explanation sounded plausible, but I had serious doubts. In any event, Francine would find out soon enough that the Tucker chart wasn't in the drawer anymore.

"By the way," I said, "do you still use a service to process your insurance claims?"

Her face blanched under the heavy makeup. "Yes." She walked toward the door and added, "Is there anything else? I have a lot of work to do."

"Just one more question. Ever hear of a company called Sunland Manufacturing?"

Francine crossed her arms and wrinkled her brow in thought.

"Did you say Sunland? It's such a common-sounding name, isn't it?" she said. "Sunland . . . Sunland . . . No, I don't think so."

"Maybe one of your patients works there?" I said.

She gave me a controlled chuckle that was meant to sound convivial but, in fact, struck me as just the opposite. "I wish I could remember every patient's employment history, but I'm afraid I'll have to disappoint you."

What disappointed me was that her nose didn't grow like Pinocchio's, because I was pretty sure she was lying.

I returned the false jolly smile. "Don't worry, we'll talk again. Maybe I can come up with something that jogs your memory."

What I didn't say was that the next time we chatted, I planned to have enough information on Sunland Manufacturing to know if Francine was lying, even without the help of a long wooden nose. Unfortunately, there was only one place, other than my office, where I could find that kind of information: Eric Bergstrom's computer. I just hoped that my ex-husband wouldn't be a pill about helping me out.

·   ·   ·

MY EX WORKS for a company with computer databases that put the FBI's to shame. The investment bankers at Cohen, Luna &

Davoodian discovered early in their careers that he who has the most information wins. If CLD didn't have information on Sunland and the other Tucker Sinclair, it didn't exist.

Eric's office is in Century City, which comprises several large square blocks of high-rise buildings between Santa Monica and Olympic Boulevards, nestled between Beverly Hills and West Los Angeles. It was the former back lot of 20th Century Fox Studios, sold to developers to recoup some of the heavy losses suffered when the big-budget movie *Cleopatra* flopped at the box office. Now it's a Westside alternative to downtown. It's organized, impeccably groomed, and self-contained, kind of like Eric. I parked in the garage and headed up the elevator to the twenty-sixth floor.

Cohen et al. is a perennial favorite on the Architectural and Design Tour of Los Angeles. Its art collection alone commands respect, even if you don't know Hockney from hackneyed. The elevator doors opened. My shoes clicked across the pink marble tiles and then sank silently into the plush rose and aqua floral carpet of the expansive lobby.

The receptionist was new, one of a long line of well-dressed young women with flawless skin and perfect makeup who typically adorned the firm's entryway. This one was slightly plump. Management must have relaxed its hiring practices. Usually the company recruited employees based primarily on low body fat. I asked for Eric. She whispered something into the telephone receiver and then told me to have a seat.

Eric and I had become friends while attending UCLA business school. I was attracted to him because he was the only man I'd ever met who could reach my good china without a step stool. I liked that in a man. By the time we realized that our relationship was closer to sibling rivalry than romantic love, we were married. But too much of our passion was channeled into career building, not relationship building, and both of us had done things we regretted. After the divorce, there had been some competitive wounding, but eventually we both realized that it took too much effort to keep track of who did what to whom, so we went back to being friends—at least, most of the time.

While I waited, I studied a brass plaque on the antique cherry reception desk that read, *No packages on the desk.* I hate whiny signage, but I didn't have time to get too worked up about it, because Eric's tall, lanky body materialized, escorting a petite woman with cinnamon-colored hair who was carrying a clunky lawyer briefcase. She was a client, no doubt. She reminded me of the sweet but frail ingenue who gets instant audience sympathy in those disease-of-the-moment movies. The elevator door had just closed when he spotted me and waved.

As he walked over, I noticed those familiar bushy eyebrows that kept his face from being branded pretty. They looked different somehow. As though they were pasted to his forehead. His warm smile looked the same, though, and that, he was flashing just for me.

"Tucker, hi. I've been wanting to talk to you."

"Me, too," I said, trying to look unrushed. "Let's go to your office."

He hesitated. "I'm expecting a new client. Maybe we could meet after work for a drink."

"That would be good, but see, I need this favor right now, and it's really, really important."

Eric rolled his eyes and raked his fingers through his Rodeo Drive haircut—usually a bad sign, but this time he surprised me. He sighed and nodded for me to follow.

The view from Eric's window was spectacular, and I wondered if I'd ever have one at Aames & Associates to match his. The early morning fog hadn't traveled as far as Century City, but the sky was overcast with puffy gray clouds dense as cigarette smoke on a flight to Tokyo.

Eric closed the door and settled into his luxurious leather chair at his pricey mahogany desk, which held his classy Mont Blanc pen and a tacky Proud-to-Be-a-Gopher coffee mug from his undergraduate days at the University of Minnesota.

"So, what gives?" he said.

I didn't want to come right out and ask to use his computer. He'd say no. So I decided to use a little investment banking patois and ask his opinion about the fake Internet idea. That would get his juices flowing. It wouldn't take him long to say fuhgeddaboudit, which was good. Eric was a bit of a pessimist, and there was nothing that improved his disposition faster than dashing somebody's hopes.

I willed my face to look earnest. "What would you say to a person who wanted to raise twenty-five million dollars in venture capital for a new high-tech company that had revolutionary medical software and plans for a splashy IPO?"

"That's a little sketchy. Is this the company's first time for venture capital financing?"

"Yep."

"Twenty-five sounds high, then. The percentage of VC dollars invested in first-time borrowers hit an eight-year low in the first quarter. It's rebounded somewhat, but I'm not even cautiously optimistic that the situation will get much better than it is, at least, not for a while."

"What about eleven million?"

"Still sounds high, but if the company's hot, I guess it's possible. Venture capitalists are cautious right now, but they're still investing four billion dollars a quarter. Most of that goes to software companies. Biotechnology is second, but money going to the medical devices sector shot up fifty-four percent in the second quarter, so who knows?"

"So, if this somebody told you he'd raised eleven million in, say, six weeks, you'd believe him?"

"I suppose he could get any amount if he asked the right people."

"Wow. That's impressive."

He looked puzzled. "So, is that the favor you wanted? If so, I don't get it. You have access to all of this information. Why are you asking me?"

"I just like to get your take on things, that's all." Eric's hands were clasped in front of him on the desk. He was looking at me with a sweet but pained expression. "Why are you staring at me like that?" I went on. "You look like you swallowed a guppy."

"I was just thinking: Here you are again, coming to me for advice. It's like when we were together."

I paused, wondering what he was up to. "Um . . . yeah," I said. "So what's your point?"

"I don't know. Don't you find that unique? Isn't that something that's usually reserved for people in committed relationships?"

I studied his face. Something was bothering me. "We have a committed relationship, Eric. We're friends."

"I know," he said, "but I mean, really committed."

"Hey, just because we're not sleeping together doesn't mean we shouldn't be there for each other."

He hesitated, as if searching for the next sentence. "It's just . . . I've been thinking a lot lately about being part of a couple. How that feels. How you don't need anybody, or, for that matter, even want anybody else in your life. I miss that, don't you?"

I didn't want to bring it up, but lately I'd been more worried about cell mates than soul mates. I tried to figure out what he was hinting at, but the only thing I could think of was that he was misinterpreting my stress about the Whitener business as "lonely and depressed woman needs man to make her life complete." I hoped he wasn't thinking of setting me up with one of his well-groomed friends.

"Frankly, Eric," I said sincerely, "I'd have to say no, I don't miss it."

"Really? You've never thought about taking the plunge again?"

I must have looked worse than I thought. Either that, or everybody in my life was flipping out.

"You have some great personal insights, Eric, but can't we talk about this some other time, because I know your client's coming in a few minutes, and I need to take a quick peek at your database."

His mouth opened and closed a couple of times, but no words jarred loose. Finally, he leaned back in his chair and let out a deep, frustrated sigh.

"You know that information is not available to the public."

"The public? Oh, come on, Eric. I'm hardly the public."

"Every time I log on it's recorded," he said. "I practically had to sign a blood oath before they gave me a password. Look at your own files."

"Yours are better," I said. "Besides, I'm on my way to an important meeting and yours are also closer."

"Well, that's certainly more creative than the truth," he said, "but the answer is still no. Luna is paranoid about privacy and leaks."

"Okay, I understand."

He paused and arched one eyebrow in mock disbelief that I was caving in so early in the game. I studied that eyebrow more closely, and that's when I knew something was wrong.

"Eric, what happened to your eyebrows?"

"Nothing." His tone was defensive.

"Something is different. What did you do?"

"Tucker, I don't have time for this nonsense. I have to get ready for my next client."

Then it dawned on me. "Omigod! You got them tweezed. Who did this to you, honey? A pet groomer? They look like corgis with a crew cut."

He let out a big, loud sigh. "You never change, do you?"

Just then, "Für Elise" interrupted our conversation. It was the ringer on Eric's cell phone. He glanced at the incoming telephone number on the display panel and answered with a cautious hello. His side of the conversation went something like this: "Uh-huh . . . I can't really talk right now. Can I call you back? . . . I don't know. Can't it wait? . . . *(sigh)* . . . Okay, just a minute." Eric stood and walked toward the door as if he'd forgotten I was in the room.

"Oh, Eric, I'm sorry," I said in mock dismay. "Please don't go. I'll be nice, I promise."

He wasn't amused. He tucked the cell phone in his armpit to muffle his reply. "Look, Tucker, I have to take this call. If you really want to be nice, you won't touch anything while I'm gone. I'll be right outside in the hallway, so don't get any bright ideas."

Eric hurried from the room, closing the door behind him. I sat in the chair for a few moments, mentally kicking myself for failing at my mission to get into his database. I hated losing my touch. In the midst of all that self-flagellation, my eyes swept the room. I couldn't help but notice that I was alone. Alone with Eric's computer. I needed that Sunland/Tucker information, and this felt like an opportunity. I slipped quietly out of the chair and cracked open the door to see if Eric was still on the phone. He not only wasn't on the phone, he wasn't even in the hallway. Liar, liar, pants on fire. I wondered who he was talking to and why he needed so much privacy. Whatever. I didn't have time to speculate, so I closed the door and jogged to his desk.

The Cohen, Luna & Davoodian logo flitted across the screen as I positioned myself in front of the computer screen. Password, password. To a less creative person this glitch might have presented a problem, but this was me figuring out Eric. I won't say he was predictable, but being married to him meant never having to say, "Oh, honey, what a surprise." Besides, I knew he kept it in a file marked *passwords,* right next to his supply of Nut Goodies candy bars. I found the file and the password right away, and while I was in the drawer, I slipped a couple of bars into my purse for Venus. Eric would never miss them, and she'd be in chocolate heaven.

The computer program was similar to mine at work, so it didn't take long to get in and find my name. There were no liens, judgments, or bankruptcies filed against me. I wasn't a sexual offender. That was good news. In fact, I had no criminal record at all—yet. My house was listed under my name with the tax assessor, but not for long if Aunt Sylvia had anything to say about it. But as far as I could see, I was the only Tucker Sinclair living in Southern California, maybe the world.

Sunland Manufacturing was a little trickier to find, but it was there. It was a privately owned company in Santa Fe Springs. The question was, why did they need a post office box in Beverly Hills, which was a good twenty-five miles away? According to its profile, Sunland manufactured and sold medical equipment under the brand name Medcomac. Some of these products, I knew from my research, were experimental and not supported by the medical community, let alone the insurance industry. Big risk. Sunland had employed about 1,150 employees nationwide until nine months ago, when they'd filed for Chapter 11 in bankruptcy court. Now they were down to a fraction of that number. The CEO was listed as Bernard Cole.

I checked my watch. Eric could be back any minute. I had to hurry. I clicked around until I located Cole's name under *Who's Who in California*. He was a bootstraps kind of guy. Vietnam vet, community activist in a slew of organizations—some sounded political; most sounded conservative. He had no ties to Milton Polk that I could find, which was disappointing. Time was running out. I was getting ready to print a hard copy when I heard two men talking in the hallway.

"You'll like Eric. Hard as nails. Nothing fazes him." I recognized the familiar lisp of Arturo Luna, Mr. Paranoia. The man with him must be the client Eric was expecting. If Luna found me here, I'd be in big trouble. I quickly logged off and hoped the sound of my heart thumping wouldn't give me away.

I eased open the door and saw the two men standing a few feet away. Luna was pointing out his latest acquisition, a large oil painting that looked like Picasso on speed. I waited until both their backs were turned, quietly slipped into the hallway, and retraced my steps through the lobby past a well-dressed man in a charcoal suit reading *The Economist*.

At the ground floor, I transferred to the garage elevator and waited alone as it silently descended three levels beneath the building until the doors opened into a cement cocoon. Fluorescent lights flickered against painted fuchsia wall graphics, creating a grotesque cheeriness. Motor oil and exhaust fumes blended into a toxic perfume.

I found my car and paid at the kiosk, but it wasn't until I eased into traffic on Century Park East that I remembered that I hadn't confirmed a time or place for my date with Eric. I didn't want to ignore his invitation and hurt his feelings, especially since, for some reason, he'd seemed so needy with all his talk about relationships and taking the plunge.

I was about to call him on my cell phone when it finally sank in. I closed my eyes and almost clipped a Rolls Royce that was running a red light at Olympic Boulevard. How could I have been so stupid? His warm smile. His invitation for cocktails. I knew what it was. Eric had been trying to tell me something. He wanted me back.

9

e and Eric. Eric and me. Part of me said, why not? and part
of me said, been there, done that. Eric and I had already
given our relationship a chance. In fact, we'd given it several
chances. We just hadn't been able to make it work. He couldn't
make me fall in love with golf or opera or keeping the toilets in
our condo Ty-D-Bol-ed, but I'd failed, too. Of course, I'd never
try to make anybody fall in love with housework, but I could
never interest him in learning tango or in laughing at the funny
dialogue I made up and whispered in his ear during perform-
ances of *Götterdämmerung*. It wasn't that I didn't love Eric. What
we had was rare and wonderful. It just wasn't that snap-crackle-
pop love that you needed to hold a marriage together. In the
end, I decided to let the invitation for drinks slide and hoped he
would, too.

It took me forty-five minutes to get from Century City to
downtown L.A., but when I arrived at work just after eleven
o'clock, everything was quiet. Eugene was away from his desk.
Gordon was in a meeting. Just as well. I wasn't anxious to tell him
that I didn't have the NeuroMed documents and that I didn't have
a clue where they might be. I checked my voice mail and was surprised to find a message from Mona Polk. I was curious to know
why the doctor's widow would be calling me, so I picked up the

phone and dialed her number. A heavily accented female voice answered. I asked to speak to Mona Polk.

"She no here."

"I'm returning her call. Can you take a message?"

"*Sí, sí.*"

I gave the woman my name and telephone number, but I had the feeling that she wasn't writing it down.

"Could you read that back to me, please?" I said, doing my best to enunciate.

"*Momento.*" She clunked down the receiver.

Several *momentos* ticked by before a barely audible voice came on the line.

"Ms. Sinclair, thank you for calling. Sorry about the mix-up. Elsa was trying to screen some of my calls." Her voice had a breathy, singsong quality to it that ran the risk of becoming irritating over time. She sounded like Marilyn Monroe singing "Happy Birthday, Mr. President."

"You left a message for my husband," she continued. "Normally, I wouldn't bother with his calls, but I don't think he called you back. I thought I should explain about the delay."

Delay? Was this woman a total banana-fish? Surely Detective Kleinman had been to see her. She had to know that her husband was dead.

"What kind of delay are we talking about here?" I said.

She didn't respond right away, so I tried the old intimidation-through-silence trick that I'd learned from the good old boys of business: I kept my mouth shut and waited. There was an uncomfortable lull in the conversation before she answered.

"He's dead, you know."

It was an offhand remark, as if she had just gotten home from the market and realized that she'd forgotten something on her grocery list. Like: "Oh, pooh! My husband is dead." Maybe she was in shock, or maybe she just didn't give a rip. I tried to think of an appropriate eulogy, but I was still mad at Polk and "your husband was a real character" didn't seem to capture the moment.

"Yes, I heard," I said. "I'm sorry."

"He was quite fond of you, you know. He thought the two of you were alike in many ways."

It would have been more accurate if she'd said that Polk and I admired each other's differences. Trying to fit the doctor and me into the same mold was like trying to squeeze a Sumo wrestler into size A panty hose.

There was a pause and a breathy sigh before she continued. "I'd like to meet with you as soon as possible. I need your advice about what to do with NeuroMed."

"I'm afraid I'll be leaving next week for a job in the Netherlands," I said, "but I'm sure one of our other consultants—"

"I promise I won't take much of your time. Can you come to my house this afternoon?" She paused and then added, "Please."

I'll admit I wanted to find out what she was up to. Plus, talking to her might help fill in the blanks of Polk's last days, as well as allow me to find out if the original NeuroMed documents were at the house. On the other hand, I couldn't give Mona Polk free advice about NeuroMed without a signed contract. Gordon was a nice guy, but he didn't encourage his consultants to be philanthropists.

"Let me discuss it with my boss," I said. "I'll get back to you this afternoon."

She hesitated as if unsure of herself. "All right. I'll be waiting for your call."

I hadn't even replaced the receiver when Venus came rushing

through the door. Her round face looked flushed amid the coils of her black hair. She had on a 1940s-style suit with out-to-here shoulder pads that she thought made her look less like a pear. She bypassed her usual chair and headed right to where I was sitting at my desk. Something was wrong with this picture. Then it registered. Venus never rushed.

"Why didn't you call me back last night?" She sounded upset and out of breath.

"Your line was busy, and then I got distracted. Why?"

"Have you checked your e-mail this morning?"

My eyes narrowed as I studied her face. It looked stormy. "Venus, what's going on?"

"Sometimes you try my patience, girl." She pressed the power key and waited for the computer to boot up. "Open your Listserv."

I opened the company's bulletin board and scanned the list of employee memos. Venus impatiently reached over my shoulder and arrowed down to one entry entitled "Project Manager Announced."

I read the message in stunned silence. It was an office news release announcing that Richard Hastings had been selected project manager for the Juliana Health Clinic and Spa chain, headquartered in Amsterdam. It went on to say that he'd be heading a team of five consultants that would blah, blah, blah. Not only was my name not listed as the project manager, it wasn't listed at all. There was no explanation why this replaced a similar announcement released weeks ago, naming me as team leader. No reference to all the work that I'd already done on the project. I felt as if I'd been sucker punched.

Venus's arms were crossed. She had a poisonous look on her face. "What's Gordon up to?"

I took a deep breath and shushed it out. "I don't know, but I'm sure as hell going to find out." I selected the Print command and waited for a hard copy to roll out of my HP.

"Has this got something to do with that doctor?" Venus asked.

It was possible, I thought. Gordon might have seen the article in the paper about Polk's death, but why panic? He still didn't know the NeuroMed file was missing.

"Maybe Hastings sent it to me as some kind of sick joke?" I said.

"Nuh-uh. I got one, too. Everybody did. Not even Hastings is stupid enough to do that."

Covington had made it known he wanted Hastings to be partner. I wondered if the firm felt pressured to put him in charge of the Juliana project to please an important client. I understood why the partners might cave in to Covington's demands, but I didn't understand why they would keep that decision from me.

"Shit," I said. "Eugene's going to freak out. I have to find him."

I rushed through the doorway, followed closely by Venus, but Eugene was back, quietly sitting at his desk, looking at a framed picture of his cat, Liza. A few seconds later, he put it into a cardboard box on the floor.

"What are you doing?" I asked cautiously.

He looked up. His lips were pressed in a straight line that he tried to pawn off as a smile.

"Packing," he said. "I've been fired."

"You've been *what*?" My words came out at a decibel level OSHA would have considered hazardous. "By whom?"

He shrugged and canted his head. "Harriet in Human Resources. They're downsizing, and I didn't make the cut."

Venus raised her eyebrows. She sat on the edge of Eugene's

desk and reached for a chocolate Tootsie Pop in a treat jar that hadn't yet made it into the packing box.

"You taking this brown baby?" she asked him. "Because if you want, I can take it off your hands."

"Venus!" I warned. "We're having a crisis here."

"I know it's a crisis, girl, but obladee, obladah."

Eugene's breath sounded ragged. The last thing I needed was for him to panic. I grabbed Liza's picture and set it back on his desk.

"It's a mistake," I said. "I'll fix it with Gordon."

"Thanks, Tucker," he said, "but it won't do any good."

"Don't go anywhere, either of you." I stomped into my office, grabbed the copy of the memo from my printer, and hurried back to Eugene's desk. "Harriet can't fire you. That's my job."

"Uh-oh," Venus said. "She's got that 'Bad, Bad Leroy Brown' look in her eye."

Eugene frowned and poked at Venus with a rolled-up copy of *Martha Stewart Living* until she finally moved her butt off his desk. Public safety issues made me question the wisdom of leaving the two of them alone, but I had to talk to Gordon—now.

I felt a little shaky as I walked down the hall to his office. Something was seriously wrong. The company wouldn't be downsizing, especially with the prospect of getting that contract from Wade Covington. Plus, it was bad form to fire my administrative assistant behind my back. Even if Eugene wasn't all mine now, everyone knew that he would be soon.

Look before you leap. There are two sides to every story. Two wrongs don't make a right. All the old clichés ran through my head as I tried to keep myself calm, tried to convince myself that there was a logical explanation for all this. But no mantra could temper the overwhelming sense of fear and betrayal that squeezed my insides until they hurt. Not telling me that Eugene had been downsized might have been unintentional, but not telling me I'd been replaced on the Amsterdam project was deliberate. With every step, I hoped Pookie had been wrong, that Gordon Aames hadn't turned against me. One thing was sure: Everything depended on how I handled myself now. The day wasn't going well, but it was early, and I was sure that I could turn it into a complete disaster if I really tried.

10

Y ou can't go in there. He's in conference."

I smiled and waved at Marsha as she rose from her chair.
What was she going to do, throw her body across the threshold?
She was devoted to Gordon, but not that devoted.

I flung open the door and saw Gordon huddled over some
papers on the conference table. Sitting next to him was Richard
Hastings, wearing a suit that reeked of the annual Barney's airport hangar sale. Hastings was in his late thirties, fastidious, and
terminally trendy. There wasn't a single hair on his head that was
out of place, not a visible hangnail or a sweaty-armpit stain. I suspected even his boxer shorts sported dry-cleaner creases. He
looked so slick, it was amazing he didn't slide off his chair.

Gordon's shirt was open at the collar, his tie loose. I wasn't
sure, but it appeared as if his bald spot had grown wider since I'd
last seen him. When he saw me, he turned the paper he was
holding facedown on the pile.

"Tucker," he said, sounding perfectly friendly. "I want to talk
to you, but I'm in a meeting. Why don't you wait outside?"

"I don't think so, Gordon. And I think you know why."

I held up the Amsterdam memo. He exchanged a look with
Hastings, who, as he rose to leave, flashed me a little smirk that I
wanted to rub off his face with a floor buffer.

"You've read your e-mail," Gordon said. It was somewhere between a question and a statement. "I was going to explain this morning, but you weren't in."

"I'm here now."

I sat at the conference table across from him and crossed my arms and my legs. I thought about my negative body language and crossed my fingers as well. Gordon buttoned his collar and tightened the tie. His skin looked sallow.

"First of all, let's get something straight, Tucker." His voice was quiet but firm. "You don't have permission to come into my office unannounced. Ever."

"Oh, but you have permission to fire my administrative assistant unannounced? Is that the deal?"

Gordon moved to his desk, placing the papers he'd taken from the conference table on his credenza, well out of my sight.

He sat in his chair, looking calm. "He wasn't fired. We're downsizing administrative staff, and he's low man on the totem pole."

I stared at him until he looked away.

"For a guy who taught me how to bullshit," I said, "you're a little rusty."

He took off his glasses and wiped them with a little chamois he pulled from his desk drawer. "This won't get us anywhere, Tucker. Let's call a truce. The reason I wanted to talk to you was that I met with our attorneys last night."

I searched my range of feelings for one that fit the occasion, and finally settled on baffled, hurt, and suspicious. "Without me? Why?"

Gordon put his glasses back on and began signing some letters, finishing off his signature with a big, round flourish surrounding his name.

"You were gone all day yesterday," he said. "I couldn't wait any longer, and when you didn't come in this morning—"

His wimpy excuse irritated me. "Marsha told me nothing was scheduled. She had my cell phone number. No one called."

"Things were happening too fast," he said. "I had to move forward, contain this mess before someone got hurt. The attorneys say it doesn't matter that we have Polk's signature on all those documents. He can still claim you changed that report, with or without his permission. They're worried we'll be inundated with lawsuits unless we can negotiate with Whitener to end this whole mess. They're working on that, but in the meantime they want you off the front lines."

My chest felt tight; my throat constricted as I waved the memo in front of him. "The front lines being Amsterdam?"

"We're making inroads into the European market. The Juliana is a high-profile project. The last thing we need is to trot you out during a criminal investigation."

"There *isn't* any criminal investigation." My words came out angry. "There's one threatening letter from somebody who made a bad decision and wants to be compensated for it."

Gordon stacked the signed letters neatly and screwed the cap on the pen before laying it on the desk. "We have to be careful how we handle Whitener, especially now that Polk is dead."

"I guess you read the article in the *Times*."

"No. Wade Covington called me last night." Gordon's lips were pinched, his jaw tight. He seemed upset now but was keeping it under control. "He wasn't exactly impressed with your smart-ass attitude when he saw you in Polk's office. He hinted it might cause a problem getting that bid."

"That's ridiculous," I said. "How could he even suggest that?"

"He said you threatened to bring him into this whole Polk business with the police. He was upset, and frankly, so am I."

An angry Wade Covington wasn't good news. I tried to re-member what I'd said to make him that way, but all I could think of was that one little remark about scuba diving. Was he humor-impaired? It was a joke.

I took a deep breath to control my growing alarm. "He must have misunderstood. I'll call him. I'll smooth things over—"

"That's exactly what you will *not* do," Gordon said, his voice strained. "You will not speak to Wade Covington. And forget Polk. His death is unfortunate, but we have to move on. The guy probably changed those reports himself, just like you said. The lawyers think so, too. They want to position the firm as the in-nocent victim."

I paused but maintained eye contact. "You keep talking about the firm. What about me?"

"There's no easy way to say this, Tucker. The only thing I'm interested in right now is putting this Whitener business behind us and getting back into Covington's good graces. After he called me, I polled the partners. They're concerned."

"I'm concerned, too. That's why I want to—"

He stood abruptly, clearly agitated. "Obviously, I'm not get-ting through to you. The partners think you're jeopardizing the firm. They want you out."

The muscles in my face felt heavy, and my mouth wouldn't close. Gordon's words buzzed around my head for what seemed like an eternity, while my eyelids blinked their way into the *Guinness Book of World Records*. I looked at his face. It was thin and angular and not particularly handsome, but it was the face of a man who'd been both a teacher and a friend, and that made his hostility toward me even more jarring. When I found my voice, it seemed as if it belonged to someone else.

"Out? You mean *out* out. Like out of the firm? Is that why I won't need an administrative assistant? The partners are firing me? You're the boss, Gordon. What do you want?"

"It's out of my hands," he said quietly. "They voted to suspend you while they look into the situation. I convinced them to let you take some time off. With pay. It's the best I could do. I'm sorry."

His words felt like a cold shower. I sucked in my stomach, hoping to keep my emotions in check, but the pain wouldn't go away. The fat lady had sung. There'd be no help from the firm with any FBI investigation now. And no partnership. No office with a view. It felt as if the final curtain had just dropped on my entire life.

"And if I refuse to go quietly?" I kept my voice icy and controlled.

Gordon's expression had changed, had become pained, as if it disturbed him to have lost his composure. He sat and started rearranging and fiddling with those letters in an attempt to keep the focus off his words and my question.

"It's only temporary," he said. "The partners will meet next week to discuss the problem. It's at the top of their agenda. By that time, our attorneys will have met with Whitener's people, and we'll be able to assess the situation. I'm sure they'll support you then."

"Gordon, why do I get the impression that you're on everybody's side except mine?"

He raised his head slowly and looked at me. His expression was an accusation, as if I'd betrayed him in some way and my disloyalty weighed heavily on him. Then he winced as if in pain. I wondered if his ulcer was acting up. I could only hope so.

"I'm sorry you feel that way," he said. "I've always been on your side—you know that—but sometimes you don't make it easy. Just stay out of it for now, and give me time to smooth things over."

When I spoke, it was with a tone that I used when I was about to say something I'd probably regret. "You don't leave me much choice, so I'll play it your way. For one week. But what you're doing is wrong, Gordon, and probably illegal. So when the partners meet, I'll be there—with my own attorney. Tell them to put *that* on their agenda."

The muscles in his cheeks twitched from clenching his jaw. He stared at the desktop, looking small, much smaller than I'd ever seen him look before. I held the Amsterdam memo in a death grip, trying to keep from bumping into anything as I crossed the room.

Before opening the door, I turned to face him. "And, Gordon? That downsizing bit is pure bullshit. You fired Eugene without cause. So I suggest you *un*fire him, or I'm going to tell him to get himself a lawyer, a good one, and sue your ass off."

I stumbled out of the office, past a stunned Marsha, down the hallway, concentrating only on a subtle leafy pattern in the beige carpet. Was the accent color cream or oatmeal? Had I imagined the past fifteen minutes? I tried to reconvene my anger, but all I felt was emptiness. I'd spent my whole career at Aames & Associates. For what? Pookie was right. I'd trusted harder, not smarter, and had only myself to blame.

Eugene's desk was in sight when I realized that I'd forgotten to tell Gordon that the NeuroMed file was gone. Just as well. The last thing I needed was to have him angrier with me than he already was. I couldn't let anything sidetrack me now, because I had less than one week to locate those missing documents, or I might find myself not only out of a job but also into a jail cell.

11

i didn't want to make Eugene more anxious than he already
was, so I downplayed my own uneasiness when I explained
what had happened in my meeting with Gordon. I knew Eugene's salary was a piddly amount compared with the cost of a
lawsuit, so I thought the firm would weigh those risks and decide to keep him on the payroll, but I wasn't sure. At first he refused to stay on without me, but I eventually convinced him it
was the best thing to do.

Regardless of what Gordon said about a temporary suspension, I felt unemployed. My entire identity had been tied up in
the firm, but now I wasn't sure that I even wanted to be rein-
stated, not under the circumstances. One thing I was sure of,
though: Whether I stayed with the firm or not, I wanted it to be
my decision, not Gordon's or the partners'. As for Covington, it
was unimaginable that he would deny Gordon a consulting contract because of my one flippant remark. I was already persona
non grata at the firm, and didn't want the blame for losing that
consulting bid heaped on me, too. Despite Gordon's warning, I
was going to call Covington—grovel if necessary—to straighten
things out.

Venus was fuming. Poor Gordon if he tangled with her today.
She and I commiserated for a while until she had to leave for a

meeting. After she was gone, I checked the firm's contact database and copied a half-dozen numbers listed for Covington onto the back of the Amsterdam memo. I was going to call him, but first I wanted to talk with Mona Polk. I had to find out who had altered the NeuroMed report and why they were blaming me. She seemed like the logical place to start my search. Besides, if things didn't work out at the firm, I might need clients of my own, and she'd be my first.

Mona picked up on the first ring. She was surprised but pleased to hear from me so soon. Yes, indeed, she said, she was eager to see me. I jotted down her address in Pacific Palisades next to Covington's telephone numbers and slipped the paper into my purse.

A pall had settled over the room. I didn't want to stay here any longer. Eugene sat at his desk in a state of agitated limbo, half packed, waiting for Gordon's call. I knew Gordon. He'd have someone in Human Resources take care of it, but not until I was gone.

The partners' meeting was next week. Whitener's deadline was Monday. I wanted to be prepared. Of course, a top priority was finding the NeuroMed documents, but I also wanted to follow up on the Tucker Sinclair–Sunland connection. If Polk or Francine had used my name for insurance fraud, I had to know what else I was facing.

I rolled up my Moorish rug and packed my tchotchkes. The lowboy would have to stay behind for now. It took several trips to load everything into the car. Nobody tried to stop me. Nobody even asked me what I was doing. By the time I was finished, there was still an hour until my appointment with Mona Polk. I decided to pace myself by taking Wilshire Boulevard instead of the freeway. By the time I'd reached Westwood Boulevard, I was still ahead of schedule, so I pulled into the Village to make a couple of telephone calls.

Westwood Village is the commercial area just south of UCLA, where I went to school. The boulevard was jammed with traffic headed onto campus. On the sidewalks, students with backpacks and men in suits with cell phones hanging from their belts barely noticed the rug sticking out of my car window as I parked at a meter near the corner of Broxton and Gayley. Across the street was one of the many coffee shops that had sprouted up in the area as part of the invasion from the Northwest. With all that caffeine, no wonder people were sleepless in Seattle.

I used my cell phone to dial the first number listed for Covington, then the second, third, fourth, and fifth. He wasn't in. Did I want to leave my name? Maybe not. What did I expect? That he'd be in and anxious to chitchat? I stared at the last number on the list. My enthusiasm was waning. Oh, what the hell. A young Valley girl answered on the third ring. Covington wasn't in. I was about to hang up when she said, "Are you RSVP'ing for the luncheon tomorrow?" She giggled.

I had no idea what she was talking about. "Yes, the luncheon," I said. "How did you know?"

"I could see it in your voice," she said. "It's a gift. Besides, I'm getting a zillion calls a minute. What's your name?"

I gave it to her, and she rustled some papers.

"Like, totally weird. You're not here."

"Guess whoever made the list doesn't have your gift. Maybe you can just add my name?"

"Yeah, okay," she said hesitantly, as if she was looking into my voice once more for some kind of sign. "Since it's, like, for charity and all."

I expected her name to be Tiffany Amber, but it was Carole.

She was a temp and the biggest gift I'd had all day. The luncheon was a fund-raiser being held at Covington's home the following day. Carole made it clear I should bring my checkbook. The suggested minimum donation was two grand. Ouch! I spelled my name—twice—and crossed my fingers hoping Tiffany Amber/Carole wouldn't screw it up. Having written down all the essential information, including Covington's address, I closed my cell phone. Things were looking up. Me, in Wade Covington's home, schmoozing in the relaxed atmosphere of an intimate charity luncheon. What more could I ask for?

I decided to test my winning streak by calling Eric. I still felt uncomfortable about the whole getting-back-together thing and hoped he wouldn't bring it up. Not that he had any really bad qualities, just annoying ones, and that wasn't even counting the universal stuff men did with toilet seats and wet towels on the bedspread, which couldn't fairly be held against him. On the other hand, neither of us had had a serious relationship since our divorce, and it did get lonely sometimes. I decided at least to keep an open mind.

I didn't have to wait long after dialing Eric's number before I heard his voice on the line. The first words out of his mouth were, "Somebody logged on to my computer. Know who that might have been?" He sounded peeved.

I felt a guilty burn on my face. "Nope," I said, "but if I think of anyone, I'll let you know."

"Yeah, I'm sure you will," he said sarcastically. Then his tone turned serious. "Look, Tucker. I'm swamped. I'll have to work at home all weekend just to catch up. So what do you want now?"

"I'll make it quick," I said. "I need a lawyer. Someone kind of civil and kind of criminal. Like the guy you play tennis with. The one with the breasts. Is he any good?"

"Sheldon Greenblatt does not have breasts." He sounded huffy, punching each syllable. "And yes, he's good. The best. But at six hundred an hour, he's not in your budget. What's going on?"

"Can I tell him you referred me?"

"Tucker, you're making me nervous. Tell me why you need a lawyer."

"Let's just say the best offense is a good defense attorney," I said. "What's his number?"

I drummed my fingers on the steering wheel as Eric weighed his desire to know more against his need to tackle the work on his desk. He was conscientious to a fault, so I knew which one he'd choose.

There was a heavy sigh, and then he said, "Let me call him first."

I smiled. "Warn him, huh?"

"Something like that." There was another short pause, and then his voice became a little softer. "Tucker, look. You can't put me off forever. We have to talk—in person—about our relation-ship."

That relationship word again. The last thing I needed was for Eric to press me on the topic right now. Still, the affection in his tone made me think about all the good times we'd had together. The PBS bug specials we'd watched, wrapped in each other's arms. The elegant dinner parties he loved to throw for our friends. The Minnesota trips to visit his aunt So-you-didn't-take-the-Bergstrom-name-then? Lena.

I kept my tone light. "Sounds scary."

"Yeah, maybe a little it is." His voice had a teasing quality about it that was very appealing. "But it could be a little won-derful, too."

Oh, what the hell. Eric deserved reciprocity for Shelly Greenblatt, so before we hung up, I agreed to meet him at six the following evening. I put the phone in my purse and glanced across the street at the shop next to Stan's Donuts. In the window was a T-shirt that read, *Jesus is coming, everybody look busy.* Sounded like good advice, so I put the car in gear and headed for Mona Polk's house.

Pacific Palisades is a hilly residential area on the coast, tucked in between Santa Monica on the south and Malibu on the west. It's as far away from the hustle and bustle of the inner city as affluence can take you. The Methodist Episcopal Church originally developed the land, and many of the streets are named after its bishops. In the early days, I guess church members felt that the high palisades got them closer to God. Nowadays, Pac Pal property owners don't claim to rub elbows with God, but they do cozy up to some pretty impressive profits when they sell.

I turned onto Bienveneda and then made a left onto a side street to a large Spanish-style house. I parked in the circular driveway and made my way to the massive wooden door. Nothing so modern as a doorbell was visible, so I used a brass lion's head to announce my arrival.

An ageless, squat woman, presumably Elsa, answered the door. She was Indian-looking, perhaps Central American, with broad brown cheeks and coarse black hair held together in a braid that cascaded down the middle of her back.

"Tucker Sinclair to see Mrs. Polk."

She gave me what looked like the evil eye before motioning me inside with a nod. The circular foyer connected to a long hallway leading to parts unknown. To the right were two intricately carved wooden doors. To the left was a stairway, which was barricaded by a wrought-iron gate that looked like chic prison bars. My leather-soled shoes made a hollow sound as I followed her across the terra-cotta tiles. She pointed to a dark, rough-hewn wooden bench that looked as if it had once served as a pew in some early California mission. The foyer was empty except for that bench and a small table near the door, which held an arrangement of exotic flowers. I sat.

Clad in thin backless slippers, the woman shuffled softly across the floor and through the iron gate, closing it solidly behind her as if worried I might follow uninvited. Then she rounded the corner of the stairway and disappeared.

After waiting for several minutes, I rose from the bench and walked over to sniff the flowers. Beyond roses and carnations, my knowledge of botany is minimal, and I couldn't identify any of those blooms. A miniature envelope was threaded through a plastic pitchfork poking out of the pot. I couldn't resist. The unsigned message on the card inside read, *For a job well done.* Didn't sound like a typical condolence message, but so far, my association with the Polks had been less than conventional.

Snooping is like guacamole. After you acquire a taste for it, it's hard to stop. I scouted the room to make sure I was alone and then moved toward the double doors, pressing down on one of the handles. The door opened into a massive living room that seemed somehow very un-Milton-like. I would sooner have expected a condo in the Marina with fake zebra beanbag chairs and a pinball machine. Instead, the room was filled with an amazing array of antiques that could have been dizzying had the pieces not been arranged with such skill. Ceramics, pottery, metal, and wood implements harmonized with the unique rugs and furniture pieces. The total effect was primitive and haunting.

The mood was broken when fingers dug into my shoulder with amazing strength. I turned to face Elsa. Her disposition had turned even surlier, if that was possible. Pointedly she surveyed the area to check if anything was missing. When she seemed satisfied that each piece was secure in its usual place, she motioned me out of the room. I returned obediently to the foyer, feeling like a child who'd been caught looking up dirty words in the dictionary.

She poked me in the back with her finger and pointed toward the stairs. "Go."

Her unblinking black eyes followed me as I slipped through the iron gate and began climbing the stairs. Even as I rounded the corner, I could feel her eyes still searing into my back with pinpoint precision, like a laser just before the bullet hits.

12

a fortyish and fashionably thin Mona Polk stood at the top of the stairs in a navy pleated skirt and white blouse that could have doubled as a school uniform. She wasn't at all what I'd expected. Milton Polk was overweight and out of shape. His wife looked like a woman who took care of herself, not the wide-eyed woman-child I envisioned from her lilting telephone voice. Her hair was blond and curly like a Nordic Betty Boop, and it framed a rather flat but pleasing face. A biceps the size of a lemon flexed as she reached out to offer me her hand. I followed her down a bare wood hallway that smelled of carnauba wax, until we reached a large room with floor-to-ceiling bookcases and leaded-glass windows that opened onto an English garden.

"Pardon the mess." She gestured toward an assembly line of papers and stamps on an industrial-strength table. "I'm program chairman for Project Rescue. We sponsor a shelter for battered women in Guadalajara. Have you heard of us?"

"Sorry," I said.

"No, I suppose not. There are so many needy causes, aren't there? I organized an awards dinner Saturday night," she said. "Now I'm working on our monthly newsletter, but with all the confusion, I got behind."

At least an awards dinner explained the cryptic job-well-done message on the flowers downstairs.

"Was that the dinner Dr. Polk was supposed to attend?" I asked.

She looked at me, seeking clarification with her pea green eyes. "He did attend. He left early, but he was there. That was the last time I saw him." She pressed a tissue to her left eye even though they both looked dry to me.

"I got the impression Dr. Polk was a no-show. Francine said he didn't pick up the tuxedo he'd planned to wear that night. She also told me you were out of town for the weekend and didn't know where he was."

Mona Polk pinched her lips together until they were small and round. "I was at the dinner, and so was he. Shortly after the event was over, I left for our place in Santa Barbara. My husband had already gone—home, I presumed. When I came back on Monday and he wasn't at the house, I wasn't alarmed. I don't always know his schedule."

"What time did he leave the dinner?"

"I'm not sure exactly. I saw him at around ten, so some time after that."

That meant Polk was still alive late Saturday night, which meant he probably died shortly after leaving the Project Rescue event.

"Dr. Polk told Francine he was meeting someone Saturday night," I said. "Do you have any idea who that was?"

She seemed slightly peeved, the first break I'd detected in her honeyed facade. "I suggest you discard half of what you hear from Francine Chalmers, and then discount the other half. That woman was very possessive of my husband. It made his life difficult at times. Do you mind if I work while we talk? There's a lot to be done."

I said sure, but I felt impatient to move ahead with my agenda. She sat at the table and began meticulously folding sheets of paper and sliding them neatly into envelopes, which she sealed with her tongue. I sat down in a chair across from her.

"I understand that Francine has been employed by Dr. Polk for quite some time," I said. "How closely did he supervise her work?"

"My husband was a doctor, Ms. Sinclair, not an administrator."

Technically, she was wrong. He was both, but I didn't want to argue the point.

"Who else might know about the Center's billing procedures?"

She paused to think. "Possibly Harold Amberg. He and my husband had known each other for years. They also shared practice space."

"Does Dr. Amberg know about his death?"

She looked momentarily pained. Then she leaned back in her chair, staring upward into nowhere. "I'm not sure." She left her mouth open for a moment as if she would say more, but nothing came out. It could have been glue buildup, but it felt more like holding back. "It isn't easy telling friends that your husband committed suicide."

Her statement threw me. "Did the police find a suicide note?"

"No, but why do you think people leave notes anyway?"

"I don't know. To get the last word. Maybe just to explain why."

She took a deep breath and blew it out slowly. "My husband and I said everything we needed to say to each other years ago. I'm sure he would have considered any further words superfluous." The tone of her statement seemed almost like a confession, as if she was acknowledging her failures before someone did it for her.

I tried to keep my tone soft and nonthreatening. "I'm surprised. He didn't seem like the type."

"As you probably found out, my husband was a take-charge kind of person. Why is it so hard to believe that he took charge of his death as well?" She paused. "I don't suppose he told you. He rarely talked about it. But we lost a son three years ago to Emery-Dreifuss. It's a rare form of muscular dystrophy. Ryan began showing symptoms at age five. We tried everything to make him better. Nothing worked. He died of a complex arrhythmia. My husband took his death rather hard."

I watched her closely as she talked about her child. Her face was placid, her tone clinical. At least their son's death helped shed light on Polk's passion for neurodiagnostic testing and, perhaps, his volatile nature as well. But three years had passed, so why commit suicide now, especially when he believed NeuroMed was on the verge of helping people like his son? Even adding Mo Whitener's threats to the mix didn't seem like reason enough for somebody as tenacious as Milton Polk to end his life.

"I'm sorry," I said. "I didn't know about your son. I guess that might explain—"

She interrupted. "I realize this may sound a little cold to you. Please don't get the wrong impression. I cared deeply for my husband, but we had an arrangement. I didn't question his comings and goings, and he gave me money to pursue my interests. I learned long ago not to hope for explanations."

She was right. Her comment did sound cold, but I tried to cut her some slack. Maybe she was simply numb from years of spousal neglect. Polk couldn't have been easy to live with. Besides, pushing the suicide theory might deflect suspicion from her. After all, wasn't the spouse always the obvious suspect in a murder case? I wondered if Mona Polk had any reason to want her husband dead. She might have gotten tired of dealing with his angry outbursts, or blamed him for not finding a cure for their son's illness. Maybe the guy just wouldn't put the cap back on the toothpaste, and she couldn't take it any longer. Of course, all that was useless speculation, because Mona Polk had an alibi for the time of her husband's murder. She was in Santa Barbara for the weekend, or so she claimed. In any event, the police would sort all that out. I had to move forward.

"Mrs. Polk, how exactly can I help you?"

"You can stamp." She held out a roll of postage stamps and a stack of envelopes.

"No, I meant—your phone call—the reason I'm here."

She handed me the stamps anyway. At least the roll she gave me was the self-adhesive variety and looked benign, so I decided to lend a hand. She flattened the pleats on her skirt and resumed folding the newsletters.

"My husband was something of a maverick, as you know," she said. "He didn't trust many people, but as I told you on the phone, he spoke highly of you. I need someone he trusted to give me a picture of what's happening at NeuroMed. For example, is it possible for me to run it, or will I have to sell?"

"How much do you know about your husband's business?"

"Nothing, really," she said. "He has a private practice, but I don't know what's left of it. So much of his energy lately went into building the Center. Frankly, my husband handled all our finances. I'm not sure where the money was coming from."

I'd met people like Mona Polk before, but I always found them difficult to understand. They seemed like intelligent, competent women until they married strong-willed, powerful men and somehow morphed into Stepford wives. Watching women play passive arm candy in a horror film is one thing, but seeing it in the real world is far scarier. Mona Polk was program chair-woman of a charity and had just planned and executed a large fund-raising dinner. The flowers in the foyer were proof of her success. Now her husband was dead, and she found herself clue-less about everything, including the source of her own income. What a waste of good brain cells.

"You're not a doctor, so you'll have to sell the neurology practice," I said. "As for NeuroMed, it would be tough to run it without some background in medicine. You'd probably have to hire a physician and an administrator. That costs money. Frankly, I'd look at selling that, too."

"Could you find a buyer for me?" she said.

I hesitated. That wasn't in my area of expertise. On the other hand, Milton Polk was dead, and I was in a lot of trouble. I had less than a week to find out who'd gotten me into this jam and why. Without Gordon's support, I was on my own. Mrs. Polk seemed like my only option at this point.

"I'm not a medical-practice broker," I said. "I can help you find one, but I have to warn you: I may not be the best person for the job."

At first she looked puzzled and then stunned as I told her about Whitener accusing me of scamming investors. I explained that certain people, including FBI agents, might interpret my fur-ther involvement with NeuroMed as proof of collusion between her husband and me. It was a long time before she spoke.

"I don't know what to do," she said.

I felt disappointed by her response. Her first big decision post-Milton, and she blew it.

"Don't worry. You'll figure it out."

I'd almost made it to the door when she said, "Wait. I need help, and I don't know who else to call."

That wasn't much of an endorsement, but it was a start. I nodded. "Okay. The practice broker will need reports and financial statements for both businesses. I have the NeuroMed data, but I'll need to do some research on Dr. Polk's private practice."

She looked relieved and asked me to start working on the reports immediately. I promised to prepare a contract for her to sign that would spell out all the details, including my fees. After that, she picked up the letters we had just neatly stacked, and threw them into a tote bag leaning against the table.

"I'm sorry to rush you, but I have another appointment."

"Okay," I said. "Just one more thing: I'm looking for something of mine that your husband may have left here. It's the original business plan I wrote for NeuroMed. It could be in a large maroon envelope."

She frowned in thought. "I haven't seen anything like that," she said, "but you're welcome to look through his desk. If it's not there, I'll ask Elsa to check around the house."

"I'll also need a signed note explaining that I'm working for you, in case anybody asks, and the address of your husband's private practice."

She rose gracefully from her chair, walked to a desk near the window, and pulled an address book and a couple sheets of personalized stationery from the drawer. She scribbled intently. Then she handed me the pages. On one, she'd written the name Harold Amberg, M.D., diagonally across the page. Underneath was an address in Sherman Oaks. Somehow, I expected Mona's handwriting to be small, tight, and controlled, but it wasn't. Hers was large but feminine, as if it belonged to a person who was not afraid to take risks to indulge her passions. Interesting, I thought.

"I'll call Harold and tell him to expect you." Mona pulled out one of the newsletters from her bag and handed it to me. "And take one of these, in case you're looking for a cause."

She led me down the hall to Polk's home office. I made a quick search through his desk drawers. The NeuroMed documents weren't there, but I kept looking. I didn't know what I hoped to find, just something—anything—that pointed me toward a solution to all my problems. When Mona checked her watch for the second time, I took the hint.

"If it's more convenient, I could look through these papers at home and bring them back in a day or so."

She said, "Fine," and from the closet she pulled a couple of canvas tote bags, imprinted with the name of a drug company. I filled both with all the files and loose papers I could find in Polk's desk.

Mona gave me a parting handshake. "I'll show you out."

"That's okay, I'm sure Elsa will make sure I find the door."

Elsa was nowhere in sight as I made my way down the stairs, though I expected to find her lurking behind a potted palm, watching my every move. I had just cleared the wrought-iron gate when I was distracted by a noise. A man somewhere in his twenties stood in the foyer; feathery black eyelashes, held at half-mast for maximum effect, framed his dreamy brown eyes. A skimpy white gym towel, wrapped tightly around his waist, exposed one dark, muscular leg. Water meandered down his body, furrowing the curly hair on his broad chest. He had black hair, an olive complexion, and symmetrical features. Women would have bought the calendar for his picture alone. He smiled and, with one last sultry flutter of those lashes, disappeared down the hall, leaving behind shimmering footprints on the tile floor, and the scent of Ivory soap. I couldn't help wondering if this smoldering towel boy was one of Mona's "interests" that Milton Polk financed, and if he was the appointment she was late for. Sometimes I have a bad habit of looking for the worst in people. More than likely, he was just a friend helping her work through her grief.

13

oments later I walked down Mona Polk's front steps and across the circular driveway, toward the Boxster. The street was deserted except for a few parked cars and the city trash and recycling containers lined up curbside. I had hoped that Mona could provide more details about her husband's whereabouts on the last weekend of his life, but finding that information was obviously going to be more difficult than I'd anticipated. At least, I knew where he'd been until ten o'clock on Saturday, the night he'd died.

Sitting in the car, I leaned back against the headrest and wondered if Polk had received Mo Whitener's letter, too, and if he knew about the fraud accusations against me. If so, he must have also known that sooner or later he'd be implicated as well.

I took a few minutes to sort through the items I'd taken from Polk's desk, and found an expensive-looking black leather appointment calendar. Unfortunately, all the pages were blank, as if it had been an unwanted gift that had never been used. Slipped inside the book were two form letters that were stuck together with something pink and squishy that could have been part of a Hostess Snowball. Both letters were hawking life insurance. There were also some overdue bills that I'd have to return to Mona for payment, a piece of paper with some circles and numbers that may have been a seating chart from the Project Rescue dinner, and a newspaper clipping. It was in Spanish and included a picture of a young woman. My high school Spanish was rusty, so I couldn't read anything but the name, Teresa García. Mona did charity work for a women's shelter in Mexico. The clipping was probably connected to that. I looked at the seating chart. Ten to a table. Fifty tables. Big event. The numbers inside the circles obviously corresponded to another register not contained in the envelope—the one that listed the names of the attendees.

The remainder of the pile included a parking ticket and a sealed envelope addressed to Polk in what looked like his own hard-to-read handwriting. When I opened it, I was hoping to find something helpful, like a Stupid Criminal Check List: (1) change report; (2) blame Tucker; (3) run away to Rio with [name of accomplice here]. No such luck. All I found was a receipt for a cup of coffee. Scrawled across the receipt were the words *write-off*. A business expense, I realized. Three dollars and fifty cents for a cup of coffee. Now, that was a crime. I found no cashier's checks from Mo Whitener with lots of zeros after the first number, so I put everything back in the two tote bags, including the Project Rescue newsletter Mona had given me. I wouldn't be reading that anytime soon. I had all the causes I could handle at the moment.

Mona had implied that Polk was a hands-off manager, at least when it came to the day-to-day operations, but that hadn't been my impression at all. From what I'd observed, he liked to control and wasn't the type to delegate, especially where money was involved. It might be convenient to let Francine shoulder the blame for any billing irregularities, but was it realistic? She didn't seem like the mastermind type, just the loyal type, someone who'd do anything for her boss. The question was, had she used my name to help him commit insurance fraud?

Technically, I was no longer unemployed. In fact, suddenly I had a lot to do. There were still a few hours before the end of the business day, so I decided to drive to Sherman Oaks, to ask Dr. Amberg some questions about Polk's neurology practice and to see if the NeuroMed documents were somewhere in his office.

I took Sepulveda to the San Fernando Valley, hoping to by-pass some of the traffic on the 405 Freeway. The clouds had thinned, so I put the top down to let the low autumn sun warm my head. With each twist and turn of the road, the car's motion whipped up the calming fragrance of sage from the hills above.

Polk's private practice occupied a modest space on the eleventh floor of a middle-aged building on Ventura Boulevard. The polished brass nameplate on the outer door announced, *Harold Amberg, M.D., Milton Polk, M.D., Neurology.* I expect doctors' offices to be filled with sick people and generally creepy, so I took a deep breath to prepare myself. Luckily, the lobby was empty. As soon as I walked in, I heard the sound of ball bearings sliding on a track. A glass window at the reception counter opened to reveal a young woman with a sweet smile and a freckled face that was surrounded by a cloud of curly raspberry hair.

"You must be Tucker," she said. "Mona just called. Have a seat. I won't be a sec."

She told me her name was Madie and pointed me toward the lobby and a mauve chair that was shaped like a cream puff. Current copies of *The New Vegetarian, Runner's Life,* and a flyer for a charity golf tournament were neatly fanned across a chrome cube table. I was just warming up to an article about how to make tofu taste like apricot macaroons when the glass door opened again.

This time Madie asked me to follow her to one of those

generic doctors' offices that look as if they had been overdeco-
rated by a well-meaning spouse. A collage of framed diplomas
covered one wall. A studio picture of a sensible-looking woman
and two beak-nosed children sat on a credenza behind a desk
that was too large for the room.

I passed on the scratchy-looking tweed chair and was study-
ing the inscription on a tennis trophy when the door opened
and a lean man in his mid-fifties entered the room. His gray
hair was moussed back, exposing a receding hairline. His skin
glowed with color, which, I assumed from the lobby magazines
and tennis trophies, came from exercise and healthy living
rather than a tanning salon. Large glasses covered his face and
were supported by a nose that confirmed that the kids in the
picture were his.

"Ms. Sinclair?" he said. "Mona called, told me you'd be
coming by. She said you needed some information. Of course
I'll help in any way I can. Poor Milt. My God. Too young to
die."

He peeled off a pair of latex gloves before shaking my hand.
His was dry and smooth. The white powder from the glove left
a residue on my palm.

"I hope you don't mind if I work while we talk," he said. "I
have to check a couple of X-rays before my next patient."

"No problem," I said.

As he gestured for me to sit on that scratchy tweed chair, a
whiff of starch from his lab coat wafted past my nose. He sat on
a stool near a box on the wall and pulled two films from a large
yellowish-brown envelope. He stuck the images into clips and
turned on a light at the side of the box.

"I know you're busy," I continued, "so I'll get right to the
point. Maybe I'm wrong, but I assume Mrs. Polk will have to sell

the neurology practice. She may have to let the Center go, too. I'm just curious if you have an opinion about any of that."

"Well," he said, stretching out the word like hot taffy, "as far as the Center is concerned, you'll have to ask someone else. I don't know anything about that."

"And the practice?"

He paused for a moment, maybe to study the frontal and side views of a skull that had materialized with the light, maybe to censor his words before releasing them into the space between us.

"Difficult." His intense focus on the light box made me unsure whether he meant the patient's medical status or my question.

"Seems like the practice would be easy to sell," I said. "Wouldn't it be advantageous for a young doctor to buy an established business?"

His head rocked sideways. "Sure, if it comes with patients. Unfortunately, Milt lost most of his. Truthfully, I think what he really lost was interest. Medicine has changed. Trying to manage patients with all the interference from insurance companies and government agencies was tough on Milt. But for him the Center wasn't medicine. It was business. He could wheel and deal to his heart's content. And that replaced medicine as his one great passion."

If the Center was Polk's one great passion, I wondered where that left Mona. Duh. With Smoldering Towel Boy, that's where.

"Do you have a list of his active patients?"

Amberg's face flushed pink as he turned from the films to look at me. "I find this a little awkward. When Milt started turning away patients, Madie gave them the choice of several other neurologists—with Milt's approval, of course. They also had the option of staying here with us. Most of them stayed. And frankly, it's not because I'm the best doc in town, either. It's because of Madie. Patients love her."

"Okay, let's see if I have this right. Dr. Polk had few or no patients left, and therefore had no income from his practice. So how did he pay his share of the rent?"

"I suppose there's still some money trickling in. But for the past several months, I paid it all, which was only fair. I had added income from taking over his patients. Plus, I was using most of the utilities and supplies. I tried to get Milt to formalize the arrangement by selling his practice to me, but he said he wasn't ready for that."

"So, are you still interested in buying it?"

"That depends. There's not much left to buy—some equipment and office furniture, but that's it. I'd consider making an offer if the number was reasonable, but frankly, it would only be out of consideration for Mona."

"I'm surprised you think the practice is worth so little. I mean, Dr. Polk must have been in business for twenty years or more. How could he lose it all so fast?"

Amberg returned his gaze to the films, but his look seemed more reflective than focused. "You have to understand," he went on. "I've known Milt since medical school. He's a brilliant man, but a bigger risk taker than I care to be. That's why we share office space but not balance sheets."

"When Dr. Polk *did* see a patient, who collected the money?"

"Madie, but she sent everything to his billing service for processing. There was some talk a while back of having Francine take over that function, but I'm not sure if that ever happened. You'll have to ask Madie."

"When was the last time you saw Dr. Polk?"

"Oh, about a week ago, I'd say. Why?"

"I just wondered if he seemed upset about anything."

He paused. "If he was upset, he kept it to himself. My conversations with Milt mostly centered around medicine."

A green button on a wall panel pinged and lit up. "My patient is here. I'll show you to Milt's office. Madie'll look in on you in case you have any questions."

He pulled the X-rays from the clips and led me down the hall to another office. As he unlocked the door, I said, "Dr. Amberg, you've known Milton Polk for a long time. I've heard a lot of theories of how he died—suicide, murder. If you don't mind my asking, what's yours?"

He looked directly into my eyes and without hesitation said, "I don't have a theory. Now, if you'll excuse me . . ."

His answer was abrupt, but I didn't take offense. The question didn't have an easy answer, but that didn't stop me from wanting to know what events in Milton Polk's life had collided so dramatically to leave him dead in the murky waters of Santa Monica Bay. I banished that image from my thoughts and opened the door.

Polk's office was smaller than Amberg's and had no pictures of a spouse or adoring progeny to greet visitors. A desk, two chairs, and a two-drawer lateral file, along with a lone diploma from Northwestern University School of Medicine hanging on the wall, were the extent of the furnishings. The office looked as if the same person who'd done Amberg's had decorated his, but Polk's was toned down as if she'd lost enthusiasm for the project. Or maybe the office merely reflected the fading passion of its occupant. In any case, any vitality that may have existed there had vacated the space long ago.

I opened drawers, hoping to find another calendar or journal that might provide any clue to Polk's recent movements. The lateral files contained more medical journals and article reprints on neurological disorders, but no maroon envelope with an Aames & Associates logo on it.

You find out a lot about a person by looking through his desk. Polk sorted paper clips. The big ones and little ones were carefully separated. However, the same compulsion didn't extend to rubber bands. Those were mixed up and tangled together like some big rubber band love-in. He was a Post-it junkie, too. Every size, color, and functional specialty—he had them all. Along with the standard medical books, he had a copy of *Truly Tasteless Jokes* and Antoine de Saint-Exupéry's *The Little Prince* (in French, no less). Amazing how much, and how little, that said about him.

Lying flat in the bottom drawer were what appeared to be several disorganized manila file folders that held the corporate books and records of NeuroMed Diagnostic Center. Mixed in with that pile were several testing protocols and more pink health insurance claim forms. Some claims were for patients examined in Sherman Oaks, and others were for those tested at NeuroMed. These days, most insurance claims were submitted electronically. I wondered why the billing service had sent hard copies to Polk.

"Finding everything okay?" Madie stood in the doorway.

"Nothing very promising."

She gave me a no-kidding look as her eyes swept the room. "No wonder. You don't have the Deep Six file."

I cocked my head in confusion. That was a term from the old Watergate scandal. I wondered what troublesome documents Polk had wanted to bury.

"Dr. Polk had a system," she explained. "The mail came. He'd look at the return address. Some letters he opened. The rest he threw in a box. The stuff sat for a month or so until he got tired of looking at it, and then he'd toss the whole thing."

"Without reading any of it?"

"Usually," she said with a chuckle. "Then he'd start another box. He always had one going. Hold on."

She disappeared down the hallway and returned minutes later, carrying a carton she'd found in the coat closet. It was heaped full of mail. I thanked her, grabbed a letter opener from the desk, and dug into the box like a pig looking for truffles. The search was tedious. There were stacks of unopened mail, some friendly and some not so friendly: past-due notices from everyone from the *Financial Times* to a bottled-water company, statements from two separate bank accounts. I thumbed through the canceled checks. Sizable payments had been made to several biotech suppliers for testing equipment, but none made out to Sunland Manufacturing. There were no recent large deposits, and no appointment calendars, either.

The last statement from Polk's insurance billing service showed that the practice was owed approximately ten thousand dollars in outstanding receivables. It wasn't much, but it might support Mona's "interests" and help me piece together an accurate income statement for the practice brokers.

I glanced at my watch. It was close to four-fifteen. I'd already been here over an hour. I estimated it would take me another half hour to get to the bottom of the box. Frankly, I didn't blame Polk for deep-sixing most of this stuff. I could guess what was in most of these envelopes, and I didn't want to open them, either. I began passing up the familiar and opening only what piqued my interest, until I found an envelope from a law office with a string of names too long to digest. Inside were three typewritten pages entitled:

MINUTES OF REGULAR MEETING OF BOARD OF DIRECTORS OF
NEUROMED DIAGNOSTIC CENTER, A CORPORATION

Snore. After a paragraph of legal yada, yada, yada, I almost
tossed it back in the hopper, but something caught my eye. It was
an announcement that Francine Chalmers had been duly elected
vice president of said corporation. All resolved, approved, and
ratified.

I thought, my, my. Neither Polk nor Francine had given me
the impression she was anything but an employee. They'd certainly never told me that she was an officer in the corporation.
My face felt warm with anger. Those sneaky liars. I should have
been told. If Francine was vice president, that information should
have been included in my business plan. Polk had obviously
wanted it kept hidden, but why?

"How's it going?"

I gulped air and crushed the pages to my chest. Madie stood
in the doorway watching me.

"I didn't mean to startle you," she said, "but Dr. Amberg's
gone, and our last patient is just leaving."

"Guess I zoned out," I said, catching my breath. "Madie, how
well do you know Francine Chalmers?"

"Pretty well. She used to work here, you know, until she left
to manage the Center."

"Did she have a financial interest in NeuroMed?"

"You mean more than her paycheck? No way. Francine never
had a dime. If she wanted to go out to lunch, she had to beg
Kenny for money."

"Kenny?"

"Her husband. The jerk. I used to tell her she should leave
him, but I think she was afraid."

"Dr. Amberg told me there was talk of Francine taking over the billing. Did that ever happen?"

"Not that I know of, but you'll have to ask her. Anyway, are you going to be much longer? Because my boyfriend's picking me up right at four-thirty."

"I'm not finished, but I can take the box with me if you don't mind."

She didn't, so I tossed the unpaid bills, along with the rest of the mail, into the Deep Six carton and followed her down the hallway. The overhead fluorescent light reflecting on her hair made her look like a Christmas tree angel. We were almost at the lobby door when I stopped at a room that had been closed off before. Inside was what looked like radiology equipment.

"You take X-rays here?" I asked.

"Some," she said. "Not as many now that Dr. Polk isn't here. That guy really liked to zap his patients, especially when he first bought the thing."

It was only a slight possibility, but if Polk had used this equipment a lot, he might have left the NeuroMed documents somewhere inside the room.

"Mind if I take a look?" I asked.

She checked her watch, and for the first time I noticed a crack in her cheerfulness. Nonetheless, she said, "No problem."

The room was cold and empty except for a modified version of a doctor's examination table and a couple of chairs. There was a loud hum from the machine's power source, and the total absence of any odor. Attached to a metal runner on the ceiling was a large X-ray head with a hose about four inches in diameter snaking to a box on the wall. The place reminded me of every horror film I'd ever seen: dimly lit laboratories, and mad scientists hovering over still bodies. Then I thought of Milton Polk lying in a morgue refrigerator. I had to squeeze my shoulders toward my ears to stop the chill that was moving up my spine.

There weren't many places to hide a maroon envelope in the room. Nevertheless, I checked the drawers of the lone storage cabinet, but found only hospital gowns and various medical supplies.

As I walked toward the door, my eyes scanned the room one last time, and that's when I spotted something on the X-ray equipment that made the skin around my jaw prickle. I pulled a chair over and stood on it until I could reach the machine's cold metal handles. A small raised plate was attached to the underside of the contraption. It was stamped with the manufacturer's name, Medcomac—the brand name used by Sunland Manufacturing.

I called for Madie and waited until her squishy rubber-soled shoes squeaked into the room.

"How long have you had this?" I asked.

"I don't remember," she said. "A year or so, I guess. Dr. Polk knew somebody at the company. He got a good deal on it. Are you done in here?"

"Yeah, for now."

Madie walked toward the back of the office to douse the lights, and I headed for the exit, trying to make sense of what I'd just discovered. The Medcomac equipment established a clear link between Polk and Sunland Manufacturing. I just didn't know what it meant. Had someone at Sunland simply sold equipment to Polk, or had that person also been involved in insurance fraud with Polk or someone else at NeuroMed—like Francine? The fact that she'd been made a VP of Polk's corporation indicated that she was closer to him than either of them had let on.

As nutty as it sounded, I wanted the X-ray equipment to be

a clue. Except, what if it turned out to be linked to Polk's death? What was I going to do then—set off with my Junior Sherlock spyglass to deduce the truth? That was more than nutty; it was suicidal. The image of a lifeless face in a blurry Polaroid picture flashed through my mind. But as the photograph came into focus, I saw not Milton Polk's face but my own.

All of a sudden, I felt as if I needed Dr. Watson and a couple of Valium. I wanted a safe haven, someplace to think, and that could be found in only one place—home.

14

orty-five minutes after leaving Amberg's office, I pulled into
my driveway and headed for the back door. From the Do-
manskis' open window next door I heard the sounds of another
boozy argument. There was something about the combination of
the gin and the sea air that made their voices carry. The marriage
seemed less than ideal to me, but it had held together for thirty
years, which was a good deal longer than mine had, so who was
I to criticize?

As I stepped inside, I was greeted by the smell of lavender, and
the clickity-click sound of toenails on tile—the white and wiry
Muldoon. When he realized who it was, something like disappointment appeared in his big brown eyes. He turned abruptly
and skulked toward the French doors and waited. After I let him
out, I unloaded the rug and tchotchkes from the car into Pookie's
bedroom, where they'd have to stay until I could figure out what
to do with them. I also brought in the tote bags from Mona's
place, and the Deep Six box.

After that, I checked my messages. There was one from Eric,
telling me that he'd asked for a return call from Sheldon Greenblatt, who had been in court when he'd called. Court, schmort.
Shelly should get his priorities straight. I needed his help now.
The other call was from Pookie.

"Hi, baby. Mommy misses you."

It sounded like something mushy a normal mother might say—not my mother, but somebody's. There was only one explanation for this uncharacteristic display of *über*affection. The sweat lodge had melted her brain.

"Kissee-kiss, lovey-boo," the message continued, "and give Tucker a big smooch, too."

Well, that explained it. "Muldoon, it's for you," I shouted.

No response. He was obviously too busy to take the call. Pookie continued with some adult stuff about the workshops and giggled about a fellow retreatoid, a sixty-year-old brain-fried Haight Ashbury survivor named Bruce, who had the hots for her. Only problem? He had trouble remembering her name, and everything else in the short term. Nevertheless, she asked me to FedEx a bottle of ginkgo biloba and her *Ravi Shankar's The Sounds of India* album. She was joking, but I could read between the giggles. She was having a good time. There was a brief pause before she added, "Have you called Sylvia yet? When you do, be careful, Tucker. That woman's not operating in the upper level of her vibrations." I hated to admit it, but I missed my mother and found myself wishing she'd left a number so I could call her back.

Somewhere off in the distance, Muldoon was barking. I opened the door and called for him.

"Is this your dog?" It was a nervous, high-pitched voice, coming from somewhere in the shadows near the house.

I stepped outside and saw that Muldoon had pinned a woman against the side of the deck. I called again for him to come, but of course, he didn't. It took at least three more times before he punctuated his one final growl with *mrrph* and then reluctantly walked back onto the deck.

As the woman stepped into the light, I could see that she was somewhere in her late fifties, with that fresh-scrubbed earnestness you see on faces in small Midwestern towns. At the moment, however, she looked as though she'd be happier at home whipping up a tuna hot dish for the Grange supper than fending off my suspicious glare.

"I knocked a few minutes ago," she said, "but nobody answered. You must have just gotten home. I hope you don't mind my looking around."

"That depends on what you're looking for," I said.

As she reached into her purse, I flinched, half expecting her to pull out an AK-47. It had been that kind of day. Luckily, I didn't embarrass myself by diving behind the fake wicker, because all she brought out was a business card. When she handed it to me, I noticed the logo of a local real estate company, and her name, Jane Ventana, agent.

"Sylvia Branch asked me to stop by," she said in a tone that was hesitant. "The woman who owns the house. She's planning to put it on the market in the next few months and wanted to get a ballpark figure of the value. Are you a renter?"

My jaw clamped shut so tight that I nearly didn't get the next sentence out. "News flash, Jane. Mrs. Branch can't put this house on the market, because she doesn't own it. I do."

"Oh, I'm terribly sorry," she said. "I must have the wrong address."

"No, you have the right address, just the wrong information. Sylvia Branch is playing games with your head. I'd blow her off if I were you."

Well, jeez, I said blow her *off,* not blow her *away,* but I guess the hard-edged tone in my voice was enough to start Jane Ventana backing away from the house the moment she interpreted my words as *crazy-woman-with-killer-dog speaks.* Ventana threw in several more nervous "excuse me's" and "I'm sorry's" before beating a path to her car.

When she was gone, I went back inside. I could feel the vein in my neck pulsing as I rummaged through some old photographs and my father's camera equipment, which were stored in Grandma Sinclair's steamer trunk, until I found the file that held all the legal papers dealing with the house.

I reread a copy of my grandmother's will. The wording was as I remembered. Anne Sinclair had left the bulk of her sizable estate to her two surviving children, Sylvia Branch and Donovan Sinclair. But the beach house, she'd left to me. My grandmother could have changed her mind, but according to Pookie, she was an astute woman with a lot of money and a lot of lawyers. Why would she bother to write a new will and then not tell anyone? Aunt Sylvia had to be up to her old tricks again.

Logically, I knew that Sylvia couldn't sell my house without owning it, and she couldn't own it until the probate judge said she owned it. She was just yanking my chain by sending that real estate agent. Of course, the sensible thing would have been to wait until morning and call her attorney to protest. Except, I'd tried that numerous times after Sylvia contested the original will. The guy never returned my calls. This time never was too long to wait. I had to confront my aunt before she pulled another Jane Ventana or something even more creative. Besides, Sylvia had left two telephone messages for me the previous day. Obviously, she wanted to talk. I decided to make her wish come true.

I copied down my aunt's address, and forty-five minutes later I was cruising past the entrance of Vista Hills, a gated community on the San Fernando Valley side of the Santa Monica Mountains, wondering how to get past security. I hadn't counted on that. If I drove up to the gatehouse, the guard would see that my name wasn't on Sylvia's list of approved visitors. He'd call her, and she'd call out the Dobermans. It was too risky. I'd come too far to be thwarted now.

I could cause a diversion and sneak through the gate when the guard wasn't looking, but that worked best with a sidekick, and Venus was nowhere in sight. I'd just have to sneak without a diversion. I parked a couple of blocks down the road and sprinted for a six-foot stucco wall that surrounded the enclave. I crouched down so I wouldn't be seen from either the road or the guard gate, and quietly made my way toward the entrance, stopping only to disentangle an oleander branch that got caught on my sweater.

As I neared the gate, I saw a well-built black man dressed in a neatly pressed uniform. He was sitting inside the guardhouse with the door closed, watching a small television. It must have been a funny show, because even from where I was hiding, I could hear his hearty guffaws. He might have been on the look-out for unauthorized cars, but he didn't seem too intent on watching for unauthorized pedestrians. I stayed close to the wall and crept past the wooden arm of the gate.

Inside, the neighborhood looked like a movie set—familiar but not quite real. It reminded me of the Forbidden City. Cars on the street—forbidden. Litter on the sidewalk—forbidden. In fact, sidewalks—forbidden. I hoped snarling Dobermans were forbidden, too.

I'd never been to my aunt's house, so I checked the curb for addresses. There weren't any. And if there were numbers on the houses, they were too far away for me to see. These people obviously didn't want to be found. The whole neighborhood must be in the witness protection program.

I couldn't wander around too much longer without attracting

attention, so I started looking for names on mailboxes. That wasn't so easy, either. Finally, I spotted a huge French chateau—pink, no less—looming at the top of a hill at the end of the cul-de-sac. I felt as if I'd just been plopped smack-dab in the middle of Disneyland's Versailles Adventure. There was a tiny brass plate on a mailbox near the driveway. Printed on it was the word *Branch*. I was out of breath by the time I jogged up the steps to the front door. I waited as the bell chimed out what sounded like "The Best of Lawrence Welk."

The more I thought about confronting my aunt, the harder my heart pounded. I was about to turn and run when a light switched on from inside the house and the door opened a crack.

An elderly man of medium height stood in the light of a huge crystal chandelier hanging from the foyer ceiling. He had tousled white hair and unmanageable eyebrows. They reminded me of Eric's brows and how they might look when he got old. The man had a slightly befuddled but kindly smile on his face. I wondered who he was. He definitely wasn't Sylvia's husband. Mr. Branch had died several years ago. Wherever he was, I bet he was resting in more peace there than by Sylvia's side in the here and now.

"I'm here to see Sylvia Branch," I said.

His smile turned to a puzzled frown. "How did you get in here? The guard didn't call."

I paused a moment to think. "I live in the neighborhood."

He nodded as if to say, *ah, that explains it.* "Sylvia's not available. She's in a meeting."

I wanted to ask if I could come in and snoop through her desk drawers until I ran across a copy of Grandma Sinclair's bogus new will, but I didn't.

"Will you see her when she gets home?"

He smiled. "She is home. The meeting is here, in the library."

Library? Wow. My aunt not only had money, she had Dewey decimals.

I smiled cordially. "I could wait."

He looked uncertain. "Maybe it would be better if you came back another time."

Who was this guy anyway? He looked too old to be a gigolo and too smart to be her boyfriend. He also looked too nice to be the conveyer of the nasty message I had for Sylvia Branch.

"Who are you talking to, dear?"

It was my aunt's voice. It seemed hollow and faint, as if she was speaking from some distance away.

"It's the neighbor girl," he said. "She wants to talk to you."

I heard the sound of shoes thumping down stairs. Shortly thereafter, the door opened wide, exposing a foyer that was as big as my bedroom. On the far wall were massive windows that were draped in enough fabric to tent my house for termites and sew new outfits for the Vienna Boys' Choir with the leftover yardage. It made me wonder why my aunt wanted my little shoebox of a house. She had no children of her own to leave it to. How much money could she possibly spend in her lifetime?

"You!" she said in a tone that could hardly be classified as friendly.

Sylvia Branch stood silhouetted by the light from the chandelier. She was an imposing woman and might even have been labeled handsome if it weren't for a deep crease between her eyebrows that made her look mean. She was tall, like me, but her dark hair had turned gray. Her fingers were long and slender, and the nails were polished a subtle pink. Everything about her reeked of wealth, from her dove gray wool slacks and pink cashmere sweater set to the three-strand string of pearls around her neck.

"Nice to see you again, Aunt Sylvia. May I come in?"

My cozy familiarity had obviously made her uncomfortable, because her frown deepened. "Since you haven't had the courtesy to return my calls, why should I invite you in?"

"Because we're family, and blood is thicker than water."

"Don't get smart with me, young lady. My lawyer warned me you'd cause trouble. He advised me to have no further contact with you."

"That sounds good to me, too, but let me ask you a question first. Why are you doing this to me?"

"Doing what?"

She said it as if she was stalling for time in order to come up with something other than the truth.

"Trying to steal my house, that's what. Why can't you accept the fact that your mother wanted me to have it?"

"You can't be serious." Her tone was indignant, but her eyes looked moist and pained. "I know my mother. She would never have left anything to you. I was the one who always took care of her. I did everything. And when she was dying, I sat by her bed, holding her hand. As far as I'm concerned, you're not part of this family. You don't deserve anything that belonged to her. You're a fluke."

I'd been called many things in my life, but never a fluke. I won't say that my feelings weren't hurt by her comment, but in truth, they weren't hurt all that much. You never get over being abandoned by your family, but after a while it just becomes part of your day. Besides, maybe she had a point. What claim did I have on anything that belonged to a woman I'd never met?

My tone wanted to be forceful, but it missed the mark. "I may be a fluke, but as hard as it is for you to accept, I'm a Sinclair fluke."

Her expression became cold and sly. "You're a Sinclair by accident only. My brother didn't want you. Your mother tricked him into marriage by getting pregnant."

Okay, I'll admit it: That one hurt. Maybe it was even the truth, but I doubted it. Sylvia was likely just being spiteful. I was still analyzing the emotional impact behind her words when she slammed the door in my face. I knocked several times, calling to her through the door, but I knew that she couldn't hear me. She'd already retreated deep into her house and into her bitter memories.

I still didn't understand why Sylvia resented me so much. Maybe she thought that after all she'd done for her mother, she should have gotten everything, including the beach cottage. Perhaps in her distorted view, getting the place away from me would even the score.

That theory had a few holes, but nonetheless, I planned to tell Sheldon Greenblatt to launch a two-pronged front to defeat both Mo Whitener and Sylvia Branch. That is, if he ever called me back.

Again I wondered about the old duffer who answered the door. I would have pegged him for hired help, except for the fact that Sylvia called him "dear." That didn't sound like something she'd say to her butler.

When I made my way back to the gate, the guard was still slapping his knee over some show on the tube. I tiptoed past him and made my way to the car.

When I finally got home, I found Muldoon standing by the refrigerator. Uh-oh, I thought. In all the confusion, I'd forgotten to buy dog food. Well, he'd have to forage just like me. There was some turkey in the meat tray, so I made us a couple of sandwiches and then carried the food to the couch.

"Okay, here's the thing, Muldoon, if Pookie asks, you don't remember any turkey sandwich. None of this happened. Deal?"

Munch, chomp, murff. Muldoon didn't seem to approve of my ploy, but he definitely approved of my sandwich. He had finished his and was now eyeing mine. In a pinch, Muldoon wasn't so bad to talk to, but it might be nice to add another human point of view to this little think tank. Someone like Eric? After all, he was smart, and he had good ideas. He was a little fussy and pessimistic sometimes, but what the heck. I wasn't perfect, either. I decided against phoning him, because I'd used up my quota of favors for one day. Still, the fact that I was considering calling him at all made me wonder if our relationship deserved another look.

Muldoon was pressuring me for seconds on the turkey, but settled for tortilla chips instead. Pookie would not be happy with the menu, but the little guy looked healthy enough, and he certainly looked happy.

I was too keyed up to sleep, so I went to get the papers I'd taken from Milton Polk's desk and separated everything into piles. The household bills, the seating chart, and the newspaper clipping, I'd return next time I saw Mona. The rest I'd keep for now.

I also spread out the contents of the Deep Six carton on the floor, putting all the insurance claim forms into a separate pile. Some of the forms actually listed Sunland as the employer, so I flagged those. I went through each mound again, carefully looking only at the addresses until—bingo.

In all that chaos I found an insurance claim for a patient named Anton Maslansky, living at a very familiar Beverly Hills address where I knew there would be posters of Brad Pitt movies hanging on the walls. I felt like saying wah-hoo. This was the evidence I needed to show that the Tucker file was not a typo as

Francine had suggested. Someone was using the Rexford Drive address as a mail drop to warehouse insurance payments. I wondered how extensive the scam was and how long it had been going on.

NeuroMed needed money—lots of it—and from the information I'd gathered from Eric's databases, so did Sunland Manufacturing. According to Madie, Polk had purchased equipment from Sunland through some special deal. Did that deal also include collaboration and conspiracy to commit insurance fraud? Maybe. I batched all the claims from patients listing Sunland as an employer and set them aside.

Tomorrow I'd pay a call to Bernard Cole. From what I'd read in Eric's database files, Cole seemed like an upstanding guy. I assumed he'd want to investigate these claims to see if someone in his organization was masterminding the scheme.

I cleaned up the few dishes in the kitchen sink. That made me feel neat and organized, but what I really wanted to feel was loved and appreciated. I sat in the overstuffed chair in the living room and thought about playing Pookie's message again—not the whole thing, just the first part, before I knew that the mommy kisses were for Muldoon and not me. But I didn't, because I was a big girl and above all that. Muldoon evidently saw that I needed cheering up, so he walked through my papers, disrupting my neat little piles. He put his front paws on my leg, looking eager.

I leaned down and looked him in the eye. "Kiss, kiss, Mommy loves—" He apparently didn't pick up on the sarcasm in my voice because he licked on the word "loves," and tongues collided.

"Eeyew."

He liked that sound even better, and round two grazed my

cheek, leaving a thin coat of slime that smelled like tortilla chips. Oh, well, at least his kisses were sincere and meant only for me. Maybe I'd been looking for love in all the wrong places. Maybe tomorrow I'd figure everything out, and people wouldn't be mad at me anymore. Tomorrow. At Tara.

Well, maybe Tara was too much to hope for, but at least I hoped that tomorrow would bring some answers to my questions about Polk and his connection to Sunland. It was risky talking to Bernard Cole, but I had no other choice. I just hoped that Sunland's CEO wasn't the person who'd helped Polk falsify my business plan, or—scarier yet—the person who'd killed him.

15

t he following morning, I put on a soft pinky-beige silk suit with a long skirt that I called my *Out of Africa* outfit, and a pair of shoes with two-inch chunky heels that pushed me dangerously close to six feet tall. Since it was a dual-purpose day, I hoped the getup looked businesslike enough to impress Bernard Cole and charitable enough to wow Wade Covington at his luncheon later in the day.

Sunland Manufacturing was located in Santa Fe Springs, a cluster of track homes, business parks, and heavy industrial sights located about twelve miles southeast of downtown Los Angeles. It's a city where more people work than live, and is better known for its workplace shootings than its drive-by shootings.

There were no neat brass nameplates on the mailboxes in the part of town that Sunland called home, so it wasn't easy finding the place. Luckily, there are two things I always keep in my car: a gym bag with a set of sweats and a pair of athletic shoes, in case I'm ever moved to exercise, which isn't often; and a *Thomas Guide,* the inch-thick map book of Los Angeles County streets that no Angeleno could do without, especially if that Angeleno wasn't fortunate to have GPS in her car. I checked the map to make sure I was on the right road.

It was nine o'clock by the time I finally spotted Sunland's

name painted on the side of a concrete building. I nosed the car onto the dusty shoulder and parked behind a roach coach, which was surrounded by the aroma of refried beans. A dozen or so men stood in line waiting to buy food.

I moved through the powdery dust along the chain-link fence to the entry gate and followed a path to a building with white letters that read OFFICE stenciled on the door. By that time, my shoes were covered with dirt. Not exactly impressive for either a chichi charity bash or a business call. A dust cloud formed around me as I stomped on a bristly mat in front of the door. Inside, the odor of stale cigarette smoke permeated the room. A stressed brown tweedy loveseat with two matching butt prints slouched against the opposite wall. I hoped Sunland's manufacturing facilities were cleaner than their office.

A heavily made-up woman in her late forties sat behind a metal desk. Her pageboy was black and heavy-handed and seemed better suited for someone with a pierced tongue. The letters on her fake wood nameplate read, *Irene Borodin, Human Resources Manager.* Smoke from a burning cigarette coiled from an ashtray on her desk. In L.A. you were barely allowed to smoke in the privacy of your own home. How'd she get away with it here? A computer terminal sat on the credenza behind her. It slept while she posted to a ledger book on her desk. She picked up the cigarette and inhaled deeply.

"What can I do for you?" she said, picking a piece of cigarette grit from her tongue with a long acrylic fingernail.

"I'm looking for Bernard Cole."

"He's not in."

"Know when he'll be back?"

"He doesn't come to the warehouse much. He's probably at the plant." She surveyed me closely, as if something was out of place but she wasn't sure what. A moment later she added, "We're not hiring."

Did I have *unemployed* written on my forehead, or what?

"I'm not looking for a job," I said. "I'd like to talk to Mr. Cole about employee benefits."

She looked bored. "Well, you'll have to talk to me about that. What are you selling?"

I'd decided to be up front with Bernard Cole, but no one said anything about Countess Dracula here. I reverted to plan B.

"I represent a medical facility used by a number of your employees," I said. "We've selected a group of people at random to help us with a survey to see how satisfied they are with the service."

"Who are you with?"

I paused. "NeuroMed Diagnostic Center."

She winked against the curl of smoke that had snaked toward her right eye. "What did you say your name was?"

I couldn't tell her my real name. It might make her suspicious, especially if she'd seen the fake Tucker Sinclair claim form. I needed a name without star quality, something bland and forgettable.

"Mary Jo Felder," I said. "The survey would be strictly voluntary and confidential, of course."

She crossed her arms over her chest defensively, as if I'd just accused her daughter of being big for her age. "Who do you want to talk to?"

I pulled out the insurance claim forms with Sunland listed as the employer and rattled off several names, including Sanjay Rhea, Anton Maslansky, and my own name.

The squint in her eye was no longer from the cigarette smoke. A definite frost had chilled our budding relationship. "I don't remember any Mary Elder working for NeuroMed," she said suspiciously.

"Felder. I'm a consultant with Aames and Associates, working for the owner, Mona Polk. It's probably Francine Chalmers you've worked with before."

She was starting to get froggy, overworking her tongue in search of saliva. "I can't tell you anything. It's confidential."

"Confidentiality is certainly the bedrock of good employee-employer relations," I said. "Of course, I could contact these people at home if you'd prefer. They're all currently employed here, is that correct?"

She must not have liked me looming over her. She stood, but she'd need more than three-inch heels to look me in the eye.

"I don't have time to answer any survey right now. I've got work to do. I'm afraid I'll have to ask you to leave." She sounded testy.

"Okay, but I'd like to leave my number for Mr. Cole."

I didn't have anything to write on, and she didn't seem in the mood to cooperate, so I picked up a piece of paper from the wastebasket and jotted down Mary Jo Felder and my cell phone number. Irene glanced at it briefly. Then she slipped it into the *Bernie* slot of a plastic message holder, which was already bulging with other messages. That didn't look promising.

By the time I left Borodin's office, the roach coach was gone, along with the men. The place looked as deserted as a lunar space station. Irene Borodin hadn't admitted knowing Francine, but she was familiar enough with the Center's personnel to know that there was no Mary Jo Felder working there. That revelation by itself was a little suspicious. My message to Bernie Cole was probably already in the wastebasket.

I was up to my ankles in dust, heading back to my car, when

I noticed a man in his thirties, wearing tight brown jeans and cowboy boots. He had short, sandy hair that was cut for utility rather than style. Baby fat padded his cheeks and chin almost as if his body had decided to grow up without telling his face.

A tool bag was propped up against the wall in front of two large gray metal doors that were standing open, exposing some kind of electrical panel. He was fiddling with the tangle of color-coded wires inside the box and humming "Climb Every Mountain." He didn't look like one of the von Trapp children, so I pegged him for a Julie Andrews groupie. That didn't sound dangerous. Maybe I'd ask him if he knew any of the people on my list.

I walked over and paused for a moment, waiting for him to notice me. His body tensed, but he didn't look my way.

I smiled anyway. "I tried to rewire my toaster once, but my mother made me stop. She thought I'd trigger somebody's nuclear warheads."

He turned his head, and his eyes swept slowly up my body, appraising me the way a lot of men do—as if they were looking for nesting birds in a palm tree. That's when I noticed the bruises on his face. I paused for a moment, wondering if maybe he was the type to settle his differences with his fists. Just in case, I stayed out of his punching range.

Without commenting, he went back to work. No flirty wink. No smile. No nothing. This was going to be tougher than I thought.

"I just came from Human Resources," I said casually. "A friend of mine who works here told me they were hiring. Maybe you know him? Sanjay Rhea?"

He didn't pause to think. Just answered in a twang from one of those southern states. "Don't know him."

"How about Tucker Sinclair?"

"Him, neither." He continued tinkering with the wires.

I waited for a moment and tried once more. "Anton Maslansky?"

He cocked his head like a dog that had just heard a high-pitched whistle. He looked at me as if he was trying to figure out what I was up to and what he should do about it.

"You got more friends than a wino with a credit card." His voice was low and resonant.

I considered my alternatives. "Okay. I'll be up front with you. I don't know those people. I don't even know for sure if they work here. In fact, I was hoping maybe you could tell me that."

He studied me with sapphire blue eyes that looked more suspicious than angry. "You're asking questions like a cop. Except you're not one or you'd a told me. So what's your game?"

"I guess you'd say it's my own private investigation."

He frowned as though he took a dim view of that. "Knowing things gets you into trouble, and I don't need any more of that."

His tone was casual, but I had the feeling there was more to the statement than I was meant to understand. But I wasn't giving up yet, because he hadn't said no when I'd mentioned Maslansky.

"I understand," I said. "So maybe you could help me out with my toaster problem. See, I'm pretty sure there's at least one bad wire in there somewhere, and if I don't find out which one, the thing's going to blow up, and more than toast will get burned, if you know what I mean."

Obviously, he didn't understand the toaster analogy, because he looked at me as if my crumb tray had just come unhinged. Okay, so it wasn't brilliant, but I didn't want to tell him anything incriminating that might get back to Irene Borodin.

"Let me be a little more direct," I said. "I'd like to hear everything you can tell me about those people I just mentioned, like if they work here now, if they ever worked here, and if they have any health problems."

He didn't respond. Just went back to fiddling with his wires. I made a few more attempts to draw him out. He remained civil but taciturn.

Finally, I said, "Maybe I'll just leave my number in case you'd rather talk when you're not so busy."

I couldn't give him my Aames & Associates business card. I didn't work there anymore. And I couldn't tell him my real name. I'd already lied to Irene Borodin about that. I still didn't have anything to write on. Just the two Nut Goodies I'd taken from Eric's desk but forgotten to give Venus. What the hell? I couldn't keep inventing new identities, so I wrote Mary Jo Felder and my cell phone number on one of the candy bar wrappers and laid it on the cowboy's tool bag. I waited for some reaction. Nothing. He didn't even try to sniff the chocolate.

I had only five more days to find Mo Whitener's money or risk getting an unwanted subscription to *Women Behind Bars*. My pitch to Wade Covington had better score some points, because I wasn't exactly making progress. With my fingers crossed, I pointed the Boxster toward the freeway and Hancock Park.

16

hancock Park is located in the midcity area of Los Angeles, just south of Hollywood and about a fifteen-minute drive from downtown. The houses were built for Los Angeles's elite back in the twenties. Rumor has it that many of the estates are still occupied by the second and third generation of what is now considered not just old money, but ancient money. Other than Wade Covington, I didn't know who else lived in the hood, but I suspected it was mostly made up of folks yearning for a butler's pantry and a decent ballroom.

Covington's address was on one of Hancock Park's A streets, where the houses are palatial, the children's educations private, and the prenups ironclad. A seven-foot hedge protected the perimeter of the estate for at least a square block and obscured any view of the house or grounds. Employees of an all-girl valet service were adjusting pink vests and matching bow ties as I drove up to the curb. I wiped my dusty shoes on the floor mat of the car, took the claim ticket offered by the valet, and headed toward the house.

Just inside the gated driveway was a long table sporting a sign that read, *Will Call*. I approached a well-dressed young woman who was manning the *R-S-T*s, and gave her my name. She searched the list twice but came up empty. Tiffany Amber/Carole had failed me.

"I was late RSVP'ing," I explained.

The woman continued searching through a stack of cards in a nearby box until she stopped suddenly and studied one of them. Then she wrinkled her nose as if something didn't smell quite right. "What did you say your name was?" I spelled it for her.

"Could this be you?" She produced a hand-lettered name tag that was mostly illegible but could have been *Dickerson Claire*. That Tiffany Amber/Carole was one creative puppy.

The woman wrote Tucker Sinclair on a new tag and asked whether I wanted to pay by check or credit card. I felt a twinge of concern because two grand was going to make a serious dent in my nest egg. I wrestled with my conscience for a few seconds and then pulled out my Aames & Associates Platinum Visa card. I figured it was about time the partners showed a little charity.

The woman handed me the new name tag. Right side, left side—decisions, decisions. I clipped the badge to my left jacket lapel and headed up the drive, where several Gourmand Performance catering vans were parked. I followed a path bordered by bent purple flowers and a box hedge. At the end of the path, two bouncer types in blue blazers that barely fit over their biceps spoke into handheld radios. Several more security people scanned the crowd. Why the private heat? I wondered. Were they expecting a riot over a pledge card shortage?

The guards glanced at my name badge and nodded me through a gate that opened onto a yard the size of a soccer field. Dotting the lawn were what looked like a hundred or so large round tables, each shaded by a blue umbrella. This was a bigger affair than I'd anticipated. With all these people, I was worried that I wouldn't be able to speak privately with Covington. I had to make sure he didn't make good on his threat and use the off-hand scuba remark I'd made in Polk's office as an excuse to deny Aames & Associates a consulting contract. I was in enough trouble at the firm as it was.

The caterer was still setting up. Several uniformed waiters were folding napkins and placing them on tables, and from somewhere near, I smelled a faint aroma of what I sincerely hoped wasn't rubber chicken.

Small clusters of people were scattered throughout the area, chatting. I recognized an actor I used to swoon over in my teens. Unfortunately, his star had fallen long before his last face-lift. Nonetheless, several groupies were preening over him. His facial muscles remained rigid as he parted his lips to smile, showing straight white teeth. Only his eyes shifted, surveying who might be noticing him.

"That's Jim Bob Boshanty. I did his smile." A quite ordinary-looking man had appeared next to me. Everything about him was medium: height, weight, and hair color. Nothing would distinguish this guy in a crowd except for an unnaturally white smile that stretched ghoulishly across his face.

"Gerald Wykowski, DDS, cosmetic dentistry," he said, pumping my hand. He handed me a business card in the shape of a molar. "Nice party." He studied my mouth until I snapped it shut self-consciously. "Call. We'll bond." Before I could say, "Isn't it time for your medication?" he was gone.

The conversational buzz ramped up a few decibels as the guests filtered in. Frankly, I was amazed to see so many WASPs in one place. It was an aberration in a city like L.A., where well over 150 languages were spoken by students in city schools. I decided to try for a chat with Covington before the party got into full swing, so I headed toward the house. The grass was damp, and my heels sank into the turf. Great! The last thing I needed was to leave a trail of divots in Covington's lawn.

The house was a massive two-story brick Tudor shrouded by heavy shrubbery. I made my way to the front door and knocked. A pretty teenaged Latina in a blue maid's uniform and a silly white cap answered the door.

"Hello," I said to her. "I'm looking for Mr. Covington."

She stared at me blankly. Then she closed the door. This wasn't going well. I knocked again but got no response. I waited for a moment or two before making my way around to the side of the house. Through a row of oleanders, I could just make out a secluded flagstone patio and French doors. I parted the branches and had started to step through when I heard a female voice say, "You can't go in there."

Busted! I turned to see a young woman in a waiter's uniform standing behind me.

"Uhh, I have to use the bathroom." My creativity is legend.

"There's one in the guesthouse. Over there." She pointed to another house across the grounds that could have held two the size of mine.

"Actually, I wanted to talk to Mr. Covington," I said. "Thought I'd kill two birds with one stone, so to speak." With snappy repartee like that, I thought she'd want to be my best bud, but no sale. Instead, she eyed me suspiciously.

"We're not supposed to let anyone near the main house," she said. "Some wacko's stalking the owner."

That was not good news. I hoped the guy didn't get to Covington before I did.

"And," she went on, "we're supposed to watch out for any-body suspicious."

She couldn't be referring to *moi,* but in hindsight, the killing-two-birds comment wasn't the best choice of words. I turned on the charm to compensate. "My goodness, I'll certainly keep my eyes open."

A stalker went a long way toward explaining why Covington had hired private security to keep folks out of his house on the same day he had invited hundreds of people to lunch on his lawn. But regardless of that, I had to speak with him, and hopefully before the luncheon started. I made a pretense of walking toward the guesthouse until the woman went back to her waiter work. Then I doubled back to a door at the rear of the house. From the food smells and the clanging of pots, I guessed it was a service entrance and the kitchen was nearby. The door was already propped open by a case of Diet Snapple. I felt invited in.

As I suspected, the kitchen was a short distance down the hall. Julia Child would have given up coq au vin and cooking sherry for this setup. The place was dripping with copper and had a machine for every occasion. A pudgy middle-aged woman with maroon hair was placing cucumber rounds on a salmon mold and barking orders to a dozen harried assistants. In the midst of a heated debate over a burnt quiche, a breathless young man sprinted into the kitchen and created the diversion I needed to skulk past without being noticed. To my right was a stairway that led up to the second floor. To my left was a hallway. Hallway, stairs . . . hallway, stairs . . . ? I hate high-pressure decisions.

Before I had time to make up my mind, the woman with the maroon hair stormed through the kitchen door with a cell phone embedded in her ear. Her whole head looked like a really bad birthmark. "Yes, I'm pissed, you idiot. I have six hundred fifty for lunch and no fucking dinner plates."

There was a lull in her conversation, and that's when she noticed me standing in the hall. "No one's allowed in here!" she shouted at me. Then she turned her back and screamed into the receiver, "Have those plates here in fifteen or you're dead meat!"

I decided not to wait for the rest of the show. I took the hall to the left and ended up in a massive living room. Let's just say the decor in there didn't invite you for a comfy snuggle on the couch in a muumuu and bunny slippers. The same young woman who'd answered the front door was now dusting a large oil painting at the far end of the room.

"Hello again," I said to her. "Remember me? I'm still looking for Mr. Covington. Is he around?"

She shrugged as if she didn't understand what I was saying, and returned to her dusting. Strike out. Down the hall a door was ajar, so I peeked inside. The room was everything that a man's den should be—a rich man's den. The space was beautifully appointed with a leather couch and chairs, dark wood paneling, hardback books, and walls covered by paintings. I'm no connoisseur, but the art looked important. An ornate desk and a floor lamp completed the furniture inventory. On the far wall, two louvered closet doors flanked a grand fireplace. The dark wood mantel held a silver cup with an inscription commemorating Covington's stint as commodore of the Marina Yacht Club. I wasn't surprised that he would hold a position like that. The MYC was well known as a place to take a client for a power lunch or for a powerboat ride, and many people at our firm were members, including Gordon.

Covington obviously wasn't around. I was about to leave when I noticed a black textured leather briefcase, probably made from some endangered species, on the floor near the chair. I couldn't be sure, but it looked like the one Covington had with him the night I saw him at NeuroMed.

I checked the hallway. No one was out there except for the

maid, who was still dusting. Maybe Covington had taken something from the Center that evening. Maybe it was still inside his
briefcase. I should check. My stomach did a flip-flop as I popped
open the case.

Inside, among some other papers, was a blue patient chart
similar to the one I'd found with my name on it. There was no
name label on this one, only NeuroMed's address stamped on the
outside. I opened the file's cover and thumbed through several
pages filled with notes I could barely read, until I came to the
registration page. It was only partially filled out, but I could
clearly see the patient's name at the top: Teresa García.

It took me a moment to realize where I'd seen that name before. García was the subject of the article in Spanish that I'd found
in Milton Polk's desk. Covington had obviously taken this patient
chart from NeuroMed, but why? I wanted to study the file, but I
couldn't do it here, and if I took it with me, that would be stealing. Well, not stealing exactly. The file had already been filched by
Covington, so I was actually recovering stolen property. That was
a good thing. More to the point, it was good enough for me. I'd
managed to fold the chart into quarters and stuff it into my purse
when I heard a man's voice coming from out in the hallway.

"María." The tone sounded pleasant enough.

I felt heat on my cheeks, probably from guilt. For the first
time since I'd arrived, I wondered if I was in the proverbial
wrong place. I tiptoed close enough to the door just to see out.
The young girl stood stiff and silent, facing a man in a dark blue
suit with unnaturally brown hair. It was Wade Covington.

My eyes were so fixed on what looked like cosmetic surgery
scars behind his ears that I didn't at first realize I was holding my
breath. Relax, Tucker, I told myself. This isn't breaking and entering. You paid big bucks for this weenie roast. Well, if you

couldn't trust your inner voice, who could you trust? I felt a little calmer, but not much. Mostly, I felt my heart pounding.

Covington's voice was low, but I thought I heard him say, "Don't touch the paintings, María."

"Sew-rhee," she said in heavily accented English. "I dust."

He took the feather duster from her hand and set it on a nearby end table. "We're having a party now. You can do that later."

"Wade, I'd like a word with you. Alone." It was a woman's voice, coming from somewhere down the hallway. A mild tremor didn't mask the nuances of culture in her speech.

The woman said something to the maid in Spanish, and the young girl disappeared down the hall. I moved quickly away from the doorway just as Covington turned toward me. An intense, irrational fear spread through my body, making my legs feel weak and shaky. The last thing I needed was for him to catch me eavesdropping. Better to exit and regroup.

I couldn't budge the French doors—some kind of security lock. There was no place to hide except under the desk—too risky—or behind the couch—too obvious. The closet was both risky and obvious, but what the heck. I grabbed my purse and dashed over to open the door. Neatly stacked firewood rose from the floor to thigh level. This was going to hurt. I pulled off my jacket and spread it over the wood to protect my legs.

I was just closing the door as Covington entered the den. The louvers created enough of a gap for me both to breathe and see the action. An anorexic-looking woman in her sixties, wearing a dressy pink suit, followed him into the room and closed the door. Her legs were pencil thin. Her hair was gray, styled in an old lady's do, and she looked as if she'd recently negotiated a quantity discount on pearls.

"I shouldn't have to remind you"—her tone was stern but respectful—"María is my responsibility. Please don't interfere."

"I don't know what you're talking about, Vivian. Why don't you have another drink? Alcohol makes you less imaginative."

She looked as if he'd physically struck her. There was sadness in her face that was magnified by the sag at the corners of her mouth. Her voice was strained, but she maintained her poise. "We had an understanding."

"I think we should go outside now, dear. The party's about to start."

"I mean it this time, Wade. You manage your empire. Let me handle the rest."

Something in Vivian's tone made me question whether the marriage would survive till their fiftieth wedding anniversary. A commotion from outside in the hallway interrupted their heart-to-heart. Covington walked over and opened the door.

"What's going on?"

"Sorry, Mr. Covington. I told her to leave." I recognized the harsh and edgy voice of Maroon Hair from the catering service. "I was on the phone with the rental company. There was nothing I could do."

Standing next to her, framed by the doorway, was a paunchy bald man in his fifties who looked as if he was a charter member of the Cholesterol 300 Club. He was wearing the blue blazer and gray slacks uniform of the security team and carrying a handheld radio.

"We have a possible intruder, sir," he said to Covington. "Entered the house about ten, fifteen minutes ago."

Covington's body stiffened. Vivian slid quietly onto the couch.

"What do you suggest?" Covington asked him.

"Better leave, sir, while we search the house. My man's right outside. He'll be with you all the way."

"All right, then," he said, nodding his wife toward the door. "We'll join our guests outside."

As the Covingtons disappeared into the hallway, the security guard parked his butt on the pricey desk and spoke into the radio. "Deeg, this is Buck. Got your ears on? Female, white, medium-length brown hair, five-eight to five-nine, thin build, age twenty-five to thirty, white over light brown skirt, a looker. Entered the main residence at approximately eleven-thirty hours. Last known location was the main kitchen area."

Wait a minute. Except for the looker part, he could be talking about me. Me, an intruder? Great! Not only was my inner voice a failure at serenity coaching, it lied. I was in trouble.

The wood pressed into my skin, and my left leg tingled. I didn't dare move for fear the shifting logs would roll me right into Buck's steely handcuffs. Luckily, air was filtering through the louvers, but it was still hot and stuffy in there. I imagined termites in search of lunch. At the back of the closet was a hinged door with a deadbolt. I'd seen this setup before. It was designed to load wood from outside, to avoid carrying it through the house. In this case, it looked as though someone had made the opening accessible from the inside only, probably for security reasons.

Buck's next official communiqué didn't exactly lift my spirits.

"I'll start upstairs. You cover the lower floor," he said as he headed for the hallway. "And, big guy? Keep your gun in the holster. Could just be a lookie-loo from the party. *Capisce*?"

Hide, run, hide, run? More decisions. Let's see, Deeg is a big guy with an itchy trigger finger and he's looking for me downstairs. I am downstairs. Well, that was easy. I allowed myself a couple of deep breaths to regain my composure, and carefully turned the deadbolt on the woodshed's back hatch to open the door. I maneuvered my buns toward the edge, careful not to upset the logs, until my feet dangled just above the ground. It was only a small leap for womankind, but unfortunately, my left leg was snoozing. It collapsed as I landed. I reached out my hand to steady myself and triggered a log avalanche. The sound was deafening.

All limbs were in working order, so I grabbed my purse and hopped away on my good leg. When I hit the grass, I pulled off my shoes and tucked them under my armpit. They'd only slow me down. Let the Deegster work for his paycheck. The prickles in my leg eased, and I ran like hell. A disguise would be good. I grabbed a blue napkin from one of the catering stations. Not exactly chic, but it would have to do. I folded the napkin in a triangle and tied it around my neck like a scarf. Even Pookie wouldn't recognize me now.

Many of the guests had taken their seats, but at least a hundred people still mingled and chatted in small groups. I slowed my pace and looked for a pod I could melt into. Jim Bob Boshanty was still holding court with a group of six or seven diehards, so I sidled to the back of the pack and tried to look enraptured.

"I loved you in *Moroccan Knights*. The Academy robbed you that year." A fleshy woman in her sixties, reeking of Shalimar, fluttered her eyelashes. Jim Bob nodded, aglow in the adoration of his fans. "Your Hassim the thief was . . ."

Blah, blah, blah. I stopped listening and scouted the grounds for Deeg and Buck. Nada. Then it hit me. What was I thinking? I was at a charity luncheon. I'd paid to get in. I hadn't done anything wrong. Why was I standing here with grass-stained feet poking out of shredded panty hose? A little voice came back with an answer: because they think you're a stalker, dummy. Okay, but I could work with that. I decided to take action, so I put on my shoes.

"Oh, look, there he is." The Shalimar lady gushed, and pointed her chubby white finger toward Covington, who was stepping up to a microphone on the dais. "Wade supports so many causes. Wonderful man." Jim Bob didn't look as if he appreciated the focus shifting to someone else, but the woman gushed on. "It's about time he got what he deserved." A few moments later, she dabbed her hankie at what I could only guess was perspiration in her cleavage, and toddled toward the seating area.

Covington spoke a few words of welcome to the crowd before settling down for lunch at the head table, next to his wife. As people stopped to shake his hand, I studied his face. Too bad nothing in that expression told me why he'd taken Teresa García's chart from the Center. The file was stamped with NeuroMed's address, so Polk or one of his technicians had obviously administered neurological tests to the girl, but how long ago, and why? I wouldn't know that until I got home and searched the file more carefully.

I was still trying to puzzle it out when I spotted Richard Hastings, sitting at one of the prime front tables. He was smiling in that smarmy, obsequious way of his as he helped the Shalimar lady settle into the chair next to him. Events weren't shaping up as I'd planned. The window of opportunity for normal conversation with Covington had closed, and Hastings's presence at the luncheon made one thing clear: I had to get out of here. I couldn't risk getting arrested for prowling with my nemesis looking on. I hurried toward the exit, but a catering van was blocking my way out. I was in the process of squeezing between the van and the hedge when I heard the ear-splitting voice of Maroon Hair.

"I'll hold the salads for fifteen, but that's the max." She handed a set of keys to the young man I'd seen running through the kitchen earlier. "Get me plates. Steal them if you have to."

The catering van's engine roared to life. I melted into the hedge to protect my toes from tire tracks as it peeled away. When the exhaust fumes cleared, I found myself face-to-face with she-of-the-maroon-hair. She stared blankly at me for a moment before screaming, "It's her. The stalker—over here!"

It was one of those defining moments when a person could choose to do the mature thing—or not. I ran toward the exit and was nearing the gate when I heard, "Stop—security!" I kept running. I heard heavy breathing behind me. When I turned around to look, my foot caught on something poking out of the grass, and my legs went flying out from under me. A moment or two later two beefy arms pulled me up and pinned me, bear-hug style, against a hard body. I tried to kick the guy's shins, but my shoes had fallen off. The best I could hope to inflict was killer grass-stains.

"You tripped me, you Neanderthal!" I shouted.

"I think not," he said, "but I'll let you go if you promise to be good."

I could feel his warm breath in my ear. "Eat shit and die."

He laughed. "You got a mouth on you."

There wasn't much wriggle room, but I tried to find some anyway. The effort caused my breath to come in short gasps. The guy was very strong and very determined. He smelled good, too. What was that fragrance?

"I can't breathe," I said.

I hoped that didn't sound as wimpy to him as it did to me, but I was starting to feel faint. He eased his grip but didn't let go. I took a couple more gulps of air and hoped we looked like prom royalty at a photo shoot and not a promo for *America's Most Wanted*. Buck the Enforcer came running up to us. His face was red. Perspiration soaked his shirtfront.

"ID'd her yet, Deeg?"

"Not yet," he said. "We're still getting to know each other. But I'm pretty sure she's not strapped."

They both snickered. Strapped? Must be some kind of bouncer lingo.

"Mind telling me who you are, ma'am?" Buck was speaking in faux-polite, looking stern and squinty-eyed.

I didn't care if the big guy's trigger finger did get itchy—I'd had enough.

"I'll get my driver's license and show you who I am, if you tell this dildo to let me go."

Deeg chuckled.

Buck eyed me suspiciously. "I'll get it for you, if you don't mind."

"Would it make any difference if I did?" I said sarcastically.

"No, ma'am," he said. "It wouldn't."

My pulse was just beginning to slow down when I remembered that Teresa García's file was in my purse. I closed my eyes and waited for disaster to strike.

As Buck pawed through my bag, I realized that the faint aroma of Deeg's aftershave was pear. I also became aware of his arms wrapped around me, and of his chin resting on my head.

Buck pulled out the crumpled file and looked at it briefly. Then he stuffed it back inside my purse. Only then did I allow myself to breathe normally. Buck inspected the two-grand credit card receipt. He checked out my driver's license, looking carefully at the photo, and then at me.

"Brown hair. Brown eyes. Five-nine. Hundred and—"

"Enough already," I said. "It's me, okay?"

"What were you doing in the house, ma'am?" Buck asked.

"I stepped inside to use the can, and the next thing I know, Deeg here is playing anaconda."

The Deegster chuckled softly again.

"So where were you going in such a hurry?" Buck continued.

"Nordstrom's half-yearly sale?"

Buck looked irked. "Let her go," he said to Deeg.

Deeg increased the pressure for a moment, almost like a hug, before releasing me. "Ahh, and just when we were getting to know each other."

"We'll do it again some time," I said to him with all the snide I could muster.

"Careful what you wish for."

When I turned to face Deeg for the first time, I realized he was definitely not one of the guys at the front gate. I would have remembered that. He was masculine and good-looking in a bionic sort of way. Six-two, lean, hard body, about 185 in his birthday suit, and I was good at numbers. He had spiky brown hair, killer blue-gray eyes, and was the kind of guy you dreamed would try to pick you up but never did. Except today, and much too literally.

While I was watching him, he was watching me with a look that wasn't at all cocky, just self-assured and perhaps too familiar for my taste. I knew his type: amusing to take as your date to a high school reunion as long as you didn't mind watching him flirt with former members of the cheerleading squad, women who'd never been your friends but were now on your hit list.

Deeg took my license from Buck's outstretched hand and read it. Then he frowned in thought. When he looked up at me, the intensity of his appraisal made me uncomfortable.

"I think we can let Ms. Sinclair go," he said.

That surprised me, and Buck, too. But where I undoubtedly looked relieved, Buck looked annoyed. The two of them exchanged some kind of bouncer telepathy, and Buck reluctantly handed me my purse.

"Sorry, ma'am," Buck said, "but we can't be too careful."

Buck walked a few feet away and spoke into his radio.

A smile turned up the corners of Deeg's mouth, engaged his eyes, and eventually his entire face. "Nice outfit," he said. "But under the circumstances, I think you should leave that here."

I realized he was referring to the napkin still tied around my neck. I removed it, and as he took it from me, his fingers lingered on mine too long to be accidental. I jerked my hand away. He responded with a funny half smile–half frown as if my gesture had given him an important clue. The guy liked to push buttons. There was something about him that made me think he was trouble—I just didn't know what kind yet. Luckily, Buck chose that time to wander back.

"I'm afraid we're going to have to ask you to leave, Ms. Sinclair," he said.

I didn't like Buck's attitude. I *had* been leaving before the two of them started hassling me.

"Yeah?" I said. "You and who else?"

"That would be me and Mr. Wade Covington, ma'am. He said if you weren't off his property in five minutes, he'd call the police."

Deeg frowned. Maybe he thought that was no way to treat a lady, or maybe he was disappointed that he wouldn't have time to invite me for a little one-on-one in the backseat of his bouncer car.

"Mr. Deegan here will escort you out," Buck continued.

Well, that made sense. At least I didn't have to ask him what kind of a bullshit name Deeg was.

"Don't bother," I said. "I know the way."

My keen sense of direction didn't deter Deegan from stepping forward and putting his hand on my elbow. Under different circumstances, it would have felt sort of silly and old-fashioned, but I didn't like being herded, especially now, so I shook him off. He grinned. The guy thought everything I did was a riot.

As we walked toward the valet, I sensed that Deegan was about to tell me something, but he must have thought better of it, because in the end, all I got was a slightly raised eyebrow when the valet brought the Boxster around. His send-off was an irreverent salute and a smile that lesser women might call sexy. I called it a waste of my time and his energy.

It wasn't until I reached the on-ramp to the freeway that I realized my jacket was missing. A sick feeling roiled through my body when I realized that there was only one place it could be: in Wade Covington's den closet, spread out like a picnic blanket on a pile of firewood, with my name tag still clipped to the lapel.

If Covington would have me arrested for merely being at his party, what would he do when he found out I'd been eavesdropping in his wood closet and stealing files from his briefcase? I was screwed.

17

as soon as I realized that I'd left my jacket in Covington's closet, I was on my cell phone with Venus. I needed someone to talk to, and she was the only friend who might seriously consider a commando raid to rescue it. But she told me no how, no way. She was tied up in meetings for the rest of the day but agreed to meet me the following morning for breakfast to debrief. That would have to do.

On the way home I tried to imagine what Deegan's first name might be, mostly to curb my nervous energy, rather than for any real interest in knowing. Maxwell or Lowell? No, too intellectual. Deegan was more the physical type. Chip? Whitey? Dude was more likely.

By the time I drove into the tunnel transitioning from the noise, grit, and endless traffic of the 10 Freeway onto Pacific Coast Highway, it was late afternoon. The small circle of light guiding me to the tunnel's exit widened to reveal palisades eroded by wind and rain, four lonely palm trees huddled together on the sand, and the Pacific Ocean stretching far away to the western horizon. I'd just passed the lime green shamrocks on Patrick's Roadhouse when my cell phone rang. It was Gordon. How was I? he wanted to know.

"Peachy-keen, and you?"

"You're still upset," he said. "You shouldn't be. This isn't life. It's business."

"Gee, Gordon, that's interesting, because it kind of feels like life to me."

"Fine, but there are no hard feelings on my part. You're still tops in my book."

His voice was gentle enough, but I really resented his kiss-and-make-up attitude. I should have known that Gordon wouldn't obsess over our argument. His style was to do what you had to, then make the best of it. As for me, refusing to speak to him wouldn't serve me well in the long run, either. It wasn't easy, but I gulped down my pride.

"Fine," I said, "no hard feelings."

"Good. I called to bring you up to speed on the Whitener situation. Right now he's not rational. Eleven million is a lot of money. We told him Polk had signed several documents that would exonerate us, but he's not buying it. He still thinks you and the doctor were in this together, and he blames the firm for failing to catch you at it. It's getting ugly, Tucker. He's demanding to see the NeuroMed file or he says we're all going down for the count. Unfortunately, we can't find it here at the office."

The light turned red at Sunset Boulevard, giving me a moment to think. To tell or not to tell? Gordon would be upset, but I couldn't keep the bad news from him any longer. He might even have some creative ideas about what to do next.

"You can't find it because it's missing," I said.

There was a long silence on the line, accompanied by deep breathing.

"Would you care to elaborate?" His voice was steady and composed.

"I searched my office with a flea comb, Gordon. The file

wasn't there. I think somebody took it, either inadvertently or on purpose. I'm not sure which." I waited for that to sink in before I added, "I think the file somehow ended up with Dr. Polk."

"Then go to his office and get it back," he said in a slightly more strident tone.

"It isn't there. Or at his house. Or at his private practice, either. I've checked."

"I don't want to know where it isn't, Tucker," he said, alarmed. "I want to know where it is. Jesus! You think negotiating with Whitener is a fucking walk in the park? It's taking everything we have. I need those documents—now."

I was glad this was a telephone call, so I didn't have to see the disappointment on Gordon's face. Hearing it in his voice was bad enough.

"What happens if I don't find them?"

"I think you goddamn well know what happens," he said. There was a pause while he took a few deep breaths; then he added in a softer voice, "Shit, I don't know, but keep looking, all right? And when you find them, call me—immediately." He hesitated. "And, Tucker? I can't tell you how much I regret what's happened. If I had it to do over again . . ." His voice trailed off. "Look," he added, "just keep me informed."

Obviously, Gordon hadn't heard about my appearance at Covington's charity bash, or he wouldn't have sounded so conciliatory. If I was lucky, he'd never find out.

When I arrived home, I tossed my shredded panty hose in the trash, showered, and changed into some sweats before I took the Teresa García file from my purse and read each page carefully. Most of the notes were illegible, but one thing was clear: Wade Covington was listed as her employer. The one-page Progress Notes stated that the girl had been evaluated for a head injury.

Milton Polk's signature appeared at the bottom of the page, but the file included no further information.

I picked up the newspaper clipping that I'd gotten from Mona and scanned the text. Living in L.A., you'd think I'd have kept up my Spanish. I hadn't, so I dusted off my old high school Spanish-English dictionary and began translating. At least one word looked vaguely familiar, so I looked it up first. It was *muerto*—dead.

Translating was tedious, but luckily, the article was short. Teresa García, age seventeen, had returned to the home of her uncle in the village of Corona, near Guadalajara, Mexico, after sustaining injuries from a fall in the bathtub while working in the United States. Within days, she'd slipped into a coma and died. It was one of those small-town obituaries with meager facts and the flowery language of grief. I assumed that Teresa García had fallen while working for Wade Covington, and he'd arranged for Polk to evaluate her. It all sounded innocent enough, except the girl had died. I wondered why she'd been sent home for treatment. It was hard to believe that Corona, Mexico, had better hospitals than Los Angeles, California.

I thought back to the chill I'd heard in Vivian Covington's voice when she found her husband with the maid, María, and wondered if Teresa García's fall was a cover-up for something more sinister. Tucker, your imagination is in overdrive again, I thought. Even if the García girl had been domestically challenged, Covington wouldn't risk a murder rap because of waxy yellow buildup. He had way too much to lose.

I took Teresa García's file to my desk and telephoned Mona Polk. I wanted to ask if she recognized the girl's name, but she was out making funeral arrangements. I checked my watch: six p.m. Seemed like an odd time to be planning a funeral, but what did I know? Wait a minute. Six o'clock? I was supposed to be in Century City, meeting Eric. Damn. I dialed the number for the restaurant. There was no telephone in the bar, but the hostess reluctantly agreed to go look for him. I waited, waited, waited. Two minutes. Then five. Waited until someone hung up the phone. Shit.

I didn't have time to change, but it didn't matter. Eric had seen me in sweatpants before. I grabbed a jacket and ran out the door. On the way into town I left a message on his machine at home, telling him I was on my way. But by the time I walked into the restaurant's bar, he was nowhere in sight.

If Murphy weren't careful, he'd have some competition in the lawmaking department—Sinclair's law: If anything can go wrong, it will. Tucker would see to that personally.

· · ·

THE FOLLOWING MORNING I arrived at a crowded Du-Par's Restaurant in the Farmers Market on Fairfax. The eatery is a Los Angeles landmark with waitresses and decor that haven't changed since the Stone Age. Venus was seated at a table, eating blueberry pancakes and reading the *Los Angeles Times.* She listened to the details of my adventures at Covington's luncheon, punctuating the tale with a few "tsk's" and a lot of "mm-mm-mm's." When I asked if she'd heard any recent gossip about Covington, she said, "Funny you should ask. I just read in the paper here about some award he got."

"Yeah?" I said. "Let me see."

Venus motioned to the waitress for more syrup. I ordered coffee and turned to the Calendar section of the paper. The Charity Scorecard column had a blurb about Covington's Man of the Year award, which had been presented Saturday at the Regent

Beverly Wilshire. Aames & Associates was listed as one of the corporate sponsors. Gordon was obviously working all the angles to win Covington's business. The article went on to say that approximately one hundred thousand dollars had been raised for a nonprofit agency that operated a shelter for victims of domestic violence. The name of the agency was Project Rescue.

Alarm bells sounded. Project Rescue was Mona Polk's pet charity. That awards dinner was the last place Milton Polk had been seen alive. I wondered if Wade Covington was the person Polk was to have met that night. I felt as if I'd just found a big stash of Easter eggs hidden behind one clump of grass.

The restaurant was noisy, but the tables were packed in close. I didn't want anyone to hear me, so I kept my voice low. "Venus, listen to this. The García girl lived near Guadalajara. Project Rescue is in Guadalajara. García worked for Covington. Covington worked for Project Rescue. Polk treated the girl just before she died. Are you starting to see connections here?"

I had brain drain from all those brilliant deductions, but Venus wasn't in the mood for my *ahas*.

She rolled her eyes. "Nine thousand cops on the LAPD, and you wanna play junior detective."

I waited for the waitress to pour my coffee and leave.

"Look," I said, "thanks to Milton Polk I could spend my remaining reproductive years doing hard time, and nobody seems to care but me." That tactic didn't seem to be working, so I changed to a tone that was just shy of pleading. "Come on, Venus. Call Waddell."

Venus came from a large, close-knit family that included lots of lawyers and cops, including a cousin named Waddell, an LAPD sergeant who, like Detective Kleinman, was assigned to the Pacific Station.

"Maybe he can ask Kleinman how the Polk investigation is going, and see if Teresa García's name comes up."

Venus looked at me as if I were some kind of moron. "You think police officers tell that kind of shit to just anyone?"

"No, but they might tell it to their favorite cousins."

Only her eyes were frowning. I took that as progress. "Trust me. The man is not going to tell me anything." She must have read the disappointment in my expression, because her standard stony expression softened. "Why am I always trying to protect you from you?" Her question was rhetorical, but I knew some serious considering was going on behind it. "Oh, all right. It's against my better judgment, but I'll try just this one time. But that's it," she said emphatically. "Don't you go asking me again."

I smiled. "Thanks, Venus. I owe you one."

She rolled her eyes. "One? Honey, I've got more invested in you than my 401(k)." Then her expression turned serious. "Tucker, you're a shit magnet, and this snooping around is just gonna bring on more trouble. I'm telling you, let somebody else handle it. Like a good lawyer."

"I'm working on getting one, Venus, but for now I'm all I've got. But thanks for worrying."

I left Venus to her pancakes and headed home. For the rest of that afternoon and evening, I waited for a callback from Mona Polk. I didn't want to intrude on her grief, should any surface, but I was eager to ask her about Teresa García, and about any progress that had been made on her husband's murder investigation.

While I waited, I typed up her fee agreement on my computer and also printed a few temporary business cards, using a desktop publishing program. After that, I phoned the company that managed the billing for Polk's neurology practice. One of their account reps told me he was still listed as an active client, though there had been no recent receivables posted. Armed with that information, I called a medical practice broker I knew, just to get a ballpark estimate of what he thought the practice and the Center were worth. He wasn't optimistic.

I wasn't optimistic, either. Eric hadn't called me. That was troubling. It meant there had been no word yet from Sheldon Greenblatt on whether he'd represent me either in the Whitener case or against Aunt Sylvia. Both matters had to be dealt with, and soon. I thought about calling Greenblatt myself, but Eric had warned me not to. I didn't want to screw this up, so I decided to wait a little longer, but not much.

Around seven o'clock, Muldoon whimpered for a walk, a cookie, or a game. Or possibly it was some dog-speak I couldn't decipher. Whatever. It reminded me that I was home—alone—dog-sitting. Without Pookie's fractured energy, the house felt silent and lonely. Pookie had trained me that melancholy was a misdemeanor and depression a felony. I could do serious time for the way I was feeling. What were Deegan and Buck up to, I wondered? Maybe Detective Kleinman wanted to take me out to dinner but was too shy to ask. Medic!

I poured a cup of herbal tea into a commuter mug and said the magic words that would send Muldoon into an altered state: "Wanna go for a walk?" At least one of us could be happy.

A bank of fog was looming offshore as I stepped out onto the deck. I zipped my down vest against the November chill and walked down the steps to the beach. At least the tea felt warm and comforting.

Muldoon was already on gull patrol. I let him roam for a bit, but once he tasted freedom, he was dragging his paws about going back inside. I coaxed him to the bottom of the steps, but evaporating wave foam fizzling on the sand distracted him, and he shot off again on another bark-o-rama. He didn't buy the "want some dinner?" ploy, either, and wouldn't budge any farther than those steps. Then I heard the phone ring.

I ran up the stairs onto the deck, juggling the tea mug and the keys, trying to get the door open, wishing I'd brought Muldoon's leash. Damn dog. I left the door ajar, hoping he would have enough sense to follow me inside. I grabbed the phone just before the recorder piped in. It was Eric.

"You're out of breath," he said playfully. "What were you doing?"

Small talk. That was good. It meant he wasn't angry with me for missing our meeting at the restaurant.

I wriggled out of my vest and threw it on the couch. "Just dog-sitting," I said. "Pookie's out of town."

"Your mother left something alive in your care?"

"Don't worry," I said. "He came with instructions. So far, so good. The only thing left for the day is dinner. And how hard can that be?" The words were no sooner out of my mouth than I realized that I still hadn't bought food for the little tyke. I groaned because I knew that there wasn't a single can of hypoallergenic, no-animal-by-products Zen dog food left in the refrigerator or the cupboards. Well, what the heck. If he'd survived this long, he'd survive until I made it to a pet food store.

Eric went on to explain that Sheldon Greenblatt was still in trial but that his secretary had promised a callback in the morning. I was anxious and a little angry about the delay, but Eric assured me that Greenblatt was worth the wait.

"So, Tucker, I got your message," he said. "Shall we try it again?"

His tone sounded a little businesslike, and that didn't seem quite right. But businesslike or not, I didn't want to talk about our relationship over the phone, and certainly not right then.

Before I had a chance to respond, he said, "Tucker? I said should we try to set up another meeting? Say, tomorrow night?"

I needed a longer reprieve. "How about Saturday night?"

He hesitated but, with a barely audible sigh, agreed. Eric sounded positively mellow, as if he'd just had sex. I almost asked him what *he'd* been doing, but if Eric were sleeping with someone else, he wouldn't be pursuing me. And he definitely wasn't the type to go solo. I figured he was just tired. We agreed to meet at a restaurant in Brentwood at seven o'clock Saturday night.

After we hung up, I called for Muldoon. No dog, just a cold draft surging around my ankles. I walked over and looked out the open door. The fog had moved in now, and nothing was visible except churning gray air.

"Muldoon? Here, pup."

He didn't come when I called. Typical male. Maybe he'd found a date and deserted me. I did a quick search of the house. No pooch. I headed out the door, carefully walking down the steps, feeling my way along the sand with my feet. The fog felt dense and claustrophobic. I felt responsible and guilty. I didn't even know if the little guy could swim. What if he got lost in the fog and wandered into a riptide? Pookie would never forgive me.

Surf I could only imagine pounded against the shore. I was a little disoriented and wandered farther down the beach than I'd planned. The lights from my deck had melted into the smoky air. I couldn't see three feet in front of me. Gee, there could be a giant rogue wave forming silently offshore, biding its time, waiting to suck me into a watery grave. I wouldn't even know what hit me. I shivered and thought of Milton Polk's last moments as he desperately gasped for air and found only water.

Tucker, Tucker, Tucker. You are working yourself into a major snit here. Forget the little scrub brush. For once, I took my own advice. I did a one-eighty and headed for home. The lights from the houses seemed dim and muted as I searched for some familiar landmark. This time I'd left without my vest, and I was freezing. I thought about my jacket in the Covingtons' wood closet. If Wade and the missus weren't into cozy fireside chats, they might not find it until the January rains. Fat chance. I heard heavy breathing, but it was only mine. No . . . something else. Another sound. Shuffling in the sand . . . near me. I stopped.

"Muldoon?" The fog encased me like a cocoon, bouncing the sound around my head. Maybe whimpering would help. It seemed to go a long way for the leg lifter. "Is that you, little guy?" Nothing. It was probably a jogger. I picked up my pace until, just ahead, the welcoming light from my deck came into view. I ran the last few yards and skipped up the stairs. Huddled next to the door, looking chilled and somewhat contrite, was Muldoon. I scooped him up, hurried inside, and locked the door, dumping him on the couch, sandy paws and all. But he didn't stay. He shot onto the floor, barking like a drover, whining, sniffing around the couch, and then racing toward my bedroom.

That's when I noticed my driver's license lying on the coffee table. It struck me as odd to find it where it never was, where it never should have been. It hadn't been there earlier. I was sure. I would have noticed. I couldn't remember the last time I'd had it out. Had I used it as ID for the check I wrote at the market? Yes, but that was days ago. Then my breath stopped and my heart pounded in my throat. A dim bulb clicked on in my head as I remembered. Covington's luncheon. Buck had taken my license. He'd given it to Deegan, but had Deegan given it back to me? No, at least, not until now. My chest felt heavy. Stupid! Stupid!

Stupid! Why hadn't I locked the door? Someone had just been in my house. Uninvited. Maybe still inside, hiding. Someone working for Covington? Buck, I could handle. Deegan? Not likely. Bad news if it turned out to be one of the other hulks on guard that day. At least Deegan had a sense of humor.

I strained to pick up any unfamiliar sounds, but all I heard was blood drumming in my ears and dog claws scratching on the floor. Run for help or take a peek myself? Another one of those pesky decisions. Using all the courage I could muster, I eased off my shoes and looked around for a weapon. Kitchen knife? In the drawer. Too noisy. Anything else? Nada. Nyet. A big fat zero. Not even an umbrella. Only Pookie's celery hat, sprouting from the end table. Lethal it wasn't; a distraction, maybe. I eased it off the table along with a blunt number-two pencil. Great. What was I going to tell these guys? "Watch out, I'm packin lead." Pookie's room was empty, as was the bathroom. Just my room, and I could sound an all clear. Muldoon was at my bedroom door, scratching to get in.

"Shhh, you dippy dog," I whispered. "You're gonna get us killed." *Bark! Bark! Bark!* The guy just couldn't take advice.

I quietly turned the knob. Muldoon barreled inside ahead of me. Growling, panting, searching, and then nothing. No yelping. Good sign. With my back against the wall, I nudged the door fully open with my heel and turned my head so I could see inside. Muldoon's front half had disappeared inside the closet, which left his hairy white butt and carrot tail aiming up at the ceiling. The closet was awfully cramped to hold a burly guy, but you never knew. Carefully I flipped on the light and stepped closer. Heart pounding, I knelt beside Muldoon and peered into the closet. Nothing. No beady eyes stared back at me. I collapsed on the floor with my back against the doorjamb of the closet and took my first deep breath in way too long. The pencil was still fixed in my fist like a bayonet. Celery greens were cocked and ready. I wanted to giggle, but my body said tremble, so we compromised.

Murff, murff. A dog with a mission.

"What now?" I said aloud.

Muldoon was still sniffing. Wouldn't let it be. I pulled him away and squinted to get a better look. In the back corner of the closet was a dark, still form. It looked like a piece of clothing that had fallen from a hanger. I reached in and pulled it out. A chill moved up my spine. Once again I scanned the room, looking for shadows, listening for sounds. I refocused my attention, staring in disbelief at the thing in my hand. It was the jacket I'd worn to Covington's luncheon. Clipped to the lapel was a name tag that read *Tucker Sinclair.*

18

It was nine-thirty the next morning, Friday, and three days from the deadline Mo Whitener had set for returning the group's eleven million dollars. The police had released Polk's body, and I was on my way to the private graveside service at Forest Lawn Memorial Park, in the Hollywood Hills. I was still shaken that an intruder had been in my house, and worried about leaving Muldoon alone. I considered asking my neighbor, Mrs. Domanski, to watch him, but for her, cocktails started at dawn, and I figured he was safer alone. As a precaution, I tucked both the Teresa García and the Tucker Sinclair medical charts inside a large box of shredded wheat, which I hid in the kitchen cupboard.

Mona finally called. She told me Elsa searched the house but didn't find the original NeuroMed package. She agreed to give me a key to the Center so I could look for it there. The documents were probably long gone, but perhaps I'd find some other evidence pointing the finger at Polk or his accomplices.

Mona also told me she didn't know anyone named Teresa García. She had no idea why a newspaper article about the girl's death was in with her husband's possessions. Apparently, she and Polk had met Covington through her work with Project Rescue. Covington had given a modest amount of time and an excessive amount of money to the cause. To her, that made him as fine a man as she'd ever met. Irony.

Just before we hung up, Mona informed me she'd received a call from the police. They were no longer focusing on suicide or accidental drowning as the cause of Milton Polk's death. They considered his death a homicide. It wasn't as if I hadn't considered the possibility that he'd been murdered, but somehow, hearing it confirmed left me feeling queasy. I couldn't tell from Mona's tone just how she felt about the news.

Forest Lawn has never been quite sure whether it's a cemetery or a theme park. It's the butt of a lot of jokes, which might lead a person to believe that nobody takes it too seriously except the people who get buried there. In reality, it's one of several Forest Lawns in Southern California. The Hollywood Hills locale is a good-looking piece of real estate with rolling lawns, gardens, and statuary. It isn't as impressive as the original, in Glendale, with its movie star mausoleums and full-scale copy of Michelangelo's *David,* but despite subdivisions with overwrought names like Vale of Hope, Tender Trust, and Starry Knoll, Forest Lawn Hollywood Hills has its own brand of serenity. Besides, it's the only real estate in Los Angeles County where you can move into a star-studded neighborhood and pay less than the cost of admission to Disneyland.

The sky looked more like Seattle than L.A.: overcast, gray, and threatening rain—funeral weather from central casting. I took Forest Lawn Drive from the freeway, past a Griffith Park equestrian event, to the front gates and got a map from the guard kiosk. I continued past the two-story colonial mortuary, through a large ornate wrought-iron gate, and past sweeping lawns dotted with drying bouquets and heart-shaped Mylar balloons. I stopped near a hearse and a long black limo that were parked along the road in an area called Hallowed Grove. I didn't see any groves, hallowed or otherwise, just a few spindly sycamore saplings, but in the scheme of things, Milton Polk's final resting place wasn't such a bad spot.

I hadn't been to many funerals, and I wasn't looking forward to this one. Still, I wanted to look my best, so before getting out of the car, I checked to make sure that there were no sandy paw prints on the only black dress I owned—a little cocktail number with sequined spaghetti straps that I'd funeralized with a dark pullover sweater. Unfortunately, when I surveyed the crowd, I noticed that nobody else was wearing black, not even Mona Polk. Obviously, I had a thing or two to learn about L.A. funeral couture.

About twelve people milled around a canopy that sheltered the raised casket. Most looked like Polk's contemporaries, men and women in their fifties and sixties, with the exception of a sullen-looking teenage girl who looked as if she'd mistaken this for a come-as-you-are party. Too bad no one wore name tags at these events. I looked around the fringes of the crowd for guys with buzz cuts, speaking into hidden microphones with Quantico accents, but I came up empty.

Harold Amberg was there with his wife, whom I recognized from the photo in his office. There was no sign of Wade Covington. Everyone looked under control except Francine, who was boo-hooing into a hankie under the glaring eye of a man who, I assumed, was her loving spouse. He was short and wiry with a deeply lined, angry face. If a Hack 'n Frizz hair salon ever opened up around here, he'd be their poster boy.

I stepped carefully across the spongy grass, dodging flat markers packed so closely together there was barely room to maneuver. Nearby, a family squatted around a grave, burning something that could have been incense but didn't smell like anything in Pookie's collection.

Mona stood at the edge of the group, looking pale but otherwise intact. Smoldering Towel Boy was at her side. I walked over and gave her my condolences. She seemed genuinely touched.

"This is Armando Baldioceda," she said, gesturing toward the hunk.

She pronounced his name with a Spanish accent, as if she liked the way it trilled off her tongue. I waited for her Introduction Etiquette 101 ice-breaking tagline. Something like "And did you know Armando won the Nookie Decathlon three years in a row?"

That never came, so I decided to take matters into my own hands. "Are you a member of the family, Armando?" I said, trilling the *r* in my head.

He didn't answer, just batted his eyelashes.

"I'm not sure he understands you," she said. "That's why he's staying with us, to learn English. I'm teaching him, but it takes time."

I felt like saying, "Yeah, and now that your husband's dead, you've got all the time in the world." Since I'd been dredging up all that old high school Spanish, I offered Armando a *"mucho gusto en conocerle,"* and hoped I hadn't just asked for a double dry nonfat cappuccino.

People were coming over to Mona to pay their respects, so I wandered off, scanning the crowd for a familiar face. Finally, I spotted Madie sitting alone in one of the chairs near the casket, her red hair aglow even in the gloomy light. A lightweight green raincoat concealed her nurse's uniform. When she saw me, she waved and maneuvered her way through the mourners, bringing with her the scent of lilies and roses from the graveside floral arrangements.

"I didn't expect to see you here." She sounded surprised but also relieved.

"Who are these people?" I asked.

"I don't know. Well, of course, I know Dr. Amberg and his wife, and Mrs. Polk. And Francine."

"Is that Francine's husband?"

She wrinkled her nose in distaste. "I can't believe he's here."

"Why? Doesn't he like funerals?"

"He doesn't like Dr. Polk, and the feeling was mutual."

"Yeah," I said. "The guy looks like a piece of work, all right."

My comment must have jarred Madie out of her candor, because she blushed and quickly changed the subject. She went on to tell me that Dr. Amberg had decided to use Polk's office as a storage room, and asked if I could pick up his personal effects—about four boxes of them, she thought. Her tone was apologetic, as if she considered banishing Polk's things before he was properly buried a sacrilege of some sort. I agreed. Nonetheless, I told Madie I'd drop by later in the afternoon to collect the stuff.

Of course, Dr. Amberg could do whatever he wanted with the office space. His practice was completely separate from Polk's. They shared only rent, and lately, Amberg claimed to have paid all of that. But it was interesting that he hadn't waited until Mona made her decision about selling. I guess Amberg already had Dr. Polk's patients, so the floor space they stood on to pay his fees was a mere formality.

"Who's the guy with Mrs. Polk?" Madie asked. "Her bodyguard?"

Her comment startled me, but it was an interesting observation. It was possible Mona needed protection. After all, her husband had been murdered. I couldn't imagine why, but maybe she thought the killer might come after her as well.

Armando hadn't left Mona's side once since I got here, and at the moment his hand was resting protectively on the small of her back. I considered the possibility that he'd graduated from some touchy-feely school of bodyguarding, but that's not what it looked like to me. It looked as though he had the hots for her—and vice versa.

I don't know why I had a bee in my bonnet about the possibility that Mona Polk was cheating on her husband. I was no prude, and Milton Polk was no angel. Maybe Mona was just teaching Armando English as she claimed, but to me their behavior smacked of an intimate relationship. If so, flaunting it at her husband's funeral seemed like a cheesy thing to do.

The minister had just begun ahem'ing and motioning the crowd toward the chairs when I heard a car door slam. I turned to see Detective Kleinman getting out of a blue Crown Victoria. When he spotted me, he smiled. Goodie, I thought. He wasn't mad at me anymore. He'd traded the houndstooth jacket for a more formal blue suit. I wasn't exactly ready to invest in matching underwear for our first date, but from a distance he didn't look all that bad. Then my head cleared, and I realized that he wasn't here to see me. He was a cop and was probably at the funeral hoping the killer would be there, too. That thought was enough to scare the bejesus out of me.

The eulogies were mercifully brief but more poignant than I expected. A dozen people had taken time out of their busy schedules to be there, but that wasn't many when you considered Milton Polk's fifty-plus years of bonding opportunities. From what I gathered, at least one person, Kenny Chalmers, may have come to gloat rather than grieve over his death. Maybe there were others.

Kleinman stood at the edge of the pack, listening attentively.

If he was watching anyone in particular, he was subtle about it. I, on the other hand, wasn't subtle at all. I scrutinized every single face in the crowd until I thought everyone looked like Jack the Ripper.

When the formalities were over, Kleinman made a beeline for Mona Polk. Fine. Let him ignore me. I wanted to corner Francine, but Kenny looked like a handful, so I waited for the guy to take a potty break, to mingle, to anything—but he stuck to her like gum on a theater seat. I considered throwing him a piece of meat so he'd get distracted and leave her alone.

I wouldn't have been surprised if Francine was trying to avoid me. Irene Borodin must have told her by now that someone, maybe an insurance investigator, had been at Sunland asking questions about those phony-baloney claims. If she'd cooked up that insurance scam, she must be sweating blood by now.

Kenny had his hands in his pockets, shuffling his feet, looking as if he was antsy to leave. Francine seemed dazed. She was holding a single red rose in her hand and staring at the casket.

I spoke just loud enough to get her attention. "Francine, we have to talk about that patient chart I found the other day. The one we discussed. It's important. I think you know why. Can I speak to you in private?"

The look of terror in her eyes told me that her answer was probably no. "Please leave me alone," she said in a frantic whisper.

Kenny bullied his way between us. "Who are you?"

"I worked for Dr. Polk," I said casually, offering my hand. "Tucker Sinclair."

He looked as if he'd just sucked a lemon. "Funeral's no place to talk business. Can't you see Francie's not herself?"

I feigned a polite smile and did my best to ignore him.

Francine looked pale and frightened as she again turned toward the casket.

I didn't want to freak her out, so I kept my voice steady and calm. "Maybe we can talk later at the Center?"

"She's not going to work today." Kenny's voice crackled with tension.

I gave him my "I wasn't talking to you, shithead" look before turning back to Francine. "What about tomorrow? I can meet you."

Without averting her eyes from the casket, she pressed the rose to her lips and gently placed it on a heart-shaped flower arrangement draped across the lid.

"What's your problem, lady?" Kenny said angrily. "She ain't going back to that shit hole, so take a hike."

All heads turned toward us as Kenny's words echoed in the still air. My senses were on full alert. Kenny was at least four inches shorter and twenty years older than I was, so I could take him—easy. Then I thought: Tucker! Get a grip. Funeral. Wrestling. Maybe not appropriate. Kenny was a bully, but his sentiment seemed genuine. He wanted to protect his wife. I decided to leave his knees intact but couldn't resist one last comment. I bent over and looked at him eyeball to eyeball.

My tone was quiet but steely. "Get out of my face, or I'll squeeze your head like a zit."

Kenny balled his fists and puffed up like a cobra but didn't say anything more.

"Hey, what's going on?" Detective Kleinman's voice sounded calm, almost lighthearted.

"Beat it," Kenny said.

Kleinman put his hands on his hips and gave Kenny a look of quiet consternation. The gesture also allowed Kenny, and anybody else who was looking, to see the gun strapped to his chest and the badge hanging from his belt.

Kenny paled. "Sorry, Officer. My wife's not herself. I was just taking her home." He started nudging Francine toward the road.

Kleinman nodded but made no move to stop them. I managed to slip Francine one of my homemade business cards, but before she got to the car, I saw Kenny take the card away from her and put it in his pocket. Great. All I needed was another creep who wanted to keep in touch.

According to NeuroMed's corporate minutes, Francine was an officer in the company, which left her vulnerable to the Center's financial and legal troubles. And how angry would that make Kenny? From what I'd just seen, pretty darned angry. Maybe Kenny had come here today to get some kind of killer thrill from seeing his victim buried. In any event, he'd just moved up on my suspect list. I wondered if he appeared anywhere on Kleinman's.

"Are you all right?" There was a tremor in Mona Polk's voice as she moved toward me. She glared as Kenny helped Francine into the passenger seat of the car.

"I apologize," I said. "I didn't mean to cause a scene."

"Don't apologize. Believe me, I'm glad they're gone." The car drove away, and Mona took a deep breath and closed her eyes. When she opened them again, her composure was back. "I'm having some people over for a buffet after the service. Will you join us?"

Time and options were closing in on me, so I said, "That's very kind of you, but I was hoping to stop by NeuroMed this afternoon."

Her eyes conveyed disappointment, but her tone was nonchalant. "Another time, perhaps."

Mona Polk seemed to take all of life's disappointments in

stride. I suspected that she held herself together by compartmentalizing and moving on. In any event, she gave me the key to NeuroMed and headed toward the limo. After that, the crowd began drifting back to their respective cars. Except for Kleinman. He stood with his arms crossed and his eyes boring into mine.

"You want to tell me what just happened here?" he said.

I shrugged. "I know you'll find this hard to believe, Detective, but sometimes I rub people the wrong way."

That produced a faint smile, which was followed in short order by a cynical frown. "You're holding out on me."

"Wrong, again," I lied.

"You know, sooner or later I'll find out if you are."

That made me a little sweaty, but I kept a genial look on my face. "Look, I wanted to talk business with Francine. Her husband objected. End of story. By the way, nice suit. Versace?"

This time his smile was committed, and it stayed on his lips for a while. "Good guess, but no cigar. It's a Sam Kleinman original."

I remembered him telling me that he'd been in the garment business before becoming a cop, so I asked if that was his dad.

"My uncle," he said.

I nodded. "So how's the investigation going?"

He paused, staring at me. "It's going."

"Any idea yet who killed Dr. Polk?"

"We're working on it."

"No big breaks in the case?"

"Not yet."

Kleinman obviously wasn't willing to share any information. And the way he was staring at me made me think that every word out of my mouth had the potential of getting me into more trouble. I decided not to press my luck. I'd just have to wait and see if Venus came up with anything helpful.

"Well," I said, "nice seeing you again. Have a good one."

Were bad clichés a sign of guilt? They must have been, because his eyes followed my every step as I cut a zigzag path through the gravestones on the way back to my car.

I wondered where Milton Polk's spirit was right now. Hovering over his new home, watching? I wanted to shout, "If you're out there and you can hear me, Milty, show me a sign." But I didn't, because that was a little too Pookie for me.

Besides, I didn't have time to wait for a big *ba-dum-bum* from the Great Beyond, because the minutes were dripping away. If I didn't find some way to prove my innocence before Monday, any semblance of my life as I'd known it would be gone forever.

Francine must know that I was on to her. So what would she do next? My guess was that she'd destroy any evidence of her guilt, if she hadn't done so already. I had to get to the Westside and search NeuroMed before Francine got there first. I jogged the rest of the way to the car, hoping that I wasn't too late.

19

the halls of Bayview Medical Center were unusually quiet and empty when I arrived, except for a stone-faced man carrying a cloyingly sweet-smelling flower arrangement wrapped in a plastic cone. A sullen little boy scuffed along behind him, marring the shiny tiled floors with black shoe marks.

I lingered in the lobby and used my cell phone to call home for messages. There was one from Eric. Shelly Greenblatt wanted to hear my pitch before deciding whether to take the case, but he was booked solid until after his golf game on Sunday. The Whitener deadline was Monday. Sunday was cutting it close, but I didn't have much choice. I needed a lawyer. Eric instructed me to meet Greenblatt at the Riviera Country Club at noon. And for me, a special deal: $550 an hour. Once again, Eric had come through for me. What a guy. He closed with "Tucker, I tried to reach you at the office. They told me you didn't work there anymore. What's happening? Get in touch, okay? I'm worried." Eric, worried? That felt good.

There was another message from Gordon Aames. It went something like this: "Hey, Tucker, Covington just called me. I hear you're off his A-list. He's using your appearance at his house as an excuse to yank my chain over the damn contract bid again."

Gordon's tone was more controlled than I'd expected. He didn't mention the Teresa García file, so Covington either hadn't noticed it was missing or hadn't yet connected its disappearance to me. There was a long pause in the message. I almost disconnected when I heard his voice again. "Tucker, for God's sake, what are you up to? I have to know. Call me."

He sounded desperate. He must be frantic to hear if I'd unearthed the NeuroMed documents. I'd already dialed Gordon's number when I decided against calling him. Better to search NeuroMed first. Hopefully, I'd find, if not the documents, then some other evidence that would get Whitener off our backs. I'd call Gordon when I had some good news for a change.

An EEG machine was parked in front of NeuroMed's door. Inside, the lobby was empty and quiet. Even the fish looked lethargic. Dolores Rodriguez stood in the reception area, flipping through a stack of papers with squiggly lines. She glanced up, but when she saw it was only me, she lost interest and returned to her work. I checked around for the Center's secretary, but her desk appeared to be deserted.

"Where's Janet?" I asked.

"She's off because of the funeral."

"Really? I didn't see her there."

Dolores shrugged. "That's her business."

She marked the EEG readout with a date and number in big swipes with her Magic Marker. Then she stacked it on a floor-to-ceiling shelf full of the same.

In my limited contact with Dolores, she'd always come across as someone who had to work but hated her job. Maybe she just hated everything. She walked to the sink in the storage room and tipped a hinged dispenser. The pungent smell of the greenish industrial soap made my nose twitch. She pulled down two brown paper towels that looked like sandpaper, and scrubbed at some black ink on her fingers.

"Did you need something?" she said. "Because everybody's out but me, and I have to leave in a few minutes."

I'd had enough of her snotty bullshit. "Obviously, Francine didn't tell you, but I'm working for Mrs. Polk now. I'm trying to help her decide if she should sell the Center." What I didn't tell her was that if Mona decided not to sell, I'd suggest that she fine-tune Dolores's attitude as her first order of business.

Dolores frowned as she tossed the used towels inside a can marked NON HAZARDOUS WASTE and said, "I hope you're not asking my opinion, because I don't want to put any notes in the suggestion box, if you know what I mean."

I had a suggestion for her, but I didn't want to get into it at the moment, so I bit my tongue and waited until the sound of the cart's wheels faded as Dolores rolled it around the corner and disappeared. The desk in Francine's office could have had a sign posted that read, *Moved, no forwarding address.* I pulled out the desk tray where the employee list had been taped. It was gone.

If Francine's desk drawers and file cabinets had once contained evidence of criminal activity, they were now stripped clean, along with any checkbooks, bank statements, or other clues to the whereabouts of NeuroMed's funds or Mo Whitener's eleven million dollars. In the storage room there was an empty gap in one row of files. Unless dust bunnies tell lies, whatever was there had been recently moved. I was too late.

Even though I didn't expect that Francine had left anything that would implicate her in either fraud, I had to be sure. It was a long, tedious, and frustrating search, but I looked through every file, every drawer, under every trashcan, and even gave the fish tank a critical eye. I found nothing.

I sat in Francine's chair with my feet resting on an open drawer, feeling very discouraged. The maroon envelope with the NeuroMed documents could be anywhere from a locker at the bus station to floating in the Pacific Ocean. I had to face the fact that they were probably gone forever, which left me with only one way to clear my name: identify Polk's accomplice, the person who helped him alter my business plan. I just didn't know where to look next.

It was hard to think with Mo Whitener threatening to turn me in to the FBI. I could see the whole scenario unfolding now. The investigation would turn up the insurance scam, too, and I'd be faced with a double whammy. I could almost imagine the opening arguments in my trial. Some politically ambitious assistant U.S. attorney would show the Tucker medical file and claim that insurance billing fraud wasn't producing enough money for my lavish lifestyle. In order to maintain the minimum balance in my numbered Swiss account, I'd created a fairy tale about NeuroMed.com and its profit potential so that Polk could bilk investors. For my creativity, I got a percentage of the money he collected. Maybe he would even suggest that a percentage wasn't good enough, so I'd killed Polk to get it all.

I was giving myself heart palpitations, so I decided to give up stream-of-consciousness thinking—and maybe any kind of thinking—just as Dolores walked through the door.

"Are you still here?" Her tone was pleasant in a cagey kind of way.

"Yeah, but not for long."

She watched as I gathered my things to leave, but before I walked out the door, she said, "If Mrs. Polk sells the Center, will the new owners keep us on?"

"I don't know," I said cautiously. "I would if it was me; that's all I can tell you."

She frowned in thought. "So if they did keep us on, they wouldn't lower my salary, would they?"

"I doubt they'd do that."

She hesitated. "So maybe you could talk to Mrs. Polk about my raise. Dr. Polk promised, but he didn't tell Francine it was supposed to be for this paycheck."

At least that explained her sudden attempt at gracious chitchat.

"I'll mention it to her," I said. "I'm sure she'll honor his promise if she can. When did you talk to him?"

Her facial muscles relaxed. "Saturday."

I felt my pulse throb in my throat. "Last Saturday?" I said slowly. "When?"

She paused when she heard the urgency in my voice, as if she was worried that the wrong response might jeopardize my promise to help her. "Just before midnight. I was on call. There was an emergency. When I got here, it looked like he'd been tearing up the place."

"Tearing up . . . ?"

"Yeah. Looking for something, I think."

"And you took that moment to ask him for a raise?" I said skeptically.

She shrugged. "You ask him when you catch him. He was supposed to give me my review on Friday, but he left early."

"Dolores, except for the killer, you may have been the last person to see him alive. Did you tell this to the police?"

"Sure," she said.

Another part of Milton Polk's last day had just clinked into place. Francine was right—the lab hadn't been broken into. Polk must have come here after the Project Rescue dinner, looking for something. But what? It didn't make sense for him to trash his own office. If he was hiding something at the Center, wouldn't he remember where?

"How did he seem?" I asked, excited now. "Did he say anything at all? Mention if he was meeting someone?"

"No. He was stressed, just like he always was," she said. "I didn't think anything about it. I asked him for a raise, and he said okay. Anyway, if I can get the money before Mrs. Polk sells, it's locked in, and I won't have to wait till my next review."

I felt as if I were looking at one of those graphic designs, the ones with a hidden picture that comes into focus if you squint just right. But even though I scrunched my eyes tight, the complete why of Milton Polk's death was still a blurred mass of lines and squiggles. Everything I'd learned suggested he'd been under intense pressure that weekend. Upset, maybe even desperate. He might have agreed to Dolores's raise to get her off his back, or maybe his final act was one of kindness. Regardless of his intentions, he'd run out of time. Sometime shortly after he'd spoken to her, Milton Polk had been murdered.

Dolores was busy putting away her machine when I thought to ask if Polk had taken anything with him when he left the Center. She seemed bored by the question.

"I didn't notice. Is it important?"

Important? I thought. No, not important. Crucial, vital, critical, life-or-death. She didn't react to the disappointment that must have registered on my face, so I thanked her and started toward the door.

"Wait," she added grudgingly. "You know, I think he did have a bunch of papers with him."

I stopped and turned slowly toward her. "What kind of papers?"

"How should I know that?" She responded as if my question showed a lack of gratitude. "All I know is, when he was done looking at the stuff, he put it inside a big red envelope."

20

after Dolores left, I tried to think of where Polk might have taken the NeuroMed file after he left the Center that night. I doubted that he'd gone home. At least, the documents hadn't been found at his house. If I could only find out where he *had* been, I might still be able to find the maroon envelope before Whitener's deadline on Monday.

Polk had left the Center just before midnight. Driven— where? Then I thought, duh. Driven. Why hadn't I thought of that before? The NeuroMed report must have been with Polk in the car. Maybe it was still in the car. Kleinman would know if it had been found. I doubted that he'd tell me, but he might tell Mona. The police would have to release Polk's property sooner or later. Maybe we could convince them to make it sooner.

I checked my watch: three o'clock. I wondered how long funeral luncheons lasted. I'd never been to one before, but how much time could it take for a guest to wolf down a few finger sandwiches and blot out every memory of dissing Polk while he was alive. I used the Center's phone to call Mona Polk. A machine picked up. Guess there was more blotting going on than I figured. I left a message, asking if the police had returned Polk's Mercedes.

I had to get home, because Muldoon was locked inside the

house with nothing but a few newspapers on the bathroom floor. On the way there, I stopped to buy dog food and treats from Aunt Patty's Pets in Brentwood, the store at the top of Pookie's preferred list. I also swung by Amberg's office, to pick up the boxes belonging to Milton Polk, and then headed for Casa de Sinclair.

When I got home, the air was thick with humidity, as it frequently is at the beach. It was the one thing I didn't like about living on the ocean, because it made my bedding and the clothes in my closet damp and mildewed. Today the mist had created a beauty all its own, draping the cliffs above Pacific Coast Highway in gradient layers of gray. Silhouetted through the haze was a lone palm tree, like an exotic bird suspended in space.

Muldoon didn't give a rip about palm trees or humidity. He was just happy to be off on his beach expedition once again. When he came back inside, I carefully closed and locked the French doors. I changed out of my funeral outfit and into chinos and my favorite fisherman's sweater before unloading the boxes from my car and stacking them on the living room floor. I wanted to make sure that I looked through everything before delivering them to Mona. Then I collapsed on the couch for a rest. Muldoon jumped up and put his front paws on my leg, holding a stuffed bear in his mouth. The look was eager, almost pleading.

"What should I do next, little guy?"

He shook the bear to make it clear he thought it was a stupid question. Muldoon was obviously not into the teamwork concept when it came to decision making, so I had to answer it myself. Make a list, of course. That always gave me time to think.

I found a blank sheet of paper and marked PRIORITIES in large letters at the top. Then, I wrote, *Number One: follow up with Bernard Cole.* Then I scratched it out. Cole hadn't responded to the message I'd left for him at Sunland and probably wouldn't, even if he'd gotten my note, which I doubted. Irene Borodin would have seen to that.

I moved on to *Number Two: Complete assessment of NeuroMed Diagnostic Center and Polk's private neurology practice for possible sale.* Then I scratched that out as well. Turning my NeuroMed research into a sales tool for a practice broker wasn't going to be difficult. Besides, who was I trying to kid? My number one priority was to find something—anything—that would lead me to the person who set me up. I eased Muldoon off my lap and joined him on the floor.

I sorted through all the boxes once more, careful to separate anything that might be backup for Mona's accountant, including the coffee receipt I'd found. Three-fifty wasn't much, but Polk had wanted it as a write-off, and every penny counted. Occasionally, Muldoon broke the tedium by mowing through my paper mounds, still trying to interest me in a game of tug.

Somewhere inside an envelope, inside another envelope, I found an insurance policy that I'd missed on my first search. Mona was listed as the beneficiary. The amount: two million dollars. Well, that was a tidy sum. I wondered if Mona knew about the insurance money. Maybe she was playing dumb, waiting for me to find the policy so she could act surprised, touched, and grateful. And what if my suspicions were correct and her relationship with Armando had moved beyond platonic? This windfall would go a long way toward keeping a boy-toy interested.

Then I thought of the Whitener group's missing eleven million dollars and where that might be. Eleven million. Now, *that* was some kind of incentive. The question was, how far would she go—they go—to get their hands on all that cash? Murder? In my mind, the money established a clear motive for both of them.

I forced aside my suspicions for the moment and continued sorting through the boxes. I didn't find anything more about Polk's activities that Saturday, but a picture was emerging of his neurology practice. It was probably worth something, and if the fraud charges could be resolved, so was NeuroMed, especially when buyers saw how easily the Center could turn a profit with pared-down services and beefed-up marketing. Of course, all that information had been in my business plan—the real one, that is. Polk should have listened. He'd wanted too much too soon, and thought he could lie and cheat to get it. It had been only a matter of time before it all came crashing down on his head. It should have felt better to be right.

I returned all the files to the boxes and stacked them near the back door. Too bad it wasn't as easy to file away the questions I had about Milton Polk's death. I tried to shake off the image of the morgue photo. That gouge in Polk's forehead looked as if it had been made with a great deal of force. Armando was a powerfully built young man. He could easily have overpowered Polk, killed him, and thrown him off a pier somewhere, with or without Mona's help. I shuddered. It gave me a bad case of the creeps, knowing I was working for her.

21

i 'd just finished stacking Polk's file boxes by the door when
Venus called. She wanted to see me, so by seven p.m., I was
pulling into the parking lot of the Dueling Burritos, a cop hang-
out in Mar Vista, a neighborhood squeezed between Culver City
to the south and Santa Monica to the north.

A woman dressed like Don Diego's mother greeted me at the
door with embarrassing familiarity. I guess she thought the
friendly reception and the buck-fifty margaritas were good
enough reasons to ignore the odors of stale cigarette smoke and
spilled beer.

The restaurant was separated by a half wall crowned with
amber crinkled plastic. To the right was a bar that consisted of ten
stools and an impressive collection of tequila bottles. On the left
were four rows of booths reserved for diners. The whole enchi-
lada, so to speak, was overseen by the restaurant's logo painted on
the back wall: two anemic mustachioed tubes that looked more
like bratwurst cruising for trouble.

The bar crowd had mostly left or moved into the dining
room except for a fat white girl in red high-heeled shoes with
ankle straps and a black hootchie-mama dress that squeezed her
ass out like an aneurysm. One of her hands held a frothy pink
drink in a tulip glass, and the other was draped over a doughy

guy in his late forties who looked as if he just wanted another tequila shooter.

Venus arrived, and we took a booth near the bar. Hanging above our table was a dust-covered piñata, swaying to the music of a roving mariachi trio crooning to diners stupefied by the age-old question: to tip or not to tip. Venus was agitated and hungry, a bad combo, so I gave her the other Nut Goodies bar I'd commandeered from Eric's desk. After that, she had a margarita and emergency chips and salsa and finally started to mellow. Before long, the limes from her drinks were lined up in formation across the table like little green soldiers guarding some kind of border.

All the booths were full now, and the bar was getting a second hit, which meant a lot of handshaking and smiling for Don Diego's mother. Venus asked if I'd heard anything from my aunt Sylvia since my visit to her house. I told her I hadn't, and that it made me nervous.

She filled me in on the office buzz. Apparently, Hastings was strutting down the halls as if his name were already on the letterhead. That was bad enough, but when she told me he'd joined the Marina Yacht Club so he could rub elbows with the right people, my jaw tensed. Gordon encouraged all his consultants to join social clubs so they could network with clients in an informal environment, but the yacht club was near and dear to his heart because he kept his boat there. I had the same opportunity to join that Hastings had, but I chose not to because I'm not a clubby kind of person. Right now that decision looked like a missed opportunity.

"Yacht club?" I said. "That's rich. I hear Hastings can't even take a shower without Dramamine."

Her signature laugh was full-bodied. It lifted my spirits, but only until she told me about the rumors floating around the of-

fice about my suspension. They were entertaining but not altogether flattering. Hearing them made me tense. I couldn't imagine what was going to happen to me, to my career, to my house.
Frankly, the idea of having someone waiting for me at home to
help sort through all my problems was sounding very appealing
right now.

"Venus, you think I should get back with Eric?"

Her head was tilted down, so when her eyes looked up at me,
they seemed bigger than usual, like coffee stains on boiled eggs.

"I'm trying to eat here," she said, using her chip to shovel
salsa into her mouth. "Just cuz you're not gettin any doesn't
mean you have to panic."

I shrugged. "Just an idea."

The space between her brows narrowed into a frown. "You
need to find you a real man."

"Like who? One of Waddell's cop friends? No, thanks."

"What about that Kleinman guy?" she said. "He sounds cute."

"He's mad at me. Claims I'm holding out on him."

"Your timing's off, honey. That's supposed to come later."

I rolled my eyes and gave her my yeah-yeah-yeah look. Luckily, her lecture was cut short by the arrival of the food, delivered
on plates as big as hubcaps. Venus was dieting, so she'd ordered
the sour cream on the side, but the waiter had forgotten. She
shrugged it off as an experiment gone bad.

"I hear Gordon's stressing out trying to get a hold of you,"
she said. "Everybody's supposed to pass the word along. Of
course, he got nothing from me."

"How's Eugene?"

She shook her head in disapproval. "He thinks Hastings is the
one setting you up, so he's snooping around like double-oh-seven.
You better talk to him before somebody stomps his little head."

I'd rejected the Hastings-as-suspect theory early on, but decided to take a moment to reconsider the possibility: Hastings changes the NeuroMed report and blames it on me to eliminate his strongest competitor for partner. No, it has to be bigger than that. Maybe this: Hastings has a close relationship with Wade Covington. He also has access to my files at work. Covington wants to buy the firm rather than continue to pay outside consultants but doesn't want to pay full price. Covington promises Hastings a partnership for helping him pull it off. Hastings agrees, alters Polk's report, tarnishes the firm's image just a tad but destroys mine; Gordon loses business because of fraud accusations and has to sell to Covington at a discount. Covington's happy. Polk's happy. Hastings is happy. Right? Wrong. Both scenarios seemed like the products of an overwrought imagination.

"I'll take care of Eugene," I said, "and don't worry about Gordon. I'll talk to him, too. I just want to track down the Neuro-Med documents first."

I fished out the lemon wedge from my iced tea and used my straw to march a couple of her lime corporals to my side of the table.

"What about Covington?" I asked. "Find out anything?"

"Waddell doesn't know squat about Covington or Teresa García—at least that's what he told me. I didn't press him, because—shit, Tucker—he could lose his job sticking his nose in where it doesn't belong."

"Damn. That's all?"

"No, that's not all. I made a call to a friend over at Covington's Wilmington operation, too."

Venus told me she'd met the senior manager during a consulting assignment and had kept in contact with her over the years. The woman denied knowing anything about Teresa García, but claimed that people who thought Covington was Mohammed, Jesus Christ, and Buddha all rolled into one had it wrong. Big deal. That wasn't news. I didn't know what I'd expected Venus to find out. Just more. It was disappointing.

"I have to know what happened to Teresa García," I said, "like if she really fell in the bathtub, and if so, why she ended up in Mexico afterwards. I also want to know if the police were involved."

"Whoa," she said. "I'm not the child's biographer. How should I know if she left town flying commercial or medevac? Besides, information like that just gets you in more trouble."

The mariachi boys in their black velvet sombreros had worked their way to our table, but they bobbed past quickly after admitting they didn't know the words to "Millie Make Some Chili" and hearing Venus say "no substitutions." I finished herding the limes to my side of the table. Now they were lined up in a perfect V flying formation, with my lemon wedge as point man.

"What about Sunland?" I said.

"Nothing you don't already know," she said.

Except for gossip and speculation, Venus had come up with a big, fat zero. That was a bad sign for my little investigation. I considered the possibility that Cole was getting a kickback from the phony insurance premiums. Maybe he and Polk split fifty-fifty. Francine and Irene probably managed the fine print, and everybody won except the insurance companies and consumers everywhere. I just didn't know how to prove it.

"Thanks anyway," I said. "I'll try another angle."

Venus stared disapprovingly at my citrus air force and said, "Why can't you just leave things be?"

Our friendship had a lot to do with bridges. Venus avoided crossing hers, and I usually left mine in flames. I thought for a moment before answering her.

"Because that would be too easy."

I left Venus to her double espresso and her flourless chocolate cake, because Muldoon was sitting at home in the dark with his legs crossed and I was beat.

As I sped north on the coast highway, I tried to think of who else might have information on Teresa García. The girl obviously had been treated at NeuroMed. Perhaps Francine knew something about the circumstances surrounding her death. I decided to ask her, even if it meant confronting Kenny again. I couldn't make up my mind whether that decision sounded more like a big mistake or some kind of death wish.

22

I'd just turned down the access road to my house when I saw a black Ford Explorer parked in my driveway. I felt a tingling sensation and a flash of fear because no one was at the side door, the normal place a visitor would be. I put the Boxster in reverse and cautiously backed up the street and parked well out of sight of the house.

I used the public beach access just south of my place, careful when opening the chain-link gate, so it wouldn't squeak. I walked down the concrete steps to a narrow asphalt path. A row of small trees with overgrown branches enclosed me in a dark and claustrophobic tunnel. After clearing the trees, I crouched low and negotiated my way carefully through the sand, taking cover behind a cluster of Adirondack chairs about fifty feet from the house.

A man stood on my deck in front of the French doors, silhouetted by light from a gap in the curtains. His back was to me, so I saw only that he was tall and wearing dark clothing: jeans and what looked like a brown jacket.

The pulse drumming in my ears and the crash and sizzle of waves breaking on the sand kept me from hearing anything, but I saw Muldoon's head poking out through the curtains. He looked as if he was barking his head off. No, Muldoon, I thought. No. No. Get away.

The man squatted and put his hand on the glass in front of the dog. My adrenaline surged, and I thought, if he hurts Muldoon, he'll pay. But for some reason, the pup quieted down. After a moment, the man stood, and as he turned toward me, I saw his face.

My stomach dropped a couple of floors. It was Deegan, the security guy from Covington's luncheon. My legs were cramped and achy from the cold, but I didn't dare move. Deegan walked down the steps of the deck and stepped onto the sand. He cautiously looked around. Then he headed up the hill behind the house as if he was going to leave. I felt giddy with relief. And that's when my cell phone rang.

For a split second I thought my heart would stop. Deegan must have heard the sound, too, because he whirled around and pressed his body into the shadows of the house. I pawed frantically through my purse to turn off the ringer. Run? Hide? Considering our last encounter, I decided to stay put. Deegan was too fast for me.

For what seemed like an eternity, he remained tucked alongside the house. Finally, he moved slowly out of the darkness, scanned the beach, and walked briskly toward his car. A short time later, I heard an engine start and saw lights flicker up the hill toward Pacific Coast Highway.

The damp sand had soaked through my chinos. I was cold, and my legs were shaky as I fumbled with the lock on the door. Muldoon was pumped up with guard-dog adrenaline and tried to wiggle out of my hug to reenact his moment of glory. As far as I knew, Deegan hadn't gotten into the house again, but just the same, I checked the shredded wheat box for the two medical charts. They were still there.

I changed into dry clothes and burned some of Pookie's incense, but that didn't help calm my nerves. I considered moving into a motel in case Deegan came back, but decided against it. No one was going to frighten me out of my house. I decided to return my life to some semblance of order, so I checked my telephone messages. There weren't any. Then I checked the mailbox.

Among the bills and junk mail was a letter with no return address. I opened it and found a copy of a legal document, stating that Sylvia Branch was petitioning the court to reopen probate on my grandmother's estate, claiming that new evidence had surfaced showing that the prior will was invalid. The document ordered me to appear at a prehearing meeting with her attorneys in two weeks.

I felt like kicking something. I was about to call Eric to see if he could reach Sheldon Greenblatt, when I remembered the telephone call on the beach. I checked the readout panel on the cell phone but didn't recognize the number. When I dialed, a man answered in a low southern twang. In the background were sounds of a heated conversation and canned TV laughter. I wondered if there was a half-finished six-pack on a TV tray next to the La-Z-Boy.

"Somebody just called me," I said.

"Mary Jo Felder?"

I froze. It had to be someone from Sunland. No one else knew that name and this number.

"Yeah," I said cautiously.

"Roy Trebeau. You were out at the warehouse a couple days ago, asking questions. Said you were some kind of PI."

It had to be the cowboy I'd met at the electrical panel.

"Well, I'm not a PI, technically speaking."

"Looky here," he said impatiently. "You don't run any games on me, and I won't run none on you. You investigating Anton Maslansky or not?"

I paused to consider the consequences of my answer, then said yes, thinking, great, now the authorities could add impersonating a private investigator to my rap sheet.

"I didn't tell you the other day," he said, "but I know the guy, and some of them other folks you talked about, too."

There was a click on the line. Roy seemed irritated by the interruption but nonetheless excused himself to take a call waiting. Within ten seconds there was another click, and he was back.

"Gotta take care of something," he said in that slow drawl. "You want to look at what I got, come by tonight."

What did he mean by "what I got"? For a moment I wondered if he was planning a meet-and-greet at the door in a leopard thong and an *AHH-EEE-AHH, you Jane.* In any event, I didn't like the direction this conversation was taking.

"It's kind of late," I said. "Maybe you could just tell me what you have, because I'm really only interested in—"

"Don't get so jumpy, Mary Jo," he said, as if he'd read my mind and placed my concerns somewhere between boring and humorous. "I don't wanna jump your bones. But I am trying to do something that might do us both some good." There was a short pause before he continued. "Tell you what: I'm goin out later. How about I leave the stuff in the mailbox? You have any questions, you call me tomorrow."

Sounded fair enough. "What's your number at work?" I asked.

"Afraid I won't be there. Got laid off today."

My appearance at Sunland hadn't exactly wowed Irene Borodin. I wondered if she'd seen me talking to Roy and punished him for it. Not likely. Even if Roy had asked a few questions that made her sweat, she wouldn't have tipped her hand like that.

"Sorry," I said, and meant it.

"Don't be. 'Laid off' was the words she used, but I got a hunch the Black Widow sent me packin on account of something else, and I think she's gonna be sorry about that. Yes, indeed, I do." There was resolve but also a tinge of triumph in his words. "I can't leave this guy hanging on the line any longer. You interested, then write this down."

As I took down his address, cautious Tucker said, "It's after ten p.m., much too late to go to a strange man's house by yourself. Ask Venus to go with you." But reckless Tucker piped in with "Oh, come on! Don't be a wimp. Trebeau is probably just a nice guy with a lot of problems—a closet gentleman. And even if he tries to surprise you at the door, you have your cell phone, and your running shoes are in the gym bag in the car. Go for it!"

There was only one snag with that last plan: Reckless Tucker had been wrong before. Just in case she was wrong again, about Trebeau, I left a note for my neighbor, Mrs. Domanski, telling her where I'd gone. I also programmed Duane Kleinman's pager number into my cell phone's memory. That satisfied cautious Tucker.

While searching the Internet for driving directions to Reseda, I found myself humming "Climb Every Mountain." I thought, gosh, if the FBI didn't buy my claims of innocence, I could always become a motivational speaker for the girls in cellblock D.

.   .   .

IT WAS AFTER eleven by the time I got to Roy Trebeau's neighborhood, which was made up of small one-story houses barricaded behind window bars and chain-link fences. The streets were dark. I drove slowly, looking for house numbers on the curb, but most of them were either painted out or worn off. I couldn't see anything.

I made a couple of passes before I found the address, partially obscured by a camellia bush. The house was a small white clapboard, no more than a thousand square feet. A red Ford pickup was parked on the lawn. It had a bumper sticker on the rear windshield that read, *You can't fix STUPID.* Something to consider, I thought.

A battered black metal mailbox, missing a nail on one side, was hanging at a tilt. It was empty. Damn! Had Roy forgotten plan A? No light shone from behind the drawn curtains, but the TV was blaring, so I knocked on the door. There was no answer. I knocked again . . . nothing. Maybe Roy was already gone, or maybe he was changing into his Tarzan getup.

I walked toward the back of the house, where a light was shining through frilly yellow and white café curtains hanging from the kitchen windows. I peeked inside. Unwashed dinner dishes filled the sink. An unopened bottle of red wine, the kind wrapped in raffia to make it seem more Italian, sat on a square wooden table next to a couple of wineglasses. Someone had put an unopened bag of Doritos in a white bowl labeled in blue letters, *Roy's Chips.* It definitely looked as though he was planning a party. I felt a little apprehensive and hoped he was expecting someone other than me.

Several sheets of paper were rolled like a newspaper and propped inside the chip bowl. Since Doritos don't come with instructions, I was guessing it was the information Roy had told me about on the phone. Either he'd forgotten to leave it in the mailbox, or he wasn't a gentleman after all.

I tapped on the glass and tried the knob . . . locked. A gray metal toolbox sat in front of a doggie door big enough for a small pony. I hoped Cujo wouldn't come out to greet me before jungle boy introduced us.

I walked all around the house, but obviously there was no one home. I'd been stood up, and I was more than a little miffed. I could have been at home with Muldoon, sharing a tofu dog cookie and a glass of my own cheap wine. Roy told me he was going out. He was probably in a hurry and forgot to leave the stuff in the mailbox as he had promised. To think that what I'd come for was probably sitting in a chip bowl on Roy's kitchen table really hiked my blood pressure.

I gave one last-chance knock on the kitchen window, staring at the rolled-up papers, wishing for X-ray vision. No Roy. No super powers. No dog. The rubber flap on the doggie door hung quietly on its hinge.

Big doggie door, I noted. Almost as big as me doggie door. I shoved the toolbox aside with my foot and studied the opening. It wasn't as if Roy hadn't invited me over. It wasn't even so much like breaking and entering as it was like crawling and reading. In and out. Five minutes max. Anyway, I should really leave a note for Roy telling him I'd been here. I'd take the high ground, let him be the creep. In fact, the more I thought about it, the better it seemed to do it this way. It would save him from making a toll call to apologize.

I was tall but also pretty skinny, so if I went in on my side and held my breath, I could just make it. I pushed my purse through the door ahead of me.

Rationalization can take you a long way past reason. Mine rolled to a stop just as the rubber door flap slapped against my thigh like a walrus flipper. Too late now. I couldn't get back out until I got all the way in, or I'd risk getting snagged on the door. Getting through was like doing the lambada, but aside from having to detach a belt loop from one of the hinges and scraping some skin, I made it. Once inside, I stood up and brushed myself off. For a simple crawl-and-read, I was feeling an uncomfortable mixture of fear, guilt, and the urge to giggle.

"Tucker, you got a screw loose," I said out loud. But I was getting back in touch with my attitude.

Now that I was inside the house, the TV sounded much louder. The screeching of a car chase could be heard from the next room. I walked to the table and pulled the papers from the chip bowl and unrolled them.

It looked like the contents of Roy Trebeau's personnel file. The layoff notice was there, along with a history of raises, and vacation and sick days taken and owed. He wasn't exactly what you'd call a fast-tracker. He'd been with the company for eight years in the same position. The cost-of-living raises had stopped two years ago, probably due to Sunland's financial troubles. Roy's employment history was uneventful except for a written reprimand for a recent altercation with another employee, Anton Maslansky, the man he'd mentioned on the phone. Roy had apparently accused the guy of stealing equipment from the warehouse. Some ethnic slurs had been exchanged, which led to a fistfight. At least that explained the bruises on Roy's face. But there was no evidence that any further action had been taken by Sunland. In fact, by all appearances, it looked like just another casualty of an overheated melting pot. There was nothing in these reports indicating that the fight was the cause of Roy's dismissal.

I flipped to an employee roster. Listed were several names I'd asked about, including Maslansky's, but nothing else. My shoulders slumped as I took a deep defeated breath. Some of those people listed on the insurance claims obviously did work at Sunland, which meant that my little theory was at least partially wrong. Unfortunately, Roy's information contained nothing whatsoever that could help me in any way. Damn. I needed to talk to him. Where was he anyway? He obviously hadn't planned on being gone long, not with the TV cranked up like that.

I rolled the papers up tightly and stuffed them back in the chip bowl. Then I looked around for a notepad. Better leave a message asking him to call me. If nothing else, I'd thank him for his efforts. There was no phone in the kitchen. No message pad. How come I never had any damn paper? That was really pissing me off. And so was the TV. Why did people leave the things on when they weren't home anyway? Since I'd already broken into Roy's house and invaded his chip bowl, why not go all the way and turn off the tube? He'd thank me when he got his next electricity bill.

I slung my purse over my shoulder and followed a hallway that led past a small bathroom with vintage tile around the sink. If Roy wasn't home, I wondered whose truck was parked on the lawn. Maybe he decided I wasn't a cheap-wine-and-Doritos kind of girl after all, and at the last minute walked to the minimart for champagne and caviar.

The hallway was dark, the television loud. The air felt warm and close. As I tiptoed along the linoleum, I began to notice a faint odor. I made a mental note to educate Roy on the finer points of potpourri. I held my breath and listened for any sounds, but there was nothing but a whiny orchestral piece, cueing the TV audience to bring on the tears.

The living room was dark except for the flicker of the screen. The odor was stronger now. I pinched my nose and breathed through my mouth. Maybe Cujo had an accident and Roy was outside setting him straight. Several bulky objects were visible in the room, but nothing moved. No Roy Trebeau. The TV screen looked dim and splotchy. I searched the room for a light source until I spotted what looked like a lamp. It took three steps, and I was there. I fumbled for the switch. When the bulb came on, it managed to cast only a dim shadow. I looked around to get my bearings, scanning the room in slow motion. Couch. Travel posters in glass and clips.

At first it seemed as if Roy was simply a victim of bad taste, because everywhere there were shades of red: the couch, the walls, the linoleum floor. But as my eyes became accustomed to the dim light, they settled on the TV. That's when I realized it was too much red, and not the monochromatic red from a designer's color wheel. It was spatters of red. And they were everywhere. I stood transfixed and horrified, unwilling to stay, unable to go, forcing my eyes to finish sweeping the room until they reached the easy chair in the far corner. There my eyes stopped.

A man's legs were sticking out from behind the chair. I recognized the jeans. It was the same brown pair Roy Trebeau had worn that day at Sunland, except now they were soaked in blood.

My body began to tremble. From somewhere deep inside me rose a groan. It was guttural and wounded and vibrated my vocal cords like bike wheels on gravel until there was no air to support it. I'd come here to find Roy Trebeau and what he knew, but now Roy Trebeau was the last person I wanted to find.

I stood for a moment in that room, not knowing what to do: check for a pulse, call the police, or get the hell out of there. I didn't see how Roy could still be alive. There was just too much blood. But I couldn't leave him there like that, either. Not until I was sure.

I backed out of the living room, backed all the way to the kitchen, barely able to breathe. Fighting to keep upright, I turned the lock and opened the door. The welcome freshness of exhaust fumes and grit filled my lungs. I ran for my car and, once inside, locked the door, relieved to be away from the sound of the TV, the smell of the blood, the image of those jeans.

I drove for several blocks, gripping the steering wheel and taking short, shallow gasps of air until my throat was dry and raw. Finally, I pulled into the parking lot of a 7-Eleven and used a pay phone to call 911, hanging up before the operator could ask my name.

Suddenly, too many people in my world were ending up dead. Questions without answers pounded my head: Who had interrupted my telephone conversation with Roy? Had it been his killer, and had the timing of my trip to Reseda that night been too convenient for him to resist? Was Trebeau's death linked in some way to Polk's? That prompted the biggest question of all: Was I being set up to take the fall again—this time for murder?

23

a weight pressed down on my head, and the overwhelming odor of must filled my nose. My arms flailed in the dark until my hand touched something coarse and hairy. I heard a muffled growl. Muldoon. Sometime while I slept he'd once again decided to share my pillow. There was no moving him, so I crab-walked to the foot of the bed until I was free. Through one blurry eye, I read the clock. Ten a.m.

My eyes were swollen from too little sleep. My head ached. I felt numb and in denial. Death looked so much more real in person than it did in a photograph. I hadn't really known Roy Trebeau, but I still felt some indefinable loss—and fear, because while I was crawling through doggie doors, a murderer might have been watching. Might know what I looked like, what kind of car I drove, and might be able to trace me to the house through my license plate number.

I took Pookie's robe from the hook on the bathroom door. It smelled of chamomile and L'Air Du Temps, but didn't offer the comfort I'd hoped for. The robe was way too small and made me feel like the Incredible Hulk, only pinker. At least it was better than nothing.

Muldoon didn't seem to notice that my eyes were puffy or that too much forearm was hanging out of Pookie's miniature bathrobe. I returned the favor by raking my fingers through his bristly white coat until he rolled over on his back, legs in the air.

Too bad contentment didn't come that easily for me. The world was a scary place to be alone in right now. And as if things weren't bad enough, now my fingerprints were all over the scene of a homicide. I'd never been printed before, at least not that I could remember, so maybe the police would never know I'd been there. Yeah, sure.

Once again, I found myself thinking of Eric and looking forward to seeing him that evening. Okay, so trying to recapture the feelings we'd once shared wasn't going to be easy, but we were already friends. Wasn't that the hard part? Hadn't he shown over and again that he cared? And right now there was nothing that meant more to me than that. Relationships were about compromise, and I was ready to make a few. I called his home number to reconfirm our meeting. He didn't pick up, so I left a message assuring him that I'd be at the restaurant on time, no excuses, and I'd be ready to talk.

While the coffee dribbled into the pot, I gave Muldoon a breath-freshening treat that looked like a macaroon, and let him out for a romp on the sand. A heavy marine layer had settled in, making the world uniformly gray and bleak. Only a slight breeze ruffled the sea grass. About a hundred feet offshore, a sailboat was swinging a slow arc on its bow anchor. I could barely see the name on the stern: *Yachta Money*. Funny. Boat names seemed to come in four flavors: (1) women's names, (2) foreign words or phrases, (3) heroic adjectives, and (4) plays on words. At least it provided boat owners an outlet for creative thinking.

While I mused, I kept a constant eye on Muldoon until he was back safely inside. I knew we couldn't stay locked up in the house forever. Mo Whitener's deadline was only two days away, and I still hadn't found out if the NeuroMed package was in Polk's Mercedes. I decided to drop by Mona's house. While I was there, I'd tell her about finding the insurance policy.

Since it was Saturday, I put on a pair of blue jeans and my favorite red alpaca sweater. When Muldoon sensed I was leaving, he became morose. He walked into Pookie's room and ducked under the bed. She was due home in three days. Not soon enough for me. I hated feeling responsible for the little guy, even if his breath was smelling sweeter. No coaxing, sweet talk, or apologies moved him from his hiding place. So at the last minute, I caved in and asked Mrs. Domanski to watch him for the day. I prodded Muldoon out from under the bed with a rag mop and carried him next door. Mrs. D. was still in her bathrobe, wearing Ray•Bans but looking sober. Good signs all.

I was cautious pulling out of the garage. Roy Trebeau's killer was probably long gone, but there was still spooky Deegan to worry about. I checked my rearview mirror frequently to make sure I wasn't being followed.

When I arrived at the Polks' house, a more accommodating Elsa led me to the English garden, where a buff-looking Mona Polk lay on a workout bench. She wore a fuchsia thong leotard and matching midthigh spandex shorts. Stomach flat. Biceps bulging. Thighs taut as frogs' legs. Armando knelt next to her, a vision in formfitting black sweatpants and white polo shirt, resting his hand territorially on her abs. The five-pound weight Mona held in each hand didn't quite account for the flush in her face. It was all so cozy. The grieving widow finds solace in the rigors of exercise.

When he saw me, he flared his aquiline nose in an impressive Valentino impersonation. Mona sat up. At first she looked confused, as if she was searching for the politically correct widow persona, but within a few seconds she relaxed her face, as if the pretense wasn't worth the effort.

She smiled and motioned me toward a carved stone bench in front of a nearby gazebo. "Well, hello, Tucker. It's so nice to see you here again." La, la, la. The music in her voice had returned. She could have been auditioning for *Hello, Dolly!*

I settled onto the bench. "Sorry I didn't call first."

"No problem," she said, "that is, if you don't mind talking while I finish my workout."

Did I mind? Certainly not. Getting sweaty with Armando sounded like much more fun than a fistful of Prozac. Gee, with all the stress I was under, maybe I should ask him to add me to his client base.

"Some of the information might be considered confidential," I said.

She glanced at him. "It's all right. You can speak freely."

A-r-r-r-r-mando flashed his white teeth in a smile of comprehension. Those English lessons must be working. Mona wiped moisture from her forehead with a pink wristband that matched the rest of her getup.

"We missed you at the luncheon," she said.

So much had happened. It was hard to fathom that Milton Polk's funeral had been held just the morning before. I nodded and mumbled something lame, but it didn't matter, because she wasn't listening. She grabbed two hand weights, spread her legs, and reached down to touch her toes. I know that I was probably developing a prison fixation, but it didn't look like a position recommended for men behind bars.

"Did you get my message about the Mercedes?" I said.

"I got your message, and the answer is no. The police haven't returned it yet. Frankly, I forgot about the car. I should call about it, though, shouldn't I?"

The new, proactive Mona Polk. Could a cure for cancer be far behind? She continued exercising while Armando went off to look for Kleinman's business card. I could have given her the detective's telephone number, but I was glad for the opportunity to speak with her alone.

"The Friday before he died," I said. "Dr. Polk was upset about something. Do you know what it was?"

She hesitated. "Not really. Something about a letter, but he discussed it with someone he trusted, and things were going to be all right. By Saturday night he was fine, even cheerful."

I wondered if the letter she was talking about was from Mo Whitener. I also wondered why Mona Polk hadn't mentioned it before. In any event, Polk certainly hadn't met with anyone at Aames & Associates Friday night. Gordon would have told me. More likely, Polk had seen a lawyer.

"I read in the paper that Wade Covington got an award that night," I said.

Mona exhaled deeply, resting the weights on the bench. "Yes, we hoped to raise a lot of money for our women's shelter that evening, but we needed extra security, and that cut into our profits. Peace of mind doesn't come cheap."

"Extra security because of the stalker?" I asked.

She paused and stared at me with an expression that mingled surprise with grudging respect. "You know about that?"

I nodded. She gazed back into the garden, which was heavy with the scent of jasmine. She inhaled deeply before she spoke.

"We got a letter at our headquarters. It wasn't signed, of course, but it warned us not to give the award to Wade. I don't recall the details. I don't want to remember."

Her statement sent another thought flitting through my mind. Maybe Polk had been upset that Friday afternoon, not by a letter from Mo Whitener but by one from the same person who was threatening Wade Covington. A person who thought Polk bore some responsibility for Teresa García's death.

"Was your husband's name mentioned in that letter?"

She looked up. Her surprise seemed genuine. "What an odd question. My husband wasn't involved in Project Rescue."

Armando returned with the detective's business card. Mona studied it for a few seconds and then set it on the bench beside her. She picked up the weights and, with Armando hovering protectively over her, began another set.

"Did you see Dr. Polk talking with anyone Saturday night?" I said. "Or see if he left with anybody?"

Mona frowned in thought. "He spoke with Wade, of course. Congratulating him, I'm sure. I didn't see him with anyone else, but I wasn't watching him all night, either. When things settled down, I looked around, but he was gone. I didn't think anything of that. My husband hated those events. Frankly, I was surprised he offered to go with me."

"Mrs. Polk, I hate to ask you this, but do you think your husband's death had anything to do with his conversation with Wade Covington?"

She looked at me. Armando looked at her. I looked at both of them. Everybody was looking and calculating.

She rested the weights on her hips. "As I told the police, my husband could be a hard man to understand sometimes, but I don't know anyone who wanted to harm him—certainly not Wade Covington. Why are you interested in all this?"

I thought carefully about her question. "Because I want to know who killed him—almost as much as you do."

"Of course, we all want that." An edge had crept into her voice, which caused Armando's body to stiffen.

"Do you know where Dr. Polk was during the day on Saturday?"

"I have no idea," she said. "I was busy, getting ready for the dinner."

She signaled a wrap-up to Armando. He gathered the gym equipment and began stowing it in a nearby black bag. Apparently, the workout and the interview were over.

"Just one more thing," I said. "When I was sorting through Dr. Polk's papers, I came across an insurance policy, listing you as the beneficiary. It was taken out fairly recently. The amount was two million dollars."

Mona exhaled with a raspy cry as the weights she was holding thudded to the ground. She stood for the longest time, holding herself together, but eventually her tranquil mask began to crumble. Her face became flushed; her eyes grew moist and red, until both were consumed with anguish. Finally, she covered her face with her hands and began to sob. I'd seen enough sorrow in my life to recognize the real thing. It was never easy to watch.

Armando dropped the gym bag he was carrying and ran to her side. He held her body against his, gently stroking her hair as if that might stop the ragged crying.

"Milton, I'm so sorry," she said.

Oddly, it was the first time I remembered hearing her refer to her husband by name. I stood motionless, watching the scene play out, waiting until her sobs softened to sniffles, then heavy breathing, then nothing. I felt intensely uncomfortable attempting to dissect her reaction, and struggled to find an exit strategy.

It's strange what triggers grief. At our first meeting, Mona Polk claimed she cared deeply for her husband, but I hadn't seen much evidence of that until today, not even at the funeral. Maybe in some strange way, she'd seen the insurance policy as a sign that Polk loved her after all. Regardless of how she'd perceived the gesture, I had to wonder if Mona's emotional pain could just as easily be attributed to guilt. Perhaps she'd not only loved her husband but, conceivably, had murdered him as well.

Since I'd left my fingerprints all over a homicide scene less than twenty-four hours before, I wasn't exactly eager to sashay into the nearest police station. But I had to find the NeuroMed documents, so I offered to follow up on the car. Mona seemed grateful. She gave me Detective Kleinman's business card, which I took even though I had one of my own. Gripping Armando's arm, she walked back along the flagstone path toward the house.

I tried to connect the dots between the events in Milton Polk's last night alive. Had his discussion with Covington been a simple message of congratulations, as Mona had suggested, or had something in that conversation led to Polk's tense search through NeuroMed and, eventually, to his death?

On the other hand, Mona may have lied when she claimed she hadn't seen her husband again Saturday night. She and Armando could easily have arranged to meet him after the dinner and killed him for the insurance money.

I also couldn't discount the possibility that Polk's death wasn't connected to anything I knew to date. It could have been a simple crime of passion committed by Kenny Chalmers. It was apparently no secret to people who knew them both that Kenny hated Milton Polk. Francine could have told him that the doctor was attending the Project Rescue charity dinner. Kenny could have waited outside the hotel that night and followed Polk until he found an opportunity to kill him.

By the time I reached the front door, I was up to my eyeballs in theories but still no closer to the truth. Armando stood at the foot of the stairs with his arms crossed over his chest, watching me. Mona lingered for a few seconds, holding my hand. All I could offer her in return was a small reassuring squeeze. If I was going to survive the next stop on my schedule—round three with my old buddy Detective Duane Kleinman—I couldn't afford to let my guard down. I was going to need all the strength I could muster.

24

t wenty minutes after leaving Mona Polk's house, I pulled into the visitors' lot at the LAPD's Pacific Station, a two-story brick building that looked like a neighborhood library except for the sea of black-and-white police cars parked in the back lot.

I felt a little jumpy as a uniformed female officer at the front desk made a call and then escorted me into a room with stained royal blue carpeting, ringing telephones, and the smell of Chinese takeout. Hanging from the ceiling above pods of metal desks were engraved wooden signs with names like Autos, Burglary, and Homicide.

We passed through that area and continued down a narrow hallway to a room no larger than a closet. It was cold inside. The carpet had been ripped up, leaving patches of glue and bits of the pad still sticking to the plywood base. The walls were covered in some kind of pockmarked beige paneling—soundproofing, maybe, because when the door closed, I was left alone in stone-cold silence. I sat at a table on one of the two chairs and looked for hidden cameras or two-way mirrors. There weren't any that I could see.

I was hugging myself for warmth and wondering why somebody didn't spring for a heating system in this dump, when the door opened and a man walked in. But it wasn't Duane Kleinman. This guy wore tight Levi's that accentuated all the major muscle groups and a brown leather jacket that looked like Bambi's mother. His hair was wet, as if he'd just stepped out of the shower. Delicate brown ringlets curled softly on his neck.

If I'd been capable of rational thought, I might have said something snappy. Instead, I sat frozen in my chair, unable to take my eyes off those curls.

"Joe Deegan," he said, extending his hand.

When he noticed how flustered I was, he flashed a grin. I could almost see the fluorescent lights glancing off his pearly white teeth. Little Red Riding Hood meets the big, bad wolf.

"Don't break my heart and tell me you don't remember me," he said.

"What are you doing here?"

"Paperwork."

"Why? Get tired of your little bouncer job and come to hang with the big dogs?"

Deegan laughed. "Not bad, but as I recall from our first date, you can do better."

I glowered at him. "I asked for Detective Kleinman."

Deegan must have noticed I was shivering, because he took off his jacket and tossed it to me. That's when I saw the badge hanging from his belt, and the holstered gun strapped to his chest.

"My partner's not here," he said, "so I guess you're stuck with me."

It took a few seconds for that to sink in, and when it finally did, I had more than a few questions: If Deegan was a cop, then why was he working security at Wade Covington's party? And exactly when had he read the notes from Kleinman's interview with me—before or after the luncheon? At this point it really didn't matter, because I was certain Deegan knew a lot more about me than I knew about him. All of a sudden, I had more cops in my life than Rodney King.

I put on his jacket because I was cold and because the knit collar smelled like cherry almond shampoo. Deegan sat down and tilted the chair back, crossing his legs in that male alpha-dog posture that said, "Here's what I got, baby. Interested?" Yeah, I thought, like that's going to happen.

"You come here to talk business," he said, "or to apologize for all those naughty things you said to me?"

I took a breath to regain my composure and switched to my calm business voice. "I'm here because Mona Polk asked me to check on her husband's Mercedes. I'd like to pick it up, today if possible."

He flashed an indulgent smile, like I was some cute but dopey kid asking for Gummi Bears before dinner.

"Definitely not today," he said.

I was getting nowhere, and time was running out. I had to know if the NeuroMed package had been found in the car, so I asked for an inventory of the Mercedes's contents, adding some stupid line about being concerned in case something turned up missing.

A muscle twitched at the corner of his mouth. His eyes said, "This one's yours, but don't think I didn't notice." The guy had that nonverbal communication schtick aced. I figured him for the type you could be married to for twenty years and not know his favorite color.

Deegan rattled off the items found inside the car, but the NeuroMed package wasn't among them. I didn't want to make him suspicious by questioning his memory, but I asked if he was sure he hadn't left anything out. He *was* sure. He'd just reviewed the report, and had listed everything that was in the car when it was recovered at LAX.

I wondered how the car got to the airport. Polk drowned in salt water, presumably in the Santa Monica Bay. That was a long way from LAX. Very odd. Maybe I'd overlooked something in his files that placed Polk at the airport that night, like an airline ticket receipt or an itinerary. It was improbable, but I still wanted to go home and take another peek. Maybe I'd call Mona and check with her as well.

Deegan didn't seem in a hurry for me to leave. I half expected him to ask more questions about Milton Polk's death, or worse, to tell me that one of Roy Trebeau's neighbors had written down my license plate number, but he didn't. Instead, his questions seemed harmless and were asked in that flirty boy-meets-girl dance, a maneuver I assumed he used to keep me off guard, like he was playing the good cop to Kleinman's bad cop.

I had to admit the guy was great-looking and kind of funny, too, but I wasn't going to get sucked into his game, because he was also a homicide detective, and right now I was up to my ass in dead bodies. I centered myself with a few silent *ommmmm*s, the kind Pookie used when she meditated, and hoped that Deegan wouldn't ask me any more questions. It must have worked, because about that time, he announced he was late for a meeting with his captain. He told me he'd call if he had more questions.

I raised my eyebrows. "Call? Why not just break into my bedroom again?"

At first he looked puzzled. Then he put his arms on the table and leaned forward, crowding my airspace.

"If I'd been in your bedroom, believe me, we both would have remembered."

I gave him my version of Venus's stony stare. "I'm serious,

Deegan. What were you doing in my house without a search warrant?"

His eyes narrowed, and his mouth set in a hard line. "What are you talking about?"

His intensity made my palms sweaty, made me want to tell him everything and nothing—mostly nothing. On the other hand, there wasn't any reason to withhold that information. I explained about leaving my jacket at Covington's, and about how it had been returned. All he'd said was, "It wasn't me," and that gave me a really creepy feeling. If Deegan hadn't been in my house, then who had?

"So what were you doing at Covington's party anyway?" I said.

"I think this'll work better if you let me ask the questions."

That irritated me, and I was about to tell him so when I noticed that he was staring at me like an entomologist with a bug pin. Then I realized he wasn't actually looking at me at all. He was thinking.

"You know what to do if somebody attacks you?" he asked.

"Blow em away with my forty-five?"

He looked annoyed. "I'm just guessing here, but I'd say you don't have a forty-five."

"Maybe I'll get one."

He had on his serious-cop mask now. "Anyone who owns a gun should be prepared to kill." He paused to make sure I was paying attention before continuing. "Two things you should do. First, if the guy's got hair, grab it and pull. Then find his neck, and hit it as hard as you can with your fist or the side of your hand."

Yeah, yeah, yeah, I thought. Why was he telling me all this? Cop paranoia?

"What's number two?" I asked.

"Kick him in the balls and don't look back."

I didn't have time to listen to a Neighborhood Watch lecture, even though his concern was sort of charming. He must have noticed my eyes glazing over, because he dropped the subject. His eyes lingered on mine for a few seconds, as if he was wondering what might have happened between us if we'd met under different circumstances.

Finally, Deegan let out a dismissive sigh and stood. "I'll call you about the car."

I gave him a nonchalant shrug. "Call Mrs. Polk. Our business is over."

A hint of amusement flickered briefly in his blue-gray eyes.

"You know what they say," he replied in a tone that I couldn't quite read. "It ain't over till it's over."

Deegan escorted me to the lobby. As I walked toward the main door, I realized I was still wearing his jacket. I took it off and tossed it back to him. On my way out I thought I heard him say, "See you around, Stretch," but I couldn't be sure. I had some bad news for Deegan. He might as well save that flirting routine for happy hour at his local pickup bar, because I wasn't in any mood to grant conjugal visits at the Gray-Bar Motel to a cop.

Besides, I had work to do. I had to get home and have another look at Milton Polk's files. Maybe he'd left me some clue after all. I just had to find it.

25

ll the way home I couldn't get my mind off Milton Polk.
From what I'd been told, he left work early on Friday afternoon. He was upset, presumably about a letter he received.
What I didn't know was whether that letter had been from Mo
Whitener, Covington's stalker, or somebody else. Later that
evening, the doctor met with someone he trusted—someone
who assured him that everything would be all right, which put
him in a better mood. Perhaps that meeting went on too long,
and Polk didn't have time to go back to the Center to pick up
his tux.

What he did all day Saturday was still a blank, but that
evening he went to the Project Rescue dinner in his brown suit,
still in good spirits. He even volunteered to go, which was out of
character for him. But perhaps that dinner was different because
he planned to meet someone important there that night. Maybe
Wade Covington. At least, I knew that he spoke to Covington
around ten o'clock and had presumably left shortly thereafter.
Within the next two hours, something or someone had upset his
equilibrium enough to trigger a mad search through his files at
NeuroMed. So where had he gone after that? I had to find out.

I still had no clue where the NeuroMed file was—or, for that
matter, Mo Whitener's money. I was feeling a little desperate. To

calm myself, I put the top down on the Boxster so I could smell the ocean, feel the wind on my cheeks, and be with my thoughts, which were now reading like one of Pookie's movie scripts:

FADE IN EXT.—MORNING, HOTEL GRAND CAYMAN. Former manager of NeuroMed, FRANCINE CHALMERS, sits by the pool on a chaise longue, wearing a skirted bathing suit and big white sunglasses. Her husband, KENNY, is crushing the umbrella from his piña colada in his clenched fist. Enter IRENE BORODIN, a cigarette dangling from the corner of her mouth, wearing a souvenir muumuu from a Shriners' luau. She carries a suitcase full of money, ill-gotten gains from the trio's crime spree.

Of course, I didn't really believe Francine was on the lam in the Caymans. She was probably at home, nursing a cold and checking for winning numbers on her Lotto tickets. But it certainly hadn't looked as if she was coming back to NeuroMed anytime soon.

I pulled into my garage and entered the house through the side door. My paranoia was still primed, so I did a little tippy-toe through each room before breathing freely. When I went to rescue Muldoon, he was sprawled on a lounge chair on Mrs. Domanski's deck, wearing a pair of yellow sunglasses and a matching cashmere sweater. I had to drag him home. Loyalty, schmoyalty. You couldn't blame the guy for liking cashmere.

I gave him some Pookie-approved canned dog food, but he wouldn't go near it. Too full of caviar and martinis, no doubt. I decided to pamper myself with a cup of tea in my good china. As I carried the step stool to the kitchen cabinet, I realized that if Eric were here, he could reach the top shelf without it.

There were three more messages from Gordon on my machine: one angry, one conciliatory, one pleading. He wanted to speak with me . . . had been lobbying on my behalf with the partners . . . thought he'd made some progress. Where the hell was the NeuroMed file? Had I found it yet?

I weighed the pros and cons of calling him. The argument was heavy on the con side, so when the phone rang, I didn't pick up until I recognized my mother's voice on the answering machine.

"How's Muldoon?" she asked. "Does he miss me?"

"Not really. Mrs. Domanski's been treating him to cashmere. He hardly even asks about you anymore."

She sighed. "I've been worried about you. Is that work thing settled yet?"

I filled the kettle with water and found the tea bags. Muldoon sensed the lull in my activity and started pawing my leg for attention.

"I'll tell you all about it when you get home," I said. "What time should I be at the airport?"

She hesitated. "Well, see, that's just it. I called my agent this morning to tell him. I'll be away a little longer than I'd planned."

"Nice to know I'm first on your call list, Pookie."

She ignored my sarcasm.

"Remember that man I told you about? Bruce?" she said. "Well, we ended up sort of hitting it off. In fact, we're roommates here. After the retreat he wants me to go with him to a kahuna workshop in Maui."

"You're sleeping with a hippie named Bruce who can't remember your name?" I said. "What are you thinking?"

"I'm only fifty-one, Tucker," she said defensively. "Sex is still an option. Besides, I'll be out of your hair. You can do your own thing for a change. Take a few days off. Go skiing."

I felt my jaw tighten. "Look, Pookie, if you want to hang ten with some guy you picked up in a sweat lodge, be my guest, but don't make it sound like you're doing me a favor."

There was a long pause before she said softly, "He makes me laugh, Tucker. I like him."

Okay, so she was an actor, and making people dredge up emotions like guilt and shame was part of her craft. So why did she have to be so damn good at it? I knew that if I told her Aunt Sylvia was taking me to court, two people were dead, my life was a shambles, and I didn't want to be alone anymore, she'd be on the next plane. But what was the point? There wasn't anything she could do.

"In that case," I said, "Muldoon and I will be fine. Aloha."

Another pause. Pookie was obviously weighing her anxiety and guilt against her hopes that, despite whatever I wasn't telling her, I'd still land butter side up.

"What will you do for Thanksgiving?" she said.

"I don't know. Maybe skiing does sound fun."

"I'll miss you, Tucker," she said softly.

"Yeah." But only after I replaced the receiver did I add, "I'll miss you, too, Mom."

The teakettle started whistling, so I pulled it off the burner and poured hot water into the cup. Muldoon had given up scratching on my leg long enough to find his stuffed bear, hoping to interest me in a game. I picked him up. He was warm and hairy, and when I laid my head against his neck, he smelled of Mrs. Domanski's heavy perfume. He wasn't such a bad guy, so it wasn't his fault that I'd never felt so alone in my life.

I hadn't called Eugene, but it was the weekend, and by Monday it wouldn't matter what spying he'd done, because I'd no longer be suspended from Aames & Associates. I'd be fired. My meeting with Shelly Greenblatt wasn't until tomorrow. Even though Gordon knew the NeuroMed report was missing, he didn't know it was probably permanently missing. I couldn't bring myself to tell him. Not yet.

I brought the tea into the living room and began looking through Polk's boxes again. Nothing resonated until I opened the file I'd put together for his accountant and noticed the coffee receipt. Polk wasn't one to pick up the tab if he didn't have to, but I wondered why he'd bothered to send this receipt to himself. The printing was hard to read, so I held it up to the light to get a better look. The server's name was Benito. The receipt also had a date and time imprinted on the paper. In faint blue letters was what looked like a water seal. Heat prickled my face when I read the name under the logo: Marina Yacht Club.

According to this receipt, fifteen minutes after midnight on Saturday, the night he'd been killed, Milton Polk was drinking coffee at the club's bar. He must have gone there after leaving the Project Rescue dinner, and after picking up the NeuroMed package.

I felt a surge of adrenaline as I called the number listed for the club and learned that Benito was due at work in three hours, at six p.m. I was too pumped to concentrate, so while finishing the tea, I picked up the Project Rescue newsletter Mona had given me. I skimmed over an article about the alarming increase in domestic violence in Mexico. The article stated that it was a crime that often went unpunished, dismissed by authorities as *crímenes pasionales*, crimes of passion. On the same page was a picture of Wade Covington holding his Man of the Year award. The award appeared to be a glass or Lucite sculpture of an angular wing in flight. It looked lethal.

I was thinking about that award when I remembered another

I'd seen recently, on the mantel in Covington's den: the silver cup in recognition of his term as commodore of the Marina Yacht Club. The implication swept over me slowly. The night Polk died, he was to have met someone. He left the Project Rescue dinner after he was seen talking to Covington. He stopped briefly at the Center and then drove on to the yacht club, where he drank a cup of coffee and, presumably, waited for his contact to arrive.

Perhaps Polk hadn't been looking for the NeuroMed package that night at all. Perhaps he'd been hunting for the thing I'd found hidden away in Wade Covington's briefcase, the thing that was, at this very moment, tucked inside a shredded wheat box in my kitchen cupboard: Teresa García's medical file.

My hopes now hinged on whether Benito remembered seeing Milton Polk or the person he was meeting Saturday night. I slipped the newsletter into my purse so I could show Benito the picture of Wade Covington.

I was feeling nervous but hopeful when the phone rang. The woman's voice on the line was hushed. When she identified herself, my heart began to pound. It was Francine Chalmers.

"I don't have much time," she whispered. "Kenny will be home from the shop any second. We have to talk."

"About what? Bail bonds?"

"I can fix everything," she whimpered. "Put the money back. I just need you to explain to *her* how it wasn't my fault."

The disdain in her voice was clear. She'd reduced Mona Polk to an emphasized pronoun.

"It's too late for that," I said. "You need a lawyer."

"You don't understand," she blurted out. "Dr. Polk couldn't make payroll, so I loaned him money, but he couldn't give it back right away. I had to return the money to our account before

Kenny found out. Please, if he comes home, he won't let me leave. Can I come to your place?"

Yeah, as if I just fell off a turnip truck.

"My roommate's here, training his rottweilers," I said. "You know how that goes."

"There's a little café in Hollywood. Gorky's. It's quiet. We can talk. I'll meet you in an hour."

I had no intention of meeting Francine anywhere. Not that I didn't trust her, but I didn't trust her.

"And tell me again why I should help you?" I said skeptically.

She paused. Then her voice became sly. "That report you wrote for Dr. Polk—somebody changed it, and you're in a lot of trouble. But there's more. Things you don't know about . . . things that could get you in bigger trouble."

She'd definitely gotten my attention now. Obviously, Francine knew about the letter from Whitener's lawyers, but did she also know who doctored the NeuroMed report? Maybe, but it was the "bigger trouble" I was worried about now.

"Okay, so tell me—"

She cut me off. "I have to go. Kenny's back." Then her voice faded to a desperate squeak.

"Francine. Wait!"

Click. Silence. Dial tone. My insides were churning. I briefly considered the wisdom of meeting Francine. But Gorky's was a public place, so what did I have to worry about? A little voice answered, "It's in Hollywood, you idiot." Well, okay, there was that.

I was getting ready to leave when I remembered my date with Eric. Damn. I had to cancel, but an impersonal message machine wasn't the way to tell him. With luck and a lead foot, it would take forty-five minutes to get to Gorky's. That left fifteen minutes to stop by Eric's condo. It wasn't much time, but enough to tell him what was on my mind.

Mrs. Domanski wasn't answering the door, so I slipped a spare door key into her mail slot, along with a note telling her where I'd be. I also hinted that Muldoon would appreciate an invitation for cocktails. Then I headed for Eric's condo.

26

Since our divorce, Eric had been leasing a high-rise condo on Wilshire Boulevard in Westwood, which had unofficially been declared a schlock-free zone. The decor was modern, the kitchen appliances European, and not even a daddy longlegs ventured closer than the neighbor's balcony. The unit had spectacular city and ocean views, but it was so neat and tidy and perfect that it felt like a model on some showroom floor, not a place where real people lived.

I rang the buzzer and rehearsed the speech I'd formed in my head on the way over. My relationship with Eric had been molded and seasoned by individual successes and combined failures, but those experiences had created an ironclad bond that was irreplaceable.

When the door opened, my mouth went dry. A woman was standing in the entryway. A woman that wasn't me, in Eric's condo. She was petite, feminine, and dressed in an outfit that was both casual and cultivated. She looked familiar, but I couldn't place her until I recognized the hair. It was the rich red-brown color of cinnamon. When I realized who she was, I felt both embarrassed and relieved. Eric had told me he'd be working at home this weekend. She was the client I'd seen with him by the elevator in his office.

When I asked for Eric, she told me her name was Becky and opened the door wider, gesturing for me to step into the foyer. But the last thing I wanted was to interrupt a business meeting.

"That's okay," I said. "I'm sort of pressed for time. Maybe you could just tell him I'm out here."

She nodded and disappeared inside. When Eric finally came to the door, his face was flushed.

"Tucker, I thought we were meeting at the restaurant."

He joined me in the hall, closing the door behind him. He kept running his hand through his hair, which was something he did when he was stressed.

"Actually, that's why I dropped by," I said. "I can't make it."

The time had come to tell him how I felt, so I gathered my courage, took a deep breath, and let it go.

"You know, when we were talking the other day? About relationships? I know what you were trying to tell me, Eric, and I've realized that I'm all for it. So much has happened, and I've learned that there's nothing more important than having people you trust and love in your life, so—"

"Someone told you, right? Damn it. You let me go on babbling the other day like an idiot, when you knew all along." Eric's words gushed out like a party balloon expelling air. "I guess it doesn't matter. I'm just relieved it's finally out in the open. It didn't feel right keeping it from you. All I can say is, thanks for understanding, Tucker. God, why was I so worried to tell you about Becky and me? I think I wasn't sure how you'd take it, you know, me being the first to get remarried and all, but Becky and I've been seeing each other for the past few months, and . . ."

I'm sure there was more, because I saw Eric's lips move and heard what sounded like a novice violinist torturing the strings of his new fiddle. I'd stopped listening altogether by the time he put his arm around my shoulder and gave me a brotherly hug. No, not brotherly exactly. More like a teammate hug.

For what seemed like an eternity there was nothing inside my head but astonishment that he could actually think I would find any comfort in that gesture. Then an inexplicable weight settled on my chest. Eric and Becky. Becky and Eric. Eric married to Becky? Maybe I didn't want to walk down the aisle again with him, but I realized that I wasn't ready to see anyone else make that trip, either.

If I'd been blessed with the gift of poetry, I could have looked deep inside myself to find some simple yet sublime words that would explain to the world, to Becky, to myself, why I felt that Eric still belonged to me, and why I wasn't yet ready to let him go. But I knew that if I tried to express those feelings, they would only come out sounding like "Roses are red; violets are blue; I'm losing Eric; boo-hoo, boo-hoo."

I might have stood there forever, searching for a graceful escape, if I hadn't spotted Becky standing at the door. The last thing in the world I wanted was to like her. Quite the opposite, in fact. I desperately wanted her to be a sneaky bitch on wheels, to be eminently hateable, but there she stood, looking somewhat confused, very much in love, and eminently likable.

I tried to convince myself that Eric had betrayed me in some way. That little bit of faulty reasoning gave me the courage to turn my leaden body toward the exit. As I stepped onto the elevator, I took one last look at the happy couple, standing hand in hand like smiling figurines atop a wedding cake. Then I dredged up a wan smile for Eric, and in what felt like a magnanimous gesture under the circumstances, I said, "Congratulations," as the door closed on our friendship.

By the time I reached the car, I'd skated past humiliation and self-loathing and transitioned at warp speed into anger. But none of those emotions helped to shake off that indelible old image of the tall, skinny girl with the geeky name whose boyfriend dumped her for her best friend in the world.

I rested my head on the steering wheel and waited for something to happen, but somehow I had already managed to bottle, cork, and get ready for aging all those unwieldy emotions. Just as well. This was no time to reopen old wounds. I had to meet Francine, so I started the car and headed for Hollywood.

• • •

GORKY'S WAS ON the ground floor of a decaying two-story building near the corner of Western Avenue and Hollywood Boulevard, in East Hollywood. I parked in the back lot, put some cash and my ID in my jeans pocket, and locked my purse in the trunk of the car. There didn't appear to be any way to get into the restaurant except through the kitchen, so I walked around to the front entrance. The café was positioned between an occult-gift shop and a liquor store. Two small round tables were set up on the sidewalk outside the café, but nobody in their right mind would eat there. Too much pigeon poop, too many empty Mickey D's boxes and scary-looking people—as though you might need a bodyguard to get to the borscht.

The interior was small, no more than eight tables. A samovar near the front was the only thing that gleamed; everything else was as dark and gloomy as a cave. It didn't seem like the kind of place Francine would hang out in, but what did I know? Two of the tables were pushed together toward the back wall and were occupied by five middle-aged men raising their glasses in a one-upmanship toast-o-rama. A half-full bottle of vodka sat on the table. I didn't understand Russian, but their toasts sounded like "and here's to when we discovered the cure for polio."

A man in his fifties approached me, wearing an outfit straight out of *The Brothers Karamazov.* He waved his arms and said, "No change for meter."

"I don't need change. I'm here for dinner."

He looked at me as if I were certifiable. Then he shrugged and led me to a table by the front window. The toasting stopped momentarily as the men gave me the once-over. I was the only woman in the place. They had to think about that for a minute. Wooman. Woodka. Wooman. Woodka. Woodka. Oh, well. I ordered a Russian beer and watched the hookers cruise by as I waited for Francine.

Ivan Karamazov brought me a Budski Lite. So much for Russian beer. The five men appeared to be a bottomless vodka pit. As the alcohol flowed, the speeches got louder, more passionate, and more slurred. Still no Francine. I was beginning to worry that Kenny had prevented her from coming. The alternative theory, that Francine was a thief and a flake and I shouldn't have come here in the first place, was shuffled into a back corner of my mind.

I was about to pay the check and leave when she came through the front door. She looked around furtively until she spotted me, and headed for my table. Her face was pale and haggard. She was wearing black stretch pants, an oversize black sweater, and little black ankle boots that made her look like a dowdy cat burglar. I offered her the menu, but she made it clear she wasn't there to eat. Despite her protests, I ordered her a beer so it didn't look like I was drinking alone.

"Kenny thinks I'm at the grocery store. I don't have much time."

"Then let's cut to the chase. What's all this trouble you were talking about on the phone?"

"First, you have to know that the whole insurance thing was Irene Borodin's idea," she said. "She promised me nobody would find out. And anyway, I was going to tell the insurance company it was just a flub and return the money as soon as Dr. Polk got his investors and paid me back."

Yeah, sure. How many cops and judges had heard that line before? I hoped Francine wasn't planning to waste my time making excuses for all her white-collar crimes.

"Did Dr. Polk know what you were up to?"

"Nobody knew," she said. "Just me and Irene, and I think her brother was in on it, too. She told me she'd been doing it for years with other doctors. Nobody had ever said boo."

"Why did you use my name?"

"Don't worry. I never turned in any claims for you. It's just that Irene promised me a higher percentage of the insurance refund for people I got on my own. Like I told you, I had to put the money back in our account before Kenny found out. He would have killed the doctor." When her brain caught up with her mouth, the reunion produced an unsettling quality to her voice. "I know what you're thinking, but that's not what I meant."

"Where was Kenny last Saturday night?"

"At home."

"With you?"

She hesitated, as if weighing the pros and cons of telling me what she knew. "I was in Bakersfield for the weekend, visiting my mother, but Kenny didn't kill Dr. Polk."

The denial was too quick, as if she had formulated the answer because she'd already asked herself the question. I was asking it, too. From what I knew, Kenny had a short fuse, an animosity toward Milton Polk, and, now, a very serious alibi problem. And according to Madie, Kenny controlled his wife and her money like a jealous Scrooge. Maybe he'd found out about the loan and confronted Polk. When the doctor couldn't come up with the cash to repay Francine, Kenny killed him.

"Francine, do you think it might have been Kenny that Dr. Polk was meeting after the Project Rescue dinner?"

"No way," she said emphatically. "The doctor was meeting somebody about those business plans of yours."

"How do you know that?"

"I'm not stupid. I can put two and two together. I know Dr. Polk was mad because those reports got screwed up and everybody was in trouble, and I know he's dead."

Obviously, Francine didn't know shit, but I decided to give her one more chance. "Could he have been meeting Wade Covington?"

"I told you before," she said firmly, "I don't know. He could have been meeting anyone—even *her*."

"I don't think Mona Polk has the expertise to fudge spreadsheets."

"Why not? It was a lousy job, wasn't it? Besides, cheating comes easy for her."

The last dig was delivered with a heavy load of sarcasm, but Francine had a point. No one had ever accused Mona of being saintly—or stupid. She kept herself fit, organized the business of a large charity, managed a husband, and kept a boy-toy on the side. A lot of people might call her gifted.

"Dr. Polk would have told you if he was meeting his wife," I said. "Why keep that a secret?"

"Maybe two people were with him that night; maybe it was

her and the boyfriend. Dr. Polk told me that he knew something bad about this person's past. If he was talking about her boyfriend, I don't think the doctor would have wanted me to know that."

"Wait a minute, Francine. You're not making sense. Who are you talking about? Armando? What do you think he did that was so bad?"

"Rape." She was on a roll, obviously grateful that the conversation had veered away from Kenny. "About a year ago Dr. Polk went on a ski trip to Aspen with Mr. Covington and some of his friends. They were gone a week, so Mr. Covington brought a maid from the city to clean and cook."

My ears pricked up. Covington. Maid. I was getting a flashback here. "Armando was on that trip?"

"Well, I don't know for sure," she said. "Dr. Polk didn't exactly give me the guest list, but he could have been there."

I ignored her pique. And since I was finished with my beer and she hadn't touched hers, I exchanged glasses.

"So what happened?" I asked.

"There was a party at Mr. Covington's ski lodge," she said. "Everybody was drinking. Dr. Polk wasn't much of a skier or a drinker, so he went to bed early. In the middle of the night, someone woke him up." She leaned forward and lowered her voice. "That maid had been raped and beaten. Dr. Polk wanted to take her to the hospital, but Mr. Covington insisted on flying her back to the city for treatment."

"What was the girl's name?"

She hesitated. "I don't know."

"Don't bullshit me, Francine. We had a deal: I help you; you help me. Remember?"

"You'll speak with Mrs. Polk and the insurance companies?"

"I can't promise it'll do any good, but yes."

She leaned back with a self-satisfied smile on her face. "The maid's name was Teresa García."

My breath came out as a soft little whistle. "Did anyone report the incident to the police?"

"No police."

So the dead girl hadn't fallen, as the newspaper article had stated. I wasn't surprised that the Colorado authorities weren't notified, but why wasn't the girl's family in Mexico asking questions? Apparently, everyone had accepted Covington's explanation of what led to her death, and I was sure he wanted to keep it that way.

Covington must have realized that with Polk dead, whoever took over the Center, as well as the police, would have access to the girl's medical file. He couldn't let that happen. He had to find that chart. Apparently, he had, probably the night I saw him at NeuroMed. At least, it had been in his briefcase a couple of days later. It was a logical little scenario until I realized that there was something missing.

The night I'd run into Covington at NeuroMed, Polk's body had just been identified—by me. I'd been the one to tell him that Polk was dead. He couldn't have known before. Or could he? That thought made my head spin.

"Anyway, that's all I know. I swear." Francine checked her watch and glanced toward the door. "I've got to go. Kenny will be home soon. Thank you for helping me. Irene warned me not to tell you anything, but I knew she was wrong about you."

I felt a flash of panic. "Irene Borodin? You didn't tell her we were meeting here, did you?"

Her concentration seemed to disengage and wander around the room. "No," she said.

I could tell she was lying. She *had* told Irene Borodin. The last thing I needed was for Countess Dracula to show up unannounced and create a scene. I had to get out of here.

I put some money on the table to cover the tab. A few minutes later, Francine left through the front door. I wanted to leave, too, but I'd had one too many brewskis, so I went looking for the restroom. No luck finding it, but I did locate the kitchen. One peek inside made me glad I hadn't ordered any food. Ivan the Terrible Waiter was standing over a bubbling pot of something. A cigarette dangled from the corner of his mouth. When he saw me, he jumped to attention and the ash plopped in the brew. He flicked the butt on the floor and covered it with his shoe.

"Excuse me," I said. "Where's the ladies' room?"

He gave me his hundred-watt smile and gestured like a magician with an invisible cape toward the back door. Great. The bathroom was probably a recycled Scud missile. Well, almost. What he pointed to was a separate building at the back of the parking lot, built of gray cinder blocks and with one small square window, high up on the wall. It looked like a Siberian gulag.

"Lights. Inside." He smiled proudly and made a flicking gesture.

I thought, ah, and here's to Mother Russia's greatest invention, electricity. As I exited the back door, I looked around to make sure I wasn't being watched. Three empty cars were parked along with mine in the back lot. There was also a white delivery van stationed near the door. Printed on the side were the words *Gorky's Catering*. It looked as if it had never been driven.

When I reached the building, I realized that where the lock should have been there was only a hole in the door. Open to the public. Yuk. I opened the metal door and reached my hand around the corner, switching on the light. Not bad. The place was cavernous compared to the restaurant but smelled of strong disinfectant and bad plumbing. No heat. Four stalls. Four sinks. Swinging soap dispensers just like those at the Center. Same pungent odor of industrial soap. Simple but effective.

The quiet of the restroom was a respite after all that toasting and passion. I checked all the stalls and finally settled on the cleanest one, the one farthest away from the door. No sanitary seat covers, of course.

Francine's theory that Armando had been on the ski trip with Covington sounded like a feeble attempt to divert attention away from Kenny. All the guys on that trip had been friends of Covington, according to what Polk had told her. That pretty much excluded Armando, I suspected.

All this mental badminton was stimulating, but I was on a schedule. Regardless of who had been at Aspen, Polk had been at the Marina Yacht Club the night he died. I could only hope that he'd had the NeuroMed file with him. I checked my watch. Benito was due at work in half an hour.

I was just calculating how long it would take me to get to Marina del Rey when I heard footsteps from the parking lot outside. The stride was long and heavy. When I flushed, the water level rose to the top and spilled over, leaving my shoes wet and squishy. I hiked up my jeans and was ready to scramble to dry land when the outside door creaked slowly open. I thought, great, one of those drunken toasters stumbled in the wrong door. Just at that moment, the lights went out. I strained to focus, to get my bearings. My pulse pumped in my throat. I tried to quiet the urge to gulp air.

I considered those footsteps I'd heard. Man? Woman? Definitely man. Well, maybe he was into energy conservation. Just turning off the lights. No harm done. Right, Tucker? Slowly, the footsteps walked into the room. Toward me. Hard-soled shoes. Slapping down on the concrete floor. A funny scraping noise. Loose nail.

The light from a nearby streetlamp filtered through the small window, casting a dim shadow on the gray floor. There wasn't much visibility, but probably enough for him to see my feet if he looked under the door. I carefully lifted the toilet seat and climbed onto the rim, making myself small. The door was high. Unless he was the Jolly Green Giant, he wouldn't be able to see over the top. Unless he jumped. Oh, boy! My eyes stayed glued to the floor, squinting in the dim light. I couldn't see anything, but I could hear those shoes as they stopped just outside the door to my stall. Mine was the only door shut. It hadn't taken much to figure that one out.

The whole stall quaked as he pulled on the door, testing the lock. The pulling became more forceful. A couple more jolts like that, and he'd have the door off. I could scream. That might spook him, but nobody would hear me over the toasting and shouting of the other merry Cossacks. The window? Forget it. Too high. Too far away. Besides all he had to do was wait outside and catch me on the way down. I was trapped. I inched off the toilet and knelt on the floor. I tried to flatten my body on the cement. It was cold and slimy from urine and soggy toilet paper. Quietly I inched my way under the stall partition. I tried not to gag or think of the new strains of microbes invading my immune system. Or to consider the stench. I tried to think about staying alive. Crawl. Don't look back. Get to the door. Run.

The entire metal panel shook and creaked from his kick. I expected the whole thing to come unhinged from the wall. Please hold until I get to the door, was my only thought. And it did hold. Almost. I was through the third stall and headed for home, the door, and freedom when the second kick broke the hinges, sending the door bouncing against the toilet bowl. It settled on the cement floor. Strong guy. Empty stall.

Metal clanged against metal as he slammed open each door along the way until he got to me. Beefy hands grabbed my ankles and started pulling. Ahh, so close and yet so far. I clung to the base of the toilet bowl, my wet hands struggling to maintain contact with the slippery porcelain. I tried to scream, but my diaphragm was pressed hard to the floor, cutting off my air. My "Don't fuck with me, you asshole" came out sounding more like "duhfummph."

He yanked, and my grip gave way. My head hit the floor. Pain riveted through my jaw, my forehead. Another yank. My ankle socket popped. I felt heat as my stomach scraped across the rough concrete. I kicked with everything I had until one foot was free. I kept kicking and finally hit home. Suddenly the other foot was loose.

I stood and ran for the door, but he grabbed me from behind, covering my mouth with his right hand, coiling his left arm around my body. But not around my right arm. That was free. Instinctively, I groped in the dark to peel his hand away from my mouth. I grabbed what felt like a thumb and pulled on it, bending it back as far as I could until I heard an angry grunt and felt his grip on my mouth loosen enough for me to bite his hand. I tasted stale cigarettes and blood, smelled beer and bad breath. He shouted out in pain. Loud, heavily accented pain. Eastern European? Russian? He pushed, and I fell to the floor like a downed telephone pole, landing on my hands and knees.

Purely by reflex, I rolled over on my butt, crab-walking away from him until I hit something solid. The wall. I waited on the cold concrete floor at Gorky's Park and Pee, thinking, what next? Round two? I thought about Pookie and Muldoon and what to do next. Then I thought of Joe Deegan.

Again, the shadowy figure lumbered across the floor toward me. I waited until he came close enough for me to smell his rancid clothing. When he stooped over to grab me, I somehow found the strength to reach up toward his head. As soon as I felt hair, I pulled it.

He tried to break my grip, but I formed a fist with my free hand and punched as hard as I could, aiming for his throat, connecting. He fell to his knees, rasping for air, trying to say something, but through my haze and his pain, I couldn't make out the words.

My nerve endings were doing Fourth of July fireworks just for me. Everything felt broken, bruised, or disabled. I had to get out of here before somebody clued this guy in that hands weren't the same as a couple of Black Talon slugs in the head, and he came back to try again. I felt weak, but forced myself up. With all my might, I kicked him in the balls. Then I ran, and I didn't look back.

When I got to my car, I took a quick inventory. Everything hurt: ankle, jaw, stomach. My lips felt like two boxing gloves, and a large knot was blooming on my forehead. No bones appeared to be broken, but I was a mess. Soggy tissue stuck to my sweater like shaving cream. Guess I should tell somebody, but who? Eric? No more. Deegan? No way. Besides, Deegan wouldn't give a rip. To him I'd be just another crime statistic. Duane Kleinman probably wouldn't care, either, but at least he'd appreciate the fact that my favorite sweater was now ruined.

It wasn't until I peeled out of the parking lot that my body began to tremble so hard, I thought it would never stop. Get it together, Tucker. All you have to do is find Benito. He'll tell you what you need to know, and then you'll be home free. Only, somehow I had this eerie premonition that it wasn't going to be nearly that easy.

27

all my body parts seemed to be working, but the adrenaline that had propelled me during the struggle was fading, leaving only weariness and awe that I'd just survived an assault that could have left me dead. I suppose the guy could have been one of the drunks from the restaurant, but I didn't think so. I suspected Francine had set me up by telling Irene Borodin where we were meeting. Borodin must have figured out that I was on to her, and knew if I reported her billing fraud to the insurance companies, the resulting investigation would end her charmed life. She had to shut me up or, at the least, scare me off. Her hit man hadn't succeeded, but that didn't mean he wouldn't try again.

I smelled like hell, but even if I'd had the strength to go home and change, I didn't have the time. I had to get to the yacht club. It was a long shot, but Benito seemed like my last best hope for finding out who Polk met with the night he died. Maybe the doctor left the NeuroMed file with Benito for safekeeping. It was a ridiculous theory, but I had too much at stake not to test it.

On the way to Marina del Rey, I regained my composure enough to piece together the few facts that Francine had told me with what I already knew. Polk witnessed the aftermath of the assault on Teresa García. He must have known she was dead, perhaps even before he received that newspaper obituary. The person who mailed the article to him might have believed Polk would help expose García's killer, or perhaps he had blackmail on his mind. On the other hand, I couldn't discount the theory that Polk's knowledge of the girl's death, mixed with his cash flow problems, could add up to his own formula for blackmail. Either way, I wondered how far Polk had gone to make his NeuroMed dreams come true.

The more I thought about it, the more I realized that Covington could easily have helped Polk alter those spreadsheets. A kaleidoscope of possibilities flashed through my mind: Rape . . . blackmail . . . murder . . . And rising up from the center of that unholy trinity was Wade Covington.

·   ·   ·

MARINA DEL REY is located on the ocean between the Los Angeles International Airport and Venice, a half hour and a world away from Hollywood. It was once a simple little marshland until the County made it into the largest man-made small-boat harbor in the world. Now, instead of migratory birds, upscale apartment houses nest along the fingers of the main channel, and multimillion-dollar homes lay claim to once open land.

The sun was setting. The moon and the city lights illuminated dark cumulus clouds. It looked like rain. I turned off Via Marina and into the Marina Yacht Club parking lot. No one was in the guardhouse. I grabbed the Project Rescue newsletter with Covington's picture in it, and the gym bag with my extra clothes from the trunk of my car. I hoped to find a public restroom where I could clean up and change before going inside. I squeezed between the hedge and the gate and made my way along the sidewalk toward the clubhouse.

I paused for a moment at a chain-link fence and looked out at all the boats. All I could see in the distance were masts against masts, and rigging lines crisscrossing like a cat's cradle. Directly in front of me I read a few names printed on the sterns. There were at least two *Ecstasy*s, a *Freedom,* and a *Sea Gal* swaying with the wind and the current.

The envelope Polk used to mail the coffee receipt to himself didn't have a return address, but it was postmarked from Marina del Rey. I suppose he might have mailed it from the marina as some sort of cryptic clue to where he'd been that night. If he managed to get a stamped envelope for the receipt, perhaps he'd gotten one for the NeuroMed package as well. I just hoped he had a chance to mail that, too, before somebody destroyed it.

A man walked toward me, pulling a blue handcart full of groceries. He wore loose khaki shorts and a heavy navy sweater. His legs were tanned dark, and his face was deeply lined, as if it had never been introduced to sunscreen. He was around fifty, I guessed, though it was hard to tell. With him was a huge four-legged animal with coiled hair like a blond Rastafarian. The critter had homed in on the smell of urine on my clothes and was starting to get fresh.

"Janus. No," the man said, grabbing the dog's collar and pulling him back. The way he said it—"YAHnoosh"—sounded foreign, but I couldn't quite place the accent. "Sorry. He's komondor."

Well, that explained it, and was I ever impressed. You didn't always find a dog with a rank that high. Not wanting to breach military etiquette, I saluted.

"Aye, aye, Commander," I said. "Permission to pass without getting sniffed."

The man laughed and shook his head. "No, that is breed,

komondor. Is Hungarian sheepdog. Janus, very good boy." He patted the doggie's head, which started his tail wagging and the thick white cords of his coat rippling like a bamboo curtain.

When I asked the man for directions to the restroom, he looked me up and down with an admiring smile. "You are new here?"

"Sort of."

"Janus and I, we take you to shower."

I guess Janus wasn't the only one with a keen sense of smell. The man introduced himself as Franco. He was a live-aboard, so I thought he might have a little yacht club gossip to share with me, maybe even about Wade Covington. As he led me around the side of the building, I decided to try a little small talk. So I asked about his boat. Before responding, he tucked in his chin and pushed out his lips as if he were going to say *woo-woo,* which made me think he might be Italian.

"*Isabella,* she is beautiful. Janus and I, we are here one month now. Soon we go to Mexico. Marquesas. But this is very nice place."

I couldn't imagine old Janus confined to a boat of any size. Muldoon got cranky cooped up in the house on a rainy day. Franco used his key to open a door near the rear of the club-house and pointed me toward the women's shower facility.

"Thanks," I said politely. "I bet *Isabella* is a knockout."

A spontaneous smile spread across his face, making him look like a young man in love. "You come tonight. I make you din-ner."

I tucked his slip number into the pocket of my gym bag and promised to stop by after I spoke with Benito. With a wave, Franco retreated down the gangway as Janus let out a bark that liquefied my internal organs. That was one major puppy.

The mirror said it all. I looked like hell. The knot on my forehead was growing larger and redder. My hair was matted. The cold air had made every muscle in my body ache. I peeled off my soggy clothes and stood in the hot shower until my muscles relaxed, at least, as much as they could.

When I finished drying off with brown scratchy paper towels from a roll on the wall, I put on the sweats and athletic shoes from my gym bag. I dried my hair under the hand dryer and then retraced my steps around to the front entrance of the clubhouse. I grabbed a wooden handrail, which was varnished to a mirror shine, and headed up the stairs.

A thin young girl with unnaturally straight teeth sat behind a reception desk near the front door. She didn't ask to see my membership card, nor did she seem the least bit disturbed by my appearance. She just smiled with that laissez-faire attitude of young people who don't need to work. In case she changed her mind about the welcome, I decided to speed up my efforts to find Benito. The bar was in the front part of the building, facing the water. Photos and paintings of sailing regattas hung on the walls, and an assortment of burgees was displayed along the crown molding. I managed to get the bartender's attention, but he didn't look impressed by my outfit or the condition of my face.

"I'm looking for Benito."

He looked bored with me already. "He's not here."

"They said he was working tonight."

"They were wrong. Today's his day off. Check out front if you want his schedule."

I put my head on the bar and tried to figure out why nothing ever went my way. When I looked up seconds later, the guy had already abandoned me for an octogenarian in a Greek sailor's hat.

Everything ached as I slipped off the bar stool and headed back to the front desk. When I asked the orthodontically enhanced receptionist to check Benito's schedule, she confirmed that he wasn't due in until the following Wednesday. That was too late to get any information for my meeting with Shelly Greenblatt the following day. Also too late for Mo Whitener's Monday deadline. I asked if she'd been working the previous Saturday night. She had, but her shift ended at nine p.m. She told me that no one was ever at the desk after that hour. As a last resort, I asked her to check the lost-and-found. She did, but she found no maroon envelope.

Naturally, the receptionist wouldn't give me Benito's home telephone number, either. I was at the end of my ability to think of the next step. I'd pinned my hopes on finding some bit of information that would end this treasure hunt, but I'd been naive to think I could figure out any of this. On the back of one of my homemade business cards, I wrote a note asking Benito to call me if he remembered seeing Polk that Saturday night. I handed it to the receptionist.

As I turned to leave, she said, "Milton Polk? We were wondering who he was."

I did a slow spin and looked at her.

"Hold on," she said, disappearing behind a door. When she reappeared, she was holding a large envelope imprinted with the yacht club's return address. It was addressed in Polk's own hand to himself at his home in Pacific Palisades.

"He must have dropped it in the mailbox outside without stamps," the girl said. "The post office won't deliver anymore without them. When it came back, we didn't know where to send it. He wasn't listed as a member. Do you know how we can get this to him?"

It was just like Milton Polk to try to stiff the U.S. Postal Service. My facial muscles hurt, but I managed to produce a big smile. "I'll take care of that for you."

She hesitated at first, but finally handed me the envelope. I gave her another smile and a heartfelt thank-you to boot. I eased onto a nearby couch and ripped open the package. An enormous weight lifted off my chest when I peeked inside and saw something gloriously maroon. I studied the documents to make sure they were the originals. When I was satisfied that they were, I hugged the envelope like a long-lost lover. My cell phone was still with my purse in the car, so I used a pay phone to dial Gordon's number. He was going to be ecstatic.

· · ·

"THAT'S THE BEST news I've heard all week," Gordon said with an audible sigh of relief.

He hadn't been home, but luckily his wife, Eleanor, had given me his cell phone number. I'd found him in his car.

I smiled. "Thought you'd be pleased."

"Pleased?" he said. "Tucker, you saved my ass."

Not to mention my own, I thought.

"I'll bring the file to the office on Monday."

"Are you out of your mind?" He chuckled. "I'm sending an armored car over right now to pick it up."

I smiled. The old Gordon was back, and that felt good.

"Seriously, Tucker," he said. "I don't want to ever go through this again. I think we should put the documents in a safe place for the rest of the weekend."

"Okay," I said, without much enthusiasm. I was tired and still had to stop by to see Franco and Janus before going home.

"I've been meaning to stop by my boat anyway," he said.

"How about if we meet for a few minutes to discuss strategy for Monday. On the way home, I'll drop the NeuroMed documents by the office and lock them in the safe."

He was right to be cautious, but frankly, all I'd wanted was to go home and nurse my bruised and battered body. The only thing that kept me from saying no was the prospect of getting back into Gordon's good graces. He and I would be a team again, confronting Whitener and the evil partners with the NeuroMed documents on Monday. That sounded just too appealing to turn down. Besides, I'd finally get the chance to see Gordon's boat. Eat your heart out, Richard Hastings, I thought.

I'd been spacing out on the couch in the yacht club's lobby for the better part of an hour when I felt someone touch my arm. Gordon Aames stood beside me, wearing chinos, a polo shirt, and a blue fleece jacket. For once, he looked completely re-laxed. I forgot about everything except how good it felt to see his kind and confident smile.

"Jesus, you look terrible," he said. "What the hell happened to your face?"

"It's a long story," I said.

"Can I do something? Get you anything?"

"No, I'm fine."

He sat down next to me on the couch. Then he sighed. "We've missed you at the office, Tucker." He seemed calm. Sincere.

"Thanks, Gordon, that's good news."

"You think that's good, get ready for better," he said. "We've been dropped from Whitener's complaint."

I felt relief and then a surge of unexpected anger. All the anxiety and pain I'd been through—for nothing.

"At least that's one thing I don't have to worry about," I said.

He hesitated. "Well, not you. Just the firm. But it frees me up to help you, and I'm glad to do it. I've been in close contact with all the partners. There are a few glitches with the Amsterdam project. Everyone realizes it was a mistake to replace you. I've convinced them to take a new look at the whole thing."

I felt both curious and wary. "Why would Whitener drop the firm and not me?"

"Don't worry," he replied. "It happens all the time. Whitener's attorneys realized they couldn't make a case against us."

Again, there was that "us" that didn't include me.

"I guarantee you," he continued, "the whole thing will blow over as soon as we produce the contracts and the original report. Where are they?"

I held the maroon document envelope up in front of him. He looked at it and smiled. Then he looked at me, and his apparent relief turned to concern.

"You're trembling," he said. "Are you sure you're okay?"

Actually, I wasn't sure and told him so.

He took my hands in his and said, "You're freezing. Let's go to the boat. Eleanor has some warm clothes on board. You can change. I'll make you a drink. Fill you in on everything. Did I tell you Hastings just joined the club? You know, I think you should join, too. I'll put you up for membership. What do you say?"

His question was rhetorical. It was a done deal. It was true, the firm had picked up a lot of business through the club, and now that I'd had more time to think about it, if that little weasel Hastings had joined, then so would I.

Gordon braced my elbow as I slipped the envelope with the original NeuroMed report into a side pocket of the gym bag so it wouldn't get smelly from my wet clothes. As he led me out the front door, he began brainstorming ideas about how to save one of Covington's financially troubled subsidiaries, and expressing his optimism that Aames & Associates would get the chance to turn the company around. His enthusiasm made me smile until I thought about Milton Polk and Teresa García, and my mind wandered. If winning the consulting contract hinged on keeping silent about Wade Covington and what I knew, it was something I couldn't do, not even for Gordon. But how could I break the news to him that the reward he coveted most wasn't worth the price, especially if it came from a man who, I suspected, was a rapist and a murderer?

28

it was dark as I followed Gordon through a chain-link gate and down the metal gangway to the boat slips. The narrow cement docks swayed from the wind and surge, leaving me feeling slightly off balance. Somewhere in the distance, a loose halyard clanked against a mast.

Gordon's boat was in the last slip just before the main channel. Darkness made it hard to distinguish details, but the size alone was impressive. It was a powerboat and at least fifty feet long. I stepped onto the swim step and then followed Gordon up a few stairs to the main salon. He disappeared into one of the staterooms and, after a few minutes, returned with a stocking cap, a heavy wool sweater, and a yellow rain slicker that looked as if it belonged to a school crossing guard. I set my gym bag by the couch, slipped into the sweater, and then zipped and Velcroed myself into the jacket. The pockets were full of everything from mittens to a roll of Tums tablets, which made the sucker awfully heavy but warm. I smoothed down my hair before pulling the cap over my head.

Gordon went to the bar and rummaged through a cabinet until he found a bottle and a couple of plastic glasses. "Scotch?"

"What about your ulcer?"

He winked. "It's for medicinal purposes. Just don't tell Eleanor."

"I don't drink the hard stuff," I said.

"Get used to it. It's part of the culture. You want to work with the boys, you drink with the boys. Besides, it'll relax you."

He poured until the glasses were nearly full, and then added ice from a small refrigerator under the counter. No mixer. He handed me one of the glasses. He took his and climbed up another ladder to the top deck. A short time later, I heard the sound of engines roaring to life. While he wasn't watching, I poured most of my drink down the sink, which probably emptied directly into the marina. I hoped the booze didn't give some sardine a hangover.

"I can't be gone more than half an hour," he said, "but I haven't used her in a while. I thought we could go out and run the engines while we're talking. And since you're going to be using the club and the boat to entertain, it'll give you a chance to learn the routine."

What was Gordon thinking? That he was going to teach me to drive this tanker tonight? Sweet of him to offer, but I didn't think so. Thirty minutes was barely enough time to plan our approach with the partners and for me to tell him about Wade Covington. There certainly wasn't time for How to Skipper a Yacht, part I.

Gordon released the lines from the bow and instructed me to do the same with those at the stern. When I cast them free, he slowly maneuvered the boat out of the slip. I joined him on the bridge, which was enclosed on three sides by stiff plastic windows. Despite the shelter they provided, the air up there was still chilly. I was glad to have all the extra clothing.

Across the basin, the palms surrounding the Marina del Rey Hotel were bending with the wind. Gordon motored slowly past a fuel dock and made way toward the breakwater. As we cleared the north entrance of the channel, he pushed the two throttles forward, and the boat picked up speed.

Covington had been an important client even before these latest contract talks, so I didn't know how Gordon would take the news that as soon as I showed Teresa García's medical chart to Detective Kleinman, Covington would be in no position to grant a consulting contract to anyone. I had to warn him before the shit hit the fan. As the two of us sat there looking out at the water, I tried to ease my way onto the subject.

"Have you heard anything from Wade Covington?" I asked.

"No, thank God," Gordon said. "I think I smoothed things over, but your going to his house was a big mistake."

"I wanted to apologize for offending him."

"That's what I told him," he said, "but, Tucker, we've got to talk about this independent streak of yours."

I'd heard that lecture before, and I didn't want to hear it again right now, so I pretended to be enthralled by the blipping lights on the half-dozen screens in front of me. I didn't understand boat electronics, but I didn't really need to. That was Gordon's job. I could tell that we were heading west, in the general direction of Malibu, but despite the moon, I couldn't see any vessels out here but ours. It was rougher in the open water than it had been in the channel. The motion of the boat was making me a little queasy.

"Gordon, there are some things about Covington—"

"Forget Covington." His voice had a slight edge to it now. "And don't change the subject. You haven't been a team player lately, Tucker. You can't be a maverick if you want to be a partner."

"In case you forgot," I said, "the partners banished me from the firm almost a week ago, so I'm not sure, exactly, what you're talking about."

"I'm talking about Mona Polk," he said. "You're working for her. That's strictly against company policy. All contracts have to be presented to the managing partners and approved before accepting a job from a client. You know that."

I tried to imagine how he'd found out about Mona. The only thing I could think of was that maybe she'd called the office looking for me. Except, that didn't make sense. Eugene would have taken the call. The last thing he would have done was tell Gordon.

"How did you find out?" I asked.

"Bernie Cole. He said you stopped by Sunland to see him about some survey you were doing for her."

I was stunned, and for a few seconds all I could do was stare at him. Finally I said, "You know Bernard Cole?"

"Sure. We're fraternity brothers."

"You went to Luther Mann with Bernard Cole?" I asked. "Didn't Wade Covington go there, too?"

"Sure. Bernie didn't graduate, and Wade was a few years ahead of us, but that's how we all met. Bernie and I skied Aspen before it started taking itself so seriously."

I felt a chill despite the heavy parka. "Was Wade Covington one of your ski buddies, too?"

He shot me a glance. "Why do you ask?"

"Just curious," I said. "I was thinking of taking a ski trip over Thanksgiving. Dr. Polk told me he stayed with Covington at his Aspen house a few times. Told me it was a good place to go."

He took a drink of Scotch and winced. Not playing well with his ulcer, I guessed. "Yeah. Aspen's still good."

"Milton Polk gave me the impression he was a real hot dog, but he didn't strike me as the athletic type," I said. "Was he any good?"

He reached up and adjusted some dials on one of the screens, and then increased the speed. "Did I say I skied with Polk?"

"I just assumed you might have run into him one time or another, since he was a friend of Covington's."

"You're very inquisitive tonight, Tucker," he said. "More so than usual." He squinted at me, then continued. "He didn't ski at all that I noticed. Mostly, he went from the refrigerator to the telephone. So how's Mrs. Polk doing?"

According to Francine, Milton Polk had been to Covington's Aspen house only once, when Teresa García was raped and beaten. If Gordon was at Aspen with Polk, it meant that he was also a witness to that crime, or at least an accessory to the cover-up. I was getting that wrong-place-at-the-wrong-time kind of feeling again.

"Tucker, I asked about Mrs. Polk. Is she okay? Suicide's a tough one."

"What makes you think he committed suicide?"

"What else could it be?"

"Oh, I don't know—murder maybe."

Gordon's facial muscles went slack. He pushed on the throttle, and the boat lurched forward. We were going really fast now. As the boat hit the swells, the bow bounced out of the water, pounding my body against the seat, making my stomach churn.

"Slow down!" I yelled. "We're going to crash."

"Don't worry. It's why we came out here. To run the engines."

From the determined set of his jaw, he looked as if he weren't going to stop until he ran this tub onto the beach at Waikiki. But a few minutes later the boat hit a swell that knocked Gordon's glass of Scotch out of its holder, splashing alcohol all over the bulkhead and all over me.

"Shit!" he snapped. "The instruments."

He slowed down the boat and pushed a button on a panel, after which the boat seemed to steer itself. He instructed me to call him if I saw any moving lights, and then he went below. The only lights I saw weren't moving. They were from the shore to the right of us, and they glimmered like Christmas bulbs strung along some distant roofline.

When Gordon returned, he handed me a stack of napkins to wipe the deck and to absorb the Scotch that had soaked into my sweatpants. My muscles were stiff and achy from the exertion at Gorky's and from the cold. I also wasn't feeling so steady on my feet. He wiped the moisture from the instrument screens, and I did my best to clean the deck. As I looked for a place to toss the soggy napkins, I noticed that they were imprinted with a name and some kind of logo. The light on the bridge was dim, but I could just make out a picture of an anchor. Beneath it were the words *Write Off.* My lips parted slightly as I willed my lungs to breathe. My arms felt like dead weights as I held the napkin up.

"Your boat?"

He flashed me a wry smile. "Eleanor's idea. I wanted to name her *Amazing Grace,* but she had veto power."

I closed my eyes while the realization crept slowly into my consciousness. I was almost sorry I hadn't joined Gordon for a drink. It might indeed have relaxed me, might have muted the fear that snaked its way through every part of my body. Milton Polk's scrawled instructions across a coffee receipt. Not write off the coffee as a business expense. That's not what he'd meant at all. *Write Off.* The name of a boat. The boat owned by the man he was meeting last Saturday night. The man who murdered him.

29

You killed Milton Polk," I said stupidly, overwhelmed by the realization.

Gordon's eyes darted around the bridge, focusing on every-thing but me, as if he didn't know what else to do. Even in the dim light, I could see the color draining from his face.

"You've always had a vivid imagination. It's been a big part of your success." His voice sounded thin and hollow.

"Polk was meeting someone the night he was murdered. Someone with a secret in his past. I believe that person was you, and the secret was Teresa García. What happened? Did the two of you miss each other at the Project Rescue dinner? The firm was one of the sponsors of that event. You must have been there. But that doesn't really matter, does it? Because you agreed to meet Polk later at the yacht club. I'm guessing he used Teresa García as leverage to get you to change the NeuroMed report. What I don't understand is why you killed him."

Gordon looked surprised, then pleased, as if he were proud of me. He didn't answer for a time, just stared ahead into the black-ness, his hands gripping the wheel. Finally, he gently returned the throttle to neutral, and the engines idled. I braced myself as the boat lurched from its wake.

Gordon's shoulders slumped. His expression was both worry-worn and resigned. "What a mess."

That was an understatement, to say the least. I sat frozen in my seat, trying to comprehend my own idiocy for sitting here, chatting with a murderer. As the boat drifted into the deep trough of a swell, it began to rock sideways. I braced myself to keep from rolling out of my seat. Between the smell of diesel fumes and the movement of the boat, my stomach was feeling really iffy.

"I didn't change that report," he said. "I gave Polk your research and told him he could do what he wanted, as long as he left the firm out of it. It made me sick when I found out what he'd done. My God, I could have lost everything."

"And Teresa García? What did she lose?"

"You have to believe me, Tucker," he said. "That was an accident. Polk was using the García business to squeeze all of us for money and favors—equipment from Bernie, investors from Wade. I gave him your work on the business plan for free, but he obviously wanted more. When he got Whitener's letter on Friday, he was frantic. He came to see me that night. When I refused to help him, he told me he had a medical file on the García girl in his office, and that he was prepared to turn it over to the police. He was trying to bully me. So stupid of him. I had to warn Wade, so I told Polk whatever he wanted to hear just to get rid of him."

"And what did he want to hear, Gordon? That you'd set me up to take the fall?"

"Yes." His tone was detached and businesslike. "After Polk left, I called Wade and told him to go to the Center with his key and find García's file."

"Ah, now I get it. Covington trashed the place looking for it. And when Polk stopped by the Center on Saturday night, he saw the mess and knew you'd betrayed him."

"Polk was livid when he realized the García file was missing. I denied taking it, but he didn't believe me. That's when I found out he also had the NeuroMed originals and that he planned to destroy them. He wouldn't tell me how he got them, but it didn't matter. I wanted them back. I persuaded him to bring the documents to the boat, and we'd cut some kind of deal."

"So you knew the NeuroMed file was missing all along?"

"Sure, but I also knew if anybody could find it, you could. Fear is a compelling motivator."

"Here's one thing I don't understand, Gordon: Why did Polk agree to meet with you? Wasn't he afraid you'd betray him again?"

"I don't think he considered that. He was too angry. He came storming onto the boat Saturday night. We argued. He pushed. I pushed back. He hit his head on the corner of the bar."

"So you took him out into the bay and threw him overboard to finish him off?"

"I thought he was dead," he said. "I panicked. It was a stupid mistake."

"Your second stupid mistake, if I'm right. Raping Teresa García was your first."

A look of disgust crossed his face. "I didn't rape that girl." He sighed and shook his head slowly. "We were at Wade's place in Aspen, getting shit-faced. Bernie and I heard screaming from the bedroom. We found Wade on top of her. She was hysterical, kicking, and yelling her head off. I tried to calm her down, but she wouldn't shut up, so I put my hand over her mouth. She bit me. Shit, I don't know—I snapped. I grabbed her by the shoulders and slammed her head against the headboard. I kept doing it and doing it until she stopped. Jesus! I thought I'd killed her."

My heart pounded. "You *did* kill her, Gordon. Teresa García died from those head injuries. But I don't have to tell you that.

Gee, two murders. That's almost serial. But don't worry, money works miracles in the legal system these days."

He smiled. It was a sad-little-boy smile that set my nerves on edge. "You know, Tucker," he said with eerie calm, "I can't let you off this boat."

A chill spiked through my body as I finished his sentence in my head—*alive.* I was starting to feel sick.

"Won't people think it odd," I said, "Milton Polk and me dying the same way?"

He considered that for a moment. The tone of his answer was chillingly matter-of-fact. "Not really. You're in a lot of trouble. Facing a federal criminal investigation. Depressed. You decided to end it. Or better yet, your face is a mess. Someone decided to teach you a lesson. A boyfriend? Maybe he finished the job."

I pointed to the knot on my forehead. "This is compliments of Irene Borodin. At least that's my guess. You probably don't know her, but she works for Sunland Manufacturing. I'm sure when the police get around to it, they'll be talking to all sorts of people. Maybe even to your friend Bernie Cole."

He looked annoyed. "I don't know what you're talking about, Tucker, and neither does Bernie. He didn't have a clue why you'd been to see him. You used your mother's real name, but I knew right away it was you." Gordon stood and motioned me toward the stairs. "Let's go below."

I scanned the bridge but didn't see anything that I could use as a weapon. Maybe there was a radio. I could call for help. It didn't matter that I couldn't see one, because I wouldn't know how to use it anyway. What were my chances up here versus down there? It didn't seem to make much difference. Gordon didn't appear to have a weapon, and he couldn't just pick me up and throw me overboard. At least, I didn't think so. Nevertheless,

I didn't let him out of my sight as I walked down the ladder to the salon. The air below was stale and smelled of mildew. I felt woozy, and my mouth was beginning to water.

"Don't worry," he said in an even tone. "The ocean's no more than sixty degrees. Twenty minutes and you'll just go to sleep."

"You knew I didn't change the NeuroMed report, but you set me up to take the blame. How could you do that to me?"

It was a silly thing to ask a man who was going to kill me, but giving my research to Polk in the first place seemed like his stupidest move of all. I thought back to that day in Gordon's office, when he'd spoken about not being able to go back and change the big mistakes. Teresa García and Milton Polk were already dead. He was right; it had been far too late to change that.

"Give me your car keys," he said.

"I guess that's what the police call an MO. Are you going to leave my car at the airport, like you did with Polk's Mercedes? How did you get back to the yacht club anyway? Taxi? Don't you know the police will be checking every cab in and out of LAX?"

"Give me your fucking keys, Tucker."

He looked around. My gym bag was lying next to the couch. As he walked toward it, I ran for the ladder to the lower deck. Each footstep sent a flash of pain to the bruises on my body.

"Why are you running, Tucker?" he shouted. "There's nowhere to go."

I was bouncing off the furniture and the walls from the violent motion of the boat but was able to scramble down the ladder and outside to the cockpit in time to lean over the side. The water looked black, cold, and very deep. This was it. I started to gag. The last moments of my life, and I was going to spend them losing my lunch.

Gordon was behind me, roughly pulling off my stocking cap.

He grabbed at the yellow slicker, trying to get it off, too, but Houdini couldn't have un-Velcroed me under the circumstances. At first, I felt too sick to think about what he was doing. Then it dawned on me: He wanted Eleanor's jacket. Screw him. If I was going to die, I was taking the evidence with me. I struggled to push him away, but all I managed to do was send his glasses sliding down his nose. The effort sent a searing pain through my shoulder.

Gordon tugged at the jacket again. The force sent my body rocking on the rail of the boat like a teeter-totter. My ribs ached as I clawed at the fiberglass bulkhead until my fingers touched something. It was about the size of a quart of milk, with a long, springy antenna. I grabbed for it and held on, hoping to gain enough momentum to roll back onto the deck. Unfortunately, whatever I was holding on to pulled loose, and I lost my balance.

For a moment I was weightless. Then a cold blast of water hit my face. I tried to hold on to that antenna, hoping it was some kind of radio, but when I felt myself sinking, I let it go. I fought my way to the surface. Salt water filled my mouth and nose. I gagged. Coughed. Fought panic.

I called for help, but no other vessels were close by, and Gordon's boat was already steaming back to Marina del Rey. I kicked frantically to stay afloat, but the weight of all those clothes kept pulling me under. My shoes were filled with water. I had to get them off. Using my arms to tread water, I pried off one shoe with the opposite foot. When both shoes were off, I scissor-kicked as I tore at the Velcro wristbands and front closure of the jacket. Each time I went under, it took every ounce of strength I had in my arms and legs to fight my way back to the surface. If I anticipated the swells and closed my mouth and eyes, I could avoid inhaling more briny water. By the time I'd shed Eleanor's slicker and heavy sweater, I was exhausted. My teeth were chattering, and my body shook violently from the frigid water of Santa Monica Bay.

Gordon's boat was barely visible now—just a single white light fading in the distance. I'd always hated swimming in the ocean, because there were things down there looking for their next meal. They could see me, but I couldn't see them. I tried to focus on anything except how cold and how frightened I was. I wondered if Muldoon liked Mrs. Domanski better than me . . . if Pookie and Bruce really had a groovy kind of love . . . if Eric could ever be happy without me . . . if Aunt Sylvia would finally get my house. I also wondered if Joe Deegan had those wet little curls on his neck every time he stepped out of the shower.

I swam toward the lights on the shore until I got tired. Then I lay back, closed my eyes, and let the swells carry me. I'd rest— just for a moment, that's all. Then I'd get my strength back, and start swimming again. At least, that's what I told myself. The bad news was, no matter what I did, I'd never make it back to land. The good news was, I didn't feel seasick any longer.

30

through a veil of pain and drowsiness, I saw the image of Joe Deegan. His arms were crossed, and his head was slightly cocked. That irreverent grin of his had been replaced by a look of concern. In my mental haze, his blue-gray eyes caressed my body. His fingertips touched the bumps and bruises on my face and began a slow journey down my neck.

"Think we should take her to Torrance Memorial?"

"Nah," Deegan said. "I'll take care of her."

My eyes fluttered open, and I saw him standing over me. I'd been dozing off and on for the past two hours, slumped in a chair at the Coast Guard Air Station near LAX. Someone had given me a blanket, but I still had on my wet clothes, minus Eleanor's yellow slicker, her sweater, and my shoes, which were all at the bottom of Santa Monica Bay.

From what I'd been told, whatever I was holding on to when I fell from the boat was called an EPIRB. I'd torn it out of its bracket, and when it hit the water, it sent a transmission to a satellite, which beamed a signal to some Air Force base in Illinois. They notified the Coast Guard Air Station in Marina del Rey. The gadget was programmed with personal data, including Gordon's phone numbers. Eleanor confirmed he was on the boat, so the Coast Guard sent a helicopter and a rescue swimmer. I'd been lucky. Only three out of a hundred distress calls are real. If they'd waited their usual twenty minutes to respond, I'd have been as dead as an oyster on the half shell.

Deegan's hair was messed up, as if he'd just rolled out of bed. He was wearing his brown leather jacket, Levi's, and a white T-shirt that had *Pacific-14* printed in small letters on the front.

He looked at my face and whistled. "Hate to see the other guy."

"Very funny."

"I hear you took a little helicopter ride," he teased.

I just rolled my eyes.

From a black gym bag he pulled out what looked like a pair of gray sweatpants, a blue sweatshirt, and a pair of socks. He tossed them on my lap. "Get those clothes off."

"Yeah, you wish."

He grinned. "Suit yourself, ma'am." He reached to take back the items, but my reflexes weren't completely shot. I grabbed the outfit and got up, intending to head to the bathroom to change. Only, I felt a little wobbly. Before I knew it, he'd scooped me up in his arms. What could I do? I had to hold on or I'd fall.

I was going to tell him to put me down, but by the time I could coax my nose out of his neck, he'd already carried me to the door of the bathroom. He stood there holding me for a moment. His forehead was slightly furrowed in concern, and his lips were pressed together in a masculine sort of pout. Finally, he put me down and placed his hand on the wall alongside my head.

"See what happens when you keep things from me?" he said. "You almost got yourself killed."

"I don't even know why you're here. I asked for Duane Kleinman."

"Yeah, and was I ever hurt." His words were soft, and his lips so near, I could feel his breath on my cheek. "I thought we meant more to each other than that."

I ducked under his arm and into the bathroom. The clothes were undoubtedly his and were a little large, but not by much. He was tall, but so was I. My hair was stiff with salt, and the knot on my forehead was turning strange colors that didn't qualify as attractive.

When I came out of the bathroom, Deegan was still leaning against the wall outside the door. His eyes twinkled, and the corners of his mouth were turned down, trying to hide a smile as he surveyed the damage. The look was intimate and made my face feel warm.

"You look like hell," he said.

He put a dry blanket around my shoulders and led me out the door.

"Where are you taking me?" I asked.

"Home."

"Yours or mine?"

He stopped and raised his eyebrows suggestively.

"Mine," I said firmly, because I hadn't meant it the way he thought.

He smiled to himself as he led me to a black Ford Explorer parked in the lot. He threw his gym bag and my soggy clothes onto the backseat. Then he fastened my seat belt. The car smelled of leather and something fruity, and soon the heater had warmed me into a mellowness that caught me off guard.

"Where's Gordon?" I asked.

"In custody. We were on our way to serve a warrant on the boat, only you got there first. Maybe I should lock you up for interfering with a police investigation. At least that way I could keep an eye on you."

"How did you know I was on Gordon's boat?"

"Some guy with a weird-looking dog was looking for you, too. He told us he'd seen you leave with Aames. He described you to a T. If I was the jealous type, you'd be answering a few questions right now."

Lights from the cars on the freeway were making my head throb, so I closed my eyes until we reached the coast highway, where the traffic slowed and the brightness dimmed. By the time we pulled into my driveway, I was fighting the urge to drift off.

"If you weren't in my bedroom, who was?" I asked.

"I can hardly wait to see this bedroom you keep talking about," he said. "I assume it was Gordon Aames. I gave Buck your driver's license, but he didn't want to drive all the way out to the beach, so he dropped it by your office. He left it with Aames's secretary. Some woman named Marsha. I don't know where he got your jacket, but probably from Covington."

Deegan helped me out of the car and got the spare key back from Mrs. Domanski, who perked up considerably when she saw him. She seemed quite disappointed when she couldn't entice him to join her for cocktails. As for Muldoon, he was beside himself sniffing. Deegan squatted, playfully rubbed the pup's ears, and said, "Hey, buddy." Muldoon rolled over on his back, making sure I was appreciating how admiration was properly bestowed.

Despite my protests, Deegan fed and walked Muldoon and then tucked me into bed. He even pulled an extra blanket from Pookie's room to keep me warm. If you asked me, the guy was starting to feel a little too comfortable in my house.

"Then who killed Roy Trebeau?" I said drowsily.

"Get some rest. We'll talk about it later."

He pulled the covers up around my chin and brushed his hand across my cheek as though he was checking for fever—just like Pookie did when I was a child. He took the extra set of car keys and told me someone would bring the Boxster home in the morning. Just before he turned out the lights, he ruffled my hair. The ruffle was brotherly, and for the first time, I wished that it weren't and that he wouldn't leave. I managed to mumble a few more words before I fell into a deep sleep.

31

i wasn't sure if Deegan stayed that whole night. The couch looked as if it had been slept on, but by the time I woke up, he was gone. Venus and Eugene arrived in the morning with food and a lot of bossy demands. They stayed all day despite my protests. Venus spent the time entertaining me with a date-from-hell retrospective while Eugene busied himself sprucing up the house with his latest knitting project: a dusting mitt, which featured a popcorn stitch he'd perfected during the week I was suspended from work.

Although the weather was unusually warm and sunny, I spent the next few days in a fog. My bruises would disappear, but there were lingering scars invisible to the eye. In time, perhaps they would fade as well.

The week after Thanksgiving, Pookie called. She and Bruce had decided to extend their stay in Maui until after New Year's. As it turned out, Bruce was living on a comfortable trust left to him by a grandfather who'd made his money in cement. Go figure. Muldoon and I missed her, but she sounded happier than she'd been in a long while. That was enough for us. As for Eric, he and I were on speaking terms, but it didn't feel the same. Not yet.

I'd missed my scheduled appointment with Sheldon Greenblatt at the Riviera that Sunday following my dip in the Bay, but we connected at his tennis club during the next week. Shelly agreed to represent me in the Whitener matter. He also held my hand through an unpleasant prehearing meeting with my aunt Sylvia and her lawyers. It was too early to say if she'd be successful in reopening probate on my house, but stay tuned. That Sylvia's no quitter. As for the identity of the man who answered my aunt's door, that was still a mystery. If he was a new boyfriend, he certainly hadn't mellowed her any.

Most of Mo Whitener's eleven million dollars turned up intact in several bank accounts Polk had opened for that purpose. The money was quietly returned to investors. Whatever shortfall there was, Mona made it up to the group with her proceeds from the sale of NeuroMed and Polk's private practice, plus the life insurance payoff. I should have had more faith in Mona. In the end, she'd taken charge of her life and been a stand-up person. I hoped that she and A-r-r-r-r-mando would find true happiness.

I heard that Kenny had taken out a loan against his machine shop to pay Francine's lawyer, who was trying to arrange for her to make restitution to keep her out of prison. There was an arrest warrant out for Irene Borodin and her brother, Anton Maslansky. Turns out, he was the guy who attacked me and killed Roy Trebeau for ratting him out to Bernie Cole over the missing warehouse equipment.

As for Covington, the night I ran into him at NeuroMed, he wasn't stealing Teresa García's medical chart as I'd suspected. He already had that. He was looking for the original NeuroMed file for Gordon.

A short time after I turned over Teresa García's file to the police, I read in the paper that Covington's lawyers surrendered him to the Colorado authorities under pressure from the girl's uncle and the Mexican government. Apparently, the uncle had been pushing for action all along. I half wondered if he'd been the one stalking Covington.

I still wasn't sure how Polk had gotten the original Neuro-Med documents out of my office. Gordon continued to deny any part in that. Maybe Polk took them, or maybe it had been Richard Hastings. If it was Hastings, he wasn't about to admit it. As the newest partner at Aames & Associates, he had a much higher-profile ass to cover.

Naturally, I'd resigned from the firm. For a long time, I'd wanted to be with Aames & Associates forever, but sometimes the price of making your dreams come true is just too high. Too bad Milton Polk hadn't come to that same conclusion. He might still be alive.

Oh—and I hadn't heard from Joe Deegan again.

In December, Venus's cousin Waddell invited us both to Pacific's employee holiday party. It was a family affair at a hotel in Marina del Rey and lots of fun, I guess. I danced a few times and grazed at the buffet. Deegan wasn't there, but Duane Kleinman was, and with a woman I wouldn't want to meet in a dark alley. Men.

The DJ took a break, and I needed one, too. I was sitting alone on a couch in the hotel lobby, lamenting my empty champagne glass, when Venus sashayed over and sat down next to me.

"Why aren't you mingling?" she said.

"Guess I should have invited Steve, the rescue swimmer. I think he had a crush on me."

She rolled her eyes and spoke in that huffy, authoritarian voice she uses whenever we discuss my failings with men. "Heard from him recently?" She paused for a moment. "Uh-huh, I didn't think so. Here's how it is, honey: They lose interest if you don't show some, too."

"Yeah, yeah, yeah, whatever," I said. "What's happening at the office without Gordon?"

"The partners are scrambling for business. Hastings comes in every day looking like Godzilla's on his ass. I sure wish you'd change your mind and come back."

"No way," I said. "I'm thinking maybe I'll start my own consulting practice. Sinclair and Associates. Does that sound like strategic thinking?"

"Sounds more like wishful thinking," she said.

"Maybe you and Eugene could come work with me?"

"You know me, Tucker. I don't mind being the last one to turn out the lights, but I don't want to pay the electric bill."

Venus hailed a waiter carrying a fresh tray of champagne and grabbed a glass for each of us.

"What do you suppose is going to happen to Gordon?" she said.

I shrugged. It was a question I'd asked myself many times in the past few weeks, but I had mixed feelings about the answer. Gordon had committed the worst sorts of crimes, and for that, someone besides me would determine his punishment.

We wandered back inside the ballroom, where I made a half-hearted effort to be sociable. At half past nine, I was gathering my things to leave when Joe Deegan came through the door with a gorgeous young honey blonde. I hated myself, but I felt a twinge of jealousy. They sat with a group of people who greeted them both warmly, as if they went way back. I could almost see the wedding picture sitting on their mantel at home. I chatted a bit longer, but I'd lost interest in the evening. I was saying my good-byes when I felt heat behind me and heard a voice whisper in my ear.

"Let's dance."

Over my shoulder I said, "I don't think your wife will approve."

He turned me around and looked into my eyes, as if he was having impure thoughts and saw no reason to apologize for them.

"Don't worry," he said. "Claudia won't mind. She knows how I am."

What an arrogant shithead, I thought, but I couldn't protest without making a scene. One dance—what could that hurt? His wife was right in the room. The DJ was playing Willie Nelson's "You Were Always on My Mind." It was slow and schmaltzy, and I was a sucker for both. Deegan pressed his hand into the small of my back and guided me to the dance floor. The lights dimmed.

"So, I guess you've been pretty busy lately?" I said.

"Mm–hm." He pulled me gently into his body, close. Too close. I started to feel like the Hershey part of a s'more.

"All done with your investigation?"

"Mm–hm."

"Nice party."

"Mm–hm."

He inhaled deeply and slowly laced the fingers of his left hand with my right, a gesture that seemed way too intimate under the circumstances. I shook it off. He looked at me with that grin of his but kept dancing. This time his lips were pressed gently to my ear. They felt soft.

But Deegan was wrong. Claudia did mind. Out of the corner of my eye, I saw her heading our way with a very determined look on her face. My heart started to pound. As she marched across the dance floor toward us, I prepared for a skirmish.

"Joe, I'm going home," she said. "I miss the baby. Hope you don't mind."

"You'll be okay alone?"

She smiled. "Yeah, I think so."

He put his hands protectively on her upper arms and kissed her tenderly on the forehead. "Kiss the rookie for me."

Her smile included both of us. "Sorry to interrupt."

Well, I thought, that was generous. After she left, Deegan started with the octopus routine again, but I squirmed out of his reach and started walking to my table. He caught my arm and pulled me back toward him.

"What's your problem now?" he said.

"I'll tell you what my problem is. I don't play footsie with married men."

He grinned. "Footsie?"

"You know what I mean."

"I'm not married."

"That's even worse. You're living with somebody, and you have a baby."

He did that pouty thing with his mouth again, but it didn't look as appealing this time.

"You're pretty curious about my personal life," he said. "I didn't know you cared."

"I don't care. I'm just making conversation."

"Not that it's any of your business," he said softly, "but Claudia's my sister. Her husband's out of town, and she's staying with me because she doesn't like to be alone. Anything else you want to know?"

I felt embarrassed, because there *were* things I wanted to know and because now he knew I wanted to know them. Life was so complicated.

"No, that'll do for now."

"Good, let's dance."

"You lied to me," I said.

He frowned as if baffled by my accusation. "How do you figure?"

"You said we'd talk about Roy Trebeau later, but you weren't there."

He rolled his eyes and started dancing again. "I'll watch myself now that I know it's one of your pet peeves."

"So, that's your sister."

"Yup." His hand started to wander slowly down my back.

"If that hand gets anywhere near my butt, you're a dead man."

He breathed a half sigh, half groan into my ear that came out sounding like "hmmm," but who could be sure.

At least I was finally getting an idea just what kind of trouble Joe Deegan was.

ML

13/84